ASK ME NOTHING

CAROL FOX

Published by Circleville Fox

ISBN 978-0-9970416-0-6

Prologue

Thursday, August 21, 2003, Rural Central Texas

Flies buzzed about the face of the corpse. The hot air was stifling. Dust motes, kicked up by the boots of the men standing in a semi-circle inside the big barn, danced in a ray of sunshine slanting down from the loft opening. Wisps of hay clung to the body.

Outside the old barn, a horse stamped, irritated by big horse flies. From the distant fields came the cry of a mourning dove.

"Looks like we hit the jackpot," said a rangy man, who looked as though he'd been born on horseback, to the other men inside the barn. He was staring down at the body: medium height, brown hair; about 35, muscular and fit; jeans, gray t-shirt, worn running shoes. The right side of the skull was smashed in, and flies crawled across the congealed blood.

From his jeans pocket he pulled out a cell phone.

"Jim here. We found him."

"What do you suppose did that? Baseball bat?" a young man in new jeans and fancy boots asked.

"Nah, something smaller. Like maybe a fireplace poker," an older man with leathery skin said, spitting tobacco juice into a plastic coke bottle he held in one hand.

"Some blow. Look how the blood gushed down his shirt. All the way to his tennis shoes."

"Yep. Head wound." The old man shifted the tobacco plug from one side of his jaw to the other.

"Bet his attacker got plenty splattered."

Jim went outside and lit a cigarette. The Central Texas sun beat down hard on his lined and weathered face, with its sharp features. He blew a stream of blue smoke into the sultry air. Empty fields surrounded the ancient barn, the corn already harvested, tan stalks awaiting the shredder. In the distance, the tree line showed the course of the San Sebastian River.

The horses of the Search and Recovery team, which Jim captained, stood patiently in the shade of the hackberry and elm trees near what once had been a yard.   An antique rose bush and a pomegranate tree flourished within a picket fence that leaned at odd angles.   Only a few rotting timbers remained of the small frame farmhouse.

A lineback dun mare shifted her weight from one hip to the other.   A paint gelding switched at flies.   The tang of horse sweat mingled with the smell of cigarette smoke.   The sun was unrelenting.

"Here, you can go inside," Jim said to a younger man standing watch near the horses. "Jeffrey," he said to a teenage boy leaning up against a stocky palomino gelding, "You look out for the horses."

"Yessir."

Trying not to show his intense curiosity, the young man sauntered toward the barn.   Jeffrey turned back to the big gelding and gently stroked his nose.

Jim took one last look around, memorizing the landscape: to the north, the San Sebastian River; to the south, the county road roughly paralleling the river.   Heading west, the county road led to a state highway, some fifteen miles distant. Close by, the big barn lay to the east of where the old farmhouse had stood, the rotting timbers of its floor joists a blueprint for the vanished frame house.   The pomegranate tree in the corner of the tumbling picket fence still bore fruit, and the rosebush bloomed.

Chapter 1

August, 1979, Graylor, Texas

It was summer and there was nothing to do. Her mother was always busy with Baby Patty now. June was no fun, always trying to boss her around. "I'll tell Daddy on her next time," Carla thought. "He likes me best 'cause I'm prettier." The television blared in the next room. Nothing good on this time of day.

"June," their mother called. "I need you to watch the baby while I take a quick shower. Then maybe we can go get your school supplies."

Carla watched from the kitchen as her mother crossed into the small living room carrying the baby and a blanket. Her mother put the blanket on the bare wooden floor in front of the small TV, next to the coffee table, then gently set Baby Patty on the blanket.

"Look at this," her mother said, shaking Patty's new rattle in front of her, smiling as Patty reached out for it. June sat down next to the baby, taking her responsibility very seriously.

"I won't be long," their mother said.

Carla sulked in the kitchen, leaning against the worn cabinets. She watched Baby Patty fling aside the rattle and turn toward the coffee table, starting to pull up for the first time. June was watching the television, fascinated by some stupid grown-up scene.

Outside in the backyard, their dog, Heinz, made a sudden leap and began worrying something on the ground. Carla ran to the back door. Heinz had a squirrel by the back of the neck. On sudden impulse, Carla ran to the living room.

"June, June, quick! Heinz is trying to kill a poor squirrel."

"Heinz!" June shouted, running into the yard. The

3

screen door banged behind her. "Stop it!"

But it was too late, and when June saw the mangled body of the squirrel, she began to cry. She sat on the grass sobbing.

Carla had not left the kitchen. She turned back and saw that Baby Patty had pulled up on the coffee table, a first. No doubt her mother would make a big deal out of that, too, Carla thought resentfully. She looked around, saw nobody, and quickly ran to the baby and knocked her feet out from under her. Patty hit her head on the edge of the coffee table and began to scream.

Carla flashed into the kitchen and out the back door. She looked with interest as Heinz tore into the lifeless, bloody body of the squirrel. June was nearly hysterical.

"Heinz tried to bite me. He growled at me when I tried to rescue the poor squirrel." She was sobbing uncontrollably.

Carla said nothing.

"June!" their mother shouted. She was holding the baby, rocking Patty in her arms. There was a red mark on Patty's forehead. "Can't I trust you to watch the baby a minute. What are you doing playing outside, leaving the baby alone in the house? She fell and hurt herself."

June jumped up.

"Oh, mother, I'm sorry. Heinz was killing . . . Oh, Patty."

June tried to take the baby from her mother's arms, but her mother just glared at her. June dropped her head and went into the house.

"Into her room, I bet," Carla thought. "She's so stupid."

Chapter 2

Monday, August 18, 2003, Rural Central Texas

The heavy wooden door banged behind Deputy Sheriff Bill Cummins as he entered the Oatville Store. He hitched up his belt, dragged down by the weight of the Glock, but it wouldn't stay above his protruding belly. He looked around the country store. A couple of men sat at one of the worn wooden tables drinking beer. Ceiling fans rotated above the tables, stirring the cool air. A few dusty cans sat on shelves against the back wall along with a few loaves of white bread. Behind the counter waited the proprietor, a middle-aged widow who was the clearinghouse for most of the local gossip. Her blonde hair was curled high on her head. She wore jeans and an azure blouse that brought out the blue of her blue gray eyes.

"You got some rope, Shirley?"

"How much you need?"

"'Bout 30 feet. Gimme a coke, too. Hot out there."

"So what's going on, Bill?"

"Oh, nothing."

"Don't tell me nothing. Some of us live alone out here. I need to know what's happening. I've seen all those horse trailers heading east. Some of those search and rescue men have stopped in here, too."

"Well, keep it to yourself. I can't talk about it, but you don't have anything to worry about."

"This has something to do with that man from Concord gone missing, doesn't it?"

"Might. But I'm not saying."

Bill winked at Shirley and took a sip of his coke.

"Let me have an almond Hershey bar, too."

"Ernest, measure out 30 feet of . . . You wanted the nylon, Bill?"

"Yeah, the half inch."

5

". . . thirty feet of half inch nylon."

"You bringing us some rain, Bill?" a strongly built farmer with a square face said.

"I wish. A few more weeks of this and my stock tank will dry up."

"The Janeceks, near me, are already hauling water for their cows."

"Can't afford to keep 'em, and at the price they're bringing, can't afford to sell 'em."

"In Hiram County they've had some pretty good rains," a younger man said. "I'm hauling hay from there. It's pretty good hay."

Ernest came from the back room with the coiled rope tied up. While Shirley rang it up, Bill finished the last bite of his Hershey bar, wadded up the wrapper and tossed it into the trash can behind the counter, hitting dead center.

Outside on the state highway, a tractor trailer rumbled past, followed by a few cars, heading south toward the small town of Graylor, through rich blackland fields of cotton, corn, and milo. A few high cottony clouds floated in an otherwise pale blue sky.

Much more traffic on the roads than when he was a boy. Well, everything was changing, Bill thought. It wasn't the same world. Images of his boyhood arose: the whole family eating hamburgers in this very store on Thursday nights, his father laughing and talking with the other farmers, his mother catching up on all the news of young folk marrying, babies being born—and in that order in those days —while he and his brothers wolfed their hamburgers, then ran outside to play. Bill thought ruefully of his own marriages, a boy by the first, a little girl by the second. His face softened as he pictured Anna, curly blonde hair framing a square little face with dimples.

His gaze fell on the door to the room where plumbing supplies were kept.

"One more thing. I need a float valve for a watering

trough."

"How's Jeffrey?" Shirley asked while they waited for Ernest to return with the float valve. "He playing football this fall?"

"Maybe."

Bill's face darkened. Mary Kay was ruining that boy, waiting on him hand and foot, not requiring anything of him. The boy was hanging out with the wrong kids, didn't want to submit to the discipline of football—to any discipline. Mad at the world, full of raging hormones. Just a matter of time before he got himself in serious trouble, if things didn't change. And he, the boy's father (and a deputy sheriff at that), had him only every other weekend. Mary Kay undercut him at every turn. He and Jeffrey had had such a good relationship in the early years, the little boy following him around, wanting to learn how to do everything. Loved his pony. Was turning out to be a fine little man.

And yeah, during that turbulent time when he and Mary Kay were fighting and fighting until finally he moved out, he wasn't paying enough attention. Went to his head, being single again in his thirties, all those women out there.

Sure enough he was in a bind now. He couldn't be the hard ass all the time or the boy wouldn't want to be around him. When you're fourteen and your mama lets you run all hours of the night, sleep all morning, and then begs to know what you'd like her to fix you to eat, then no, why would you trade that for someone who says, "Get up and get to work"?

"Twenty-three thirteen."

Bill started, saw Shirley looking at him funny. He pulled out his wallet, paid.

Bill took one last look around the Oatville Store, then strode across the worn and pitted concrete floor, hitching his pants one last time and bracing himself for the blast of hot air that awaited him outside the cool, comfortable store.

Chapter 3

August, 1989, Graylor, Texas

"Sweetheart," her daddy said, looking up from his newspaper as Carla twirled into the living room in her majorette uniform. The big shabby arm chair dominated the small room. "What have you got?"

Carla held out an official-looking letter to him.

"An invitation to join the honor society in the fall," he said. "Beautiful and smart!"

"Daddy, can I spend the weekend with Rhonda? Her parents have a cabin up at the lake, and I'm invited."

"I don't really know the Jeffersons. They're new here."

"But Daddy, Rhonda is my best friend. I'll be careful. You know I can take care of myself."

"You do have a good head on your shoulders, I'll say that. Okay, but let your mother know when you'll be back."

"Oh, thank you, Daddy." She kissed him on the cheek and pirouetted out of the room.

It was so easy, she thought, as she skipped down the steps of the tiny frame house she, her two sisters, and her parents were crammed into. Her mother worked all the time, sewing clothes for the three girls, cleaning, cooking, washing. Every time she thought of her mother, she seemed to see her bent over the ironing board set up in the small living room.

Not me, Carla thought. She walked down the tree-lined street of the small town toward Rhonda's house, carrying a few clothes in a backpack. The sidewalk was uneven, tilted and broken in places, and where it ended, Carla descended into the street itself. There was little traffic on the pitted and pot-holed asphalt.

Rhonda lived six blocks north, where the houses were large two-storeys and the grounds spacious and well kept, heritage of Graylor's cotton boom time. Carla climbed the stone steps of the large brick two-storey house and crossed the deep-set porch. Pale pink roses climbed a trellis at the end to her right, lightly perfuming the warm air; the other looked out over a wide side yard. Old-fashioned lacy white wrought iron chairs and matching table sat near a neglected goldfish pond in the shade of tall pecan trees. In the sunlight honeybees hovered among the variegated orange and yellow marigolds bordering the lawn of thick green carpet grass. Carla glanced around, taking in everything.

Rhonda was sitting in the living room with her backpack, flipping through a fashion magazine.

"Dad will be down in a minute to take us to Barbara's."

Carla looked around the room, once again noting the Duncan Phyfe sofa, the heavy silver candlesticks on the sideboard, all pieces the Jeffersons had bought at auction. Too old-fashioned for me, she thought. She sat down on the love seat next to Rhonda and looked at the magazine with her while they waited. Both girls were fascinated by the models and their various outfits.

"You girls have a good time," Rhonda's dad said as he dropped them off at Barbara's house on the north edge of town.

Carla admired the brick ranch house with its sliding glass patio doors in the living room that looked out past the shorn grass of the small back yard to open fields of corn and milo. Even more, she loved to look at the shiny modern appliances in the well-furnished kitchen: the Microwave, the Osterizer, the fancy coffeemaker, the big refrigerator/freezer with its ice maker and filtered water spout, and the electric stove with its double ovens that dominated the work space. Such a contrast with the small wood frame house that Carla and her two sisters were squeezed into, with the worn linoleum in the kitchen, the ancient gas stove, and the scarred and noisy refrigerator. One day she would have a modern gleaming kitchen of her own.

"Why are you carrying backpacks?" Barbara asked.

"Oh, for my bathing suit and stuff. I told Daddy we were going swimming," Carla said.

"Why won't he let you date Leroy?"

"He doesn't like him, maybe because his dad's a farmer. I don't know. Daddy doesn't really want me to go out with anybody. It's so unfair."

Barbara looked sympathetic. She was glad her daddy wasn't so mean.

"Here they come," Rhonda said, as Leroy and Tim drove up in an old Chevy sedan.

"Thanks a bunch, Barbara," Carla said.

"Yeah," Rhonda added.

Carla slid across the front seat next to Leroy, while Rhonda snuggled up to Tim in the back. Leroy headed east, then took the highway north. In the fields, a combine was discharging a steady stream of golden yellow corn into the bed of a waiting truck. The dun stalks would be shredded afterwards. On the other side of the highway, the cotton grew green and sturdy, the bolls open and heavy with white. It looked to be a good year, Leroy thought, intently observing the farmland.

A few miles farther on, he turned right onto a paved county road heading east. To their left, rolling pasture land, and beyond that, the thick green tree line indicated the course of the San Sebastian River. Most of the infrequent farmhouses were small wood frame ones, but an occasional brick ranch house with well-kept barns and sturdy pens indicated a successful farmer.

"How did you swing it?" Leroy asked, draping his arm around Carla and pulling her close.

"Rhonda's parents are going to Dallas for the weekend, and I told Daddy I was going to the lake with Rhonda and her parents. Rhonda said she was spending the weekend with Barbara. Barbara just thinks we're sneaking out for a date, 'cause Daddy won't let me go out with you."

Leroy looked at her admiringly.

"Your daddy doesn't even know you know me," he said, shaking his head.

Where the road made a sharp curve, they passed a large stone two-storey house set back from the black-top. The oldest house in the area, it spoke of former land wealth, and its massive thick walls of protection from marauding Indians. The house was well kept, but its mesquite-choked fields indicated an owner who made his living another way.

A couple of miles farther east, on the other side of the county road, a large square two-storey with upstairs and downstairs porches running the width of the home sat desolate in the broad, flat fields. Long abandoned, it must once have seen carriages rolling up the drive conveying ladies in full skirts, with spirited young men on equally spirited horses trotting alongside, arriving for festive barbecues, and from the spacious grounds, the unending rows of cotton rolling to the horizon.

"Where are we going, Leroy?" Rhonda called out from the back seat. Tim had his arm around her. He was a big blond, strong-looking farm boy whose size made him a good match for Rhonda. She was tall and large-boned, but with the slenderness of youth.

"You'll know when we get there. It's not that far."

Once this land was open prairie with grass belly-high to a horse, a rich and fruitful land crossed by crystal clear streams. Buffalo roamed these prairies, fish coursed the rivers, and small game hid in the thickets. Each season offered its gifts: dewberries in spring followed by wild plum, then summer grapes and cactus pears, and fall nuts and seeds and mesquite beans.

The road angled east, southeast, veering slightly away from the river. Now farmland lay on either side of the narrow county road, with alternating fields of tall dun-colored cornstalks, mid-height russet milo, and short dark green plants with open bolls of white cotton.

It was near sunset when they turned left onto a dirt road that led to the abandoned frame house in the cotton fields. The old barn, still in use, was larger than the farm house. In the distance, the dark tree line showed the course of the San Sebastian River. The boys had cleaned out two rooms of the old house and made up a bed in each of them: sheets and a coverlet on thick foam rubber on the floor. Outside near a hackberry tree they had set up a grill. Four aluminum chairs sat in a semi-circle under the tree. A cooler beneath an antique rose bush held soft drinks. The last rays of the sun touched the red-orange fruit of a pomegranate tree nestled into the corner of the picket fence.

Leroy wrapped his arms around Carla from behind.

"My princess."

Carla half turned and tilted her head up. Leroy stroked her dark hair.

"You are so beautiful." He leaned down and kissed her, gently at first but with growing passion. He cupped a breast in one hand and squeezed. Carla's breath came short, and she turned and pressed against him. He reached behind, underneath her blouse, and began to work at the bra clasp.

Carla pulled away.

"Not now."

Leroy caught his breath and got hold of himself.

"Tim, have you started the fire yet? We need to get those burgers on. Carla's hungry."

Leroy walked over to the cooler, flushing Tim and Rhonda from behind the hackberry, Rhonda hastily buttoning her blouse. She was a good-natured, fun-loving girl, and though she came from a family with much more money than his, she made Tim feel at ease.

The boys set to work and soon had a crackling fire. Pecan smoke drifted through the air. The girls sat on lawn chairs under the hackberry tree, listening to the summer sound of crickets and tree frogs.

In the west, the sky had turned pink and orange above the darkening land. The girls sipped their cokes while the guys tended the meat patties and cracked jokes. A big wooden wire spool served as a table holding sliced tomatoes, lettuce, pickles, and the condiments. A large bag of potato chips next to paper plates and napkins completed the arrangement.

By the time they finished eating, the stars were out and a lone owl hooted nearby. Carla shivered slightly and pressed up against Leroy.

"It's just an owl," he said reassuringly, holding her close. Carla leaned her head trustingly against his shoulder.

Tim and Rhonda were just behind them as they followed the beam of the flashlight into the dark interior of the house. In the innermost room, Leroy led Carla to the bed made up on the floor. Slowly he unbuttoned her blouse and unfastened her bra. As the clothing fell to the floor, he kissed her breasts, first one, then the other, gently at first, then nipping and sucking at them until he heard Carla's cries of pleasure. He pulled Carla's jeans down until she could kick them off, then slipped his hand into her panties, caressing the swell of her buttocks until she was trembling, then sliding his finger into the soft warm folds of her innermost parts, swollen and overflowing with moisture. He felt her contract against his searching finger and heard her cry out. Gently he lowered her onto the bedding and quickly shed his own clothes.

Holding himself above her with one arm, he softly touched her with his penis, lightly exploring the inner folds, moving all around. He heard her breathing quicken, and she arched her back. He played some more, gliding over the silken tissue, just barely entering her, pulling back, moving all around just inside the entrance. Carla's pelvis was thrusting uncontrollably when finally he lowered himself into her. For a moment he was still; then he began to thrust into her, deeper and deeper, harder and harder. She bucked underneath him, both of them in a frenzy now. Faster and faster, harder and deeper, until she screamed out and he fell on her convulsing.

A waning gibbous moon had risen, and the faint light from the open window softly illuminated her pale face framed by the dark tangle of hair spread out on the pillow. Propped up on one elbow, he gazed down at her.

"I love you so much," he said. "I would do anything in the world for you."

Chapter 4

Monday, August 18, 2003, Rural Central Texas

The tree frogs were loud in the darkening twilight and as the light dimmed, fireflies appeared, first one, then another and another until they pricked the darkness in an uneven dance. In the distance, invisible now, lay the shallow waters of Graylor Lake, just where the San Sebastian lost its identity as a river. The men sitting around the fire grilling hamburgers and hotdogs sipped their beers and reviewed the day, all except Jim, who nursed a bottle of water and sat silent. They had found nothing. But for most of the men it had been a satisfying day nonetheless—outdoors, on horseback, rough new territory. After a long day in the saddle in the August heat, a cold beer tasted fine, and the camaraderie of the fire was a welcome break from their everyday commonplace lives.

Jim, too, had once liked his beer, but after Susan's death he had liked it way too much. In fact, he had stayed drunk for most of a year.

A spurt of flame leapt up from the coals where grease had dripped onto the glowing embers. The pop of someone's beer top sounded loud in the momentary silence.

"I ain't never seen a coyote big as that one," one of the men said.

"Some of them must be breeding with dogs, big dogs."

"He didn't seem near 'fraid enough," the first man said. "Bad sign."

"Didn't look like anybody had been on those trails lately," another said.

"Too hot for most people. The campers just hang out by the lake fishing or watching the kids swim."

Jim looked up and spoke for the first time.

"What would you do if you had a dead body to get

15

rid of? You wouldn't be dragging it through the underbrush. At night you couldn't see where you were going and in the daytime someone might see you."

"Well, yeah," one of the men said. "So why are we fanning out from the river in all those thickets?"

"The sheriff's department thinks we should start from the highway and head east on this side of the river all the way to the next north/south road, then repeat on the north side of the river. Some men's minds just work that way."

An insurance adjuster in his working life, Jim had always been a keen observer and a careful thinker. After Susan's murder, he had had to find things out for himself, the hard way. Big city murders were too common, police departments understaffed, and suspicion usually fell on the husband. It had been a close call.

The flames flickered as someone poked the glowing embers, and in the distance an owl hooted. Jim shuddered as he imagined a big steel door clanking shut, locking him into a narrow cell, forever separated from the night sky on the edge of a lake, the whuffle of his horse as he approached with a bucket of oats, the scent of moist earth underneath yellow autumn leaves, the gray of a winter sky above an open pasture, a sea of bluebonnets framed by pale green leaves of distant oak and elm.

By the grace of God he had been spared. Had that file clerk not smuggled his lawyer a copy of the file with the evidence the D.A. had withheld, he might still be withering in a cell like that poor bastard who served twenty-five years for a murder he didn't commit.

That's when he dedicated his life to helping others. After he sobered up, that is.

In the distance a coyote wailed, the refrain picked up by another and another until a chorus of canine voices yapped and howled and chattered, gradually diminishing as the pack faded away. There was momentary silence, as the thread connecting men to the mystery tugged.

The fire burned and warmed the men in their solidarity.

"Well, time to turn in," one of the men said, breaking the spell.

Another tossed his beer can in the general direction of a trash bag.

"Early start tomorrow."

Men checked their horses, most tied to the back of a trailer. Some retired to fancy vehicles with sleeping quarters in the front, stall for the horses behind. One climbed into the back of his pick-up where he had broken a bale, spread out his horse's hay, and placed a sleeping bag on top. Another retreated into a small REI tent set some distance from the circle of firelight. Only Jim remained where he sat, staring into the fire.

Murderers usually went with what they knew. In a rural community like this one, most people knew the lay of the land pretty well. Those high school years, when kids had cars and time and energy, they explored every inch of their world, learning the best places to park and make out, who would let them build a fire to roast wieners—or who wouldn't know about it. Kids seemed aimless, driving around, thrilled with their independence, but they were learning all the same.

This man, the missing man, Jim had been told, was a successful realtor, maybe a little battered by the economic downturn, but not in financial trouble as far as anyone knew. Could he have been involved in drugs? Always a possibility, Jim thought. Terrible what some of these drugs did to you, like meth for example. He just didn't understand these young people—and some not so young. Everybody knew what meth did to you, to your body. Thirty-year-olds looking like ancient crones or toothless old men, all covered in disgusting sores. But who am I to judge, he suddenly thought, remembering the pain that drove him into the depths of a bottle. He wasn't thinking about his liver then.

By all accounts, the missing man had been fit, the

kind that worked out in gyms and ran. Didn't understand that himself. A hard day's labor kept you strong—and accomplished something besides. But because he took care of himself didn't mean the man wasn't mixed up in drugs. People today weren't satisfied with a decent living and a loving family. It was all about possessions and show. Drug money was big and easy—and treacherous.

On the other hand, it could be about a woman. His wife had left him for another man. And there was a big custody battle over their little girl. When it came to murder, those closest to the victim were always suspect. Like with Susan. Unless it was a serial killer. As had turned out with Susan.

Great as his grief was, imagine the bitterness of that family whose wife and mother was murdered in an eerily similar fashion to Susan's death. While the DA was busy concealing evidence and his own trial was delayed, the killer moved on down the road and bludgeoned another woman to death, not twenty miles away. The blood-spotted bandana had contained the DNA found at both murder sites. Jim wondered how the DA and chief investigators could live with themselves.

So back to the problem at hand, the missing man. In all likelihood they were looking for a corpse. Most likely the victim knew his killer. No break-in at his house. The only sign of a struggle blood on the sidewalk. Car in the garage. Someone had lured him out, doubtless someone familiar with the area. In this tidy farming community, the land surrounding the San Sebastian River, taken by the government after the dam was approved, was the wildest. Feral hogs rooted in its brushy bottoms, a few deer bounded into its glades, and coyotes roamed far and wide.

A body is an awkward thing to carry. Access by car, at least most of the way, would be important. Start with the most likely places first, then expand the grid. Those same feral hogs and coyotes would make short work of a corpse.

Tomorrow he'd have to speak to that Deputy Sheriff Cummins.

Chapter 5

August, 1991, Graylor, Texas

"Did you hear Barbara and Joe broke up?" Rhonda spilled red snow cone syrup on her white shorts as she spoke. "Oh, God damn it!"

Carla looked disapprovingly at her.

"Oh, nobody can hear," Rhonda said, glancing around the swimming pool. It lay in the middle of a park, the land donated by a prominent citizen, long deceased, who wanted to provide the children of the town with a refuge in nature. Ducks and geese paddled on a small lake, a pavilion provided space for community events, and small children enjoyed old-fashioned swings and seesaws in the shade of native pecan and elm and an occasional exotic silver leaf maple. The benefactor's idea of natural beauty had been lost in succeeding generations, with open spaces filled in with putt-putt golf and such, but families still gathered by the lake to feed the ducks, the pavilion hosted dances and church fund-raisers, and children of all ages still flocked to the pool. Rhonda and Carla sat on large beach towels spread out on the clipped carpet grass. Rhonda cut her eyes toward the Joe in question, sitting in the lifeguard's chair, and continued. "I don't know what you see in him. He's not nearly as cute as Leroy."

"It's just one of those things. No one knows why two people are drawn to each other. It's like destiny."

Rhonda licked at her snow cone. "Well, whatever. Let's go. The pool's about to close anyway."

"Not yet."

Rhonda didn't argue. Carla was a lot of fun, but she would have her way. Rhonda watched mothers gathering their kids from the pool, some coaxing, some pleading, and some with fire in their eyes, the children of these last coming promptly out of the water.

"Joe's kind of funny, though," Rhonda said

thoughtfully. "Rumors were going around that Barbara was dating one of those Concord boys on the sly. They got into it, and Barbara got mad, said if he didn't have any more trust in her than that . . . Then he got cold and mean and said some nasty things."

"Well, she was spending a lot of time in Concord, seems like almost every weekend."

"Yeah, with her aunt who has cancer. And her cousin Jimmy running around drinking every night, not much help with his mother. I bet they get back together soon, they've gone together for so long."

"Oh," Carla said, suddenly rummaging through her things. She headed quickly to the lifeguard's chair. "Oh, Joe, I've lost my sunglasses, my new sunglasses. My daddy will kill me. Please let me know if anyone turns them in."

Her large dark eyes grew moist.

"Sure thing, Carla, but they're just sunglasses. Don't be so upset."

"But they're very expensive sunglasses. I begged my daddy for them. He'll be so mad if he finds out I've lost them."

"I'll be sure to check."

"Oh, thank you. You're so sweet."

As Carla headed back toward Rhonda, she briefly looked back at Joe and gave him her most dazzling smile.

"Wait, Carla."

Carla paused, half turned toward Rhonda, who was ostentatiously folding her towel and collecting her suntan lotion.

"What are you doing this evening? Maybe I could stop by after I finish up here."

"If you like," Carla said, with a little bit of a flounce.

"Well, you certainly didn't waste any time," Rhonda said as she and Carla walked down the sidewalk together toward Rhonda's house. The sun had lowered, the fierceness of its rays abated, but still the shade of the pecan and elm trees lining Rhonda's street was welcome.

"It was just meant to be."

Carla put her arm through Rhonda's as they walked side by side down the quiet residential street. On the other side, a middle-aged woman cleaning out a flower bed stood up, stretched, and smiled at the sight of the two glowing teenagers walking arm in arm, one tall, one petite, both dark haired and vibrant.

"What will you tell Leroy?"

"Nothing for a while. All he does is work on that farm. I'm so sick of his mother always wanting to show me how to can or something. Have you seen her in that ridiculous old sunbonnet, always slaving away in her garden? Not me."

"Well, ever since his father died, Joe's had to be the man of the family. Good thing he at least graduated."

"What difference does it make? All he'll ever do is work from daylight to dark on that old farm and expect his wife to be just like his mother. No thanks."

"It'll be hard on Leroy. He worships the ground you walk on."

"He'll get over it."

Chapter 6

April, 1992, Austin, Texas

Rich black deep loam gives way to thin soil over caliche and limestone; fields of cotton, corn and milo and pastures of grazing cattle to subdivisions and then to the rolling hills of Austin, some forty miles southwest of Graylor. Even the light is different. Sharp and clear in the daylight, violet just as dusk turns to dark. It was dark now along Town Lake, where Carla and Leroy lingered in the soft spring air.

"But why can't you tell your father about me? Why can't I meet him?" Leroy stood erect. He was deeply tanned and seemed leaner than in his high school days, his body wiry, his arms sinewy and work-hardened. His face, with its regular features and full mouth, was still handsome, but had lost its carefree expression. "I've done well with the farm, and I can support you and my mother both now. I have no reason to hide. I want to meet him man to man. I want to ask for his daughter's hand in marriage."

"Oh, Leroy, you're so old-fashioned."

"All right. Tell him that we plan to be married."

"You just don't know my daddy. I never told you, but . . ." Carla's eyes welled with tears. She choked back a sob.

"What, honey?" Leroy immediately pulled her to him and held her tight.

"You just don't know . . ." Leaning into him, Carla sobbed uncontrollably. She swayed on her feet.

"Here, honey, here," Leroy said soothingly.

He eased her onto a bench looking out over Town Lake. A bull frog croaked, a solo amid the chorus of tree frogs, and a slight wind stirred the moist air. They had been strolling along the lakeside trail, right in the middle of the city. Now that he was doing well with the farm, Leroy liked to make the occasional trip to Austin to treat Carla to a movie and a special meal in a nice restaurant, unavailable in Graylor.

One would never guess, standing underneath tall oak and pecan trees, gazing at the moonlight reflected in the dark waters of Town Lake, cypress and willow sheltering its bank, that up above pulsed and throbbed the heart of a vibrant city.

"You know you can tell me anything." He held her until she ceased crying, except for an occasional shuddering sob.

"I had to . . ." She paused, then took a deep breath and leaned into his chest. "I had to lock my bedroom door every night from the time I was thirteen to keep him away from me."

Leroy went rigid. "That bastard! Did he ever touch you?"

"He tried, but I got away from him. After that, I made sure I was never alone with him."

"I'll take you out of there right now—and tell that son of a bitch why. He had better not try to stop me."

"No, Leroy, no. It would kill my poor mother. She doesn't know. I had to keep it from her all these years."

Leroy was on his feet, pacing. "It all makes sense now, why you always had to lie, why you acted so scared of your father. I just thought he was too stern, too protective of his little girl. God, how could you have kept it in all this time?"

"I had to, Leroy, I had to."

"Oh, Carla, what you've had to go through. And I thought I knew every beat of your heart." Leroy held her gently and stroked her hair, tangling his fingers in the dark ringlets. "I love you so much."

A breeze shivered the leaves of the trees and rippled the waters of the lake, making the reflected moonlight dance. A faint perfume of honeysuckle mingled with the primeval scent of muddy lakeshore.

"You'll graduate in a few months. We can marry in June. I'll keep you safe on the farm forever."

Carla shuddered one last time, but leaned into Leroy's arms.

Chapter 7

Tuesday, August 19, 2003, Rural Central Texas

At first light, men stood around the renewed fire, inhaling its incense and sipping coffee from enameled tin cups.   Horses stamped at flies, chewed their oats, and contemplated the morning.   Jim sat cross-legged, an aerial map spread out across his lap.

"Y'all pick up where you left off yesterday," he said. "I'm going to catch up with Cummins and see if we can't change our approach.   There are a few places it looks like a dirt road goes all the way to the river.   And on some of these farms only outbuildings are left, no houses.   We've got to get permission to go on private land, but I think it's our best bet."

Bacon sizzled in a giant cast iron frying pan, and a middle-aged man flipped pancakes on an improvised griddle balanced precariously over the fire.   Jim staked his horses out in the shade of a hackberry tree, unhooked the trailer from his pickup.   Ignoring the food, he poured a second cup of black coffee, climbed into the cab of his gray F250, and started off for the county seat, some twenty-five miles distant.

The dull red of the eastern sky had paled to faint orange, then faded into a colorless gray.   Now the vast cloudless sky grew bluer above Jim as he traveled down the county road, mostly farmland to his left, pasture to his right. Half a dozen black Brangus cattle were drinking from a stock pond; water dripped from the muzzles of two of the cows, who looked up and stared, hearing the noise of the vehicle.

After Jim rounded the curve by the old McDonavan house rising above its mesquite-threaded pasture, the county road straightened and slightly descended to the railroad track and the state highway beyond.   A red-tailed hawk rose from its perch on a weathered fence post and soared above the pasture toward the San Sebastian in the distance.

Once Jim crossed the north/south state highway,

another state highway roughly followed the meanderings of the San Sebastian River flowing from the west, its two forks joined together at the county seat.   Jim took in the countryside. On his left, just beyond pasture alternating with crop land, a thick line of trees indicated the course of the San Sebastian River.   On his right, crop land, rising slightly, extended north to the horizon. The road turned and twisted, but forged west. It crossed the San Sebastian so that now the river was on Jim's right, but concealed from view. Sprawling subdivisions of manufactured homes or moderately upscale ones, the inevitable gas stations—watering holes of the automobile age—all announced the imminent appearance of Williamsville, the county seat.

Several blocks west of the century-old Greek Revival county courthouse, a characterless new annex housed most of the county offices, including that of the sheriff.

"Morning," Jim said as he stepped through the office door.

Deputy Sheriff Cummins, leaning back in his chair, feet propped on top of the desk, picked at his teeth with a toothpick. "Morning," he replied, slightly moving the toothpick to one side of his mouth. His greying dark blond hair was cropped close, emphasizing his large head and square face.

Jim felt the old antagonism rise up. He worked with law enforcement people, had to, and for the most part respected them. But he couldn't forget the outright bias that had nearly ended his freedom. No, he hadn't broken down when the officers told him about Susan. His hawk-like face gave nothing away. A proud man, he had grown up in an era of self-contained emotions, when self-control was required of a man. And too, he was in shock. "It's not true, it's not true!" kept reverberating in his head, even as he stared at the officer without speaking. Susan was sleeping peacefully when he had left that morning.

Disbelief, horror, grief fought over him. And stinging

regret, for they had argued fiercely that night. Now he would never be able to apologize, make up . . . hold her in his arms once more . . . No, his face had been a stone mask.

The two men stared at each other.

"What can I do for you," Cummins finally said.

Jim got a grip on himself.

"I've been looking at this map, here," he said, making an effort to soften his tone and unrolling the map as he spoke. "And I've been thinking about the best way to go about this."

Bill gazed at the lean man before him, wondering about his intensity. This man was not from around here. What did he care about local murders?

Cummins had lived all his life in the area, gone to Graylor High, married a local girl and when eventually that didn't work out, married another local girl. His was the insularity of a man who knows his own world well, but nothing outside it. No one could be a better neighbor, but he was suspicious of outsiders.

Bill swung his feet heavily off the desk and rolled his chair forward.

Jim spread the map, just where Bill's big feet had been. He leaned all the way across the desk, picked up a paperweight and a pen holder and placed one at either end of the map.

"This is how far we got yesterday—heavy going, and no sign of anything. I'm thinking we might check out these roads first, then investigate these barns and other outbuildings."

Bill watched as Jim traced the points on the map with his finger. For a while he said nothing.

Then, "Have to get permission to go on private property. Don't need it to go on that stretch of government land. Best hiding places there, too, wild as it is. Don't want to overlook something."

"Well, that's just the problem. Pretty hard to carry a body, especially into that thick undergrowth. Couldn't hardly

27

get a horse in there, and the trail alongside the river didn't look like anybody had been on it in a while. Now if we skipped to these dirt roads, checked if they'd been driven on lately, looked into the old barns . . . . We can always come back to the wilderness area, pick up where we left off, if we don't find anything."

Personally, Jim didn't believe a body had been stowed in those thickets, at least not any distance from a dirt road a vehicle could drive on. His men had canvassed the government land, starting from the state highway. A hiking trail followed along the course of the river, the wilderness area varying in width as it paralleled the river. A man could park at the trail entrance and carry a body a little way, veering off the trail and stashing it in a thicket. But the men had searched that area thoroughly, and in fact had gone several miles down the trail, fanning out on either side to examine the underbrush minutely. It didn't make any sense to think a man would lug a corpse for miles and miles. More likely, he would pick one of those dirt roads, drive as far as he could, then cross the landowner's fence and haul the corpse into the underbrush near the river. Even that would be a lot of work. Below the dam, private land went all the way to the river. But then there wasn't that broad swath of undergrowth, either, most landowners keeping their land cleared except for a thin line of trees along the river bank. If he were concealing a body, Jim thought, and knew the land like a local, he would go for an abandoned barn.

Bill stared at Jim, not even trying to conceal his distaste. Who did he think he was, anyway? Yeah, he'd heard good things about the Search and Rescue team, but this wasn't a lost child or a wandering Alzheimer's patient, where you gladly took all the help you could get. His men could find a dead body; it wasn't going nowhere.

It hadn't been his call, even though he was in charge of the search. The sheriff had connections in the north part of the state, where Search and Rescue was based. Bill figured the sheriff was aiming for higher office, wanted to make a little show in the county, maybe get statewide attention, or at least expand his base. Well, he was the one who had to deal with this tense, sharp-featured man. But he also had a job to do.

"Keep going on the government land. I'll get hold of some of these landowners."

Bill swung his chair around to face his computer, tapped it out of sleep mode, started checking email. Conversation over.

"Will do." Jim paused. "And hope the hogs and coyotes don't beat us to the body."

He turned and walked out, leaving the map spread across the desk.

Bill swung back around, studied the map. Then he picked up the phone and started making calls.

Chapter 8

April, 1992, Graylor, Texas

"It looks like Abby will be valedictorian and Joe salutatorian," Rhonda said one afternoon. It was an irresistible spring day, and she and Carla had sneaked out of their last class and were sitting on a bench in the shade of the old pecan trees behind the Graylor High gym. A few high cottony clouds floated in an achingly blue sky. Sunlight, just hot enough to increase the languor of the afternoon, lit up the bright green new grass, while murmuring bees probed the yellow pollen of pink buttercups.

"It doesn't matter. Joe already has an offer from that new tech company. They're even going to pay for him to take classes at Concord so he can get his Associate's."

"Think you'll like living in Wirtz?"

"Anything would be better than this dump. Besides, Joe's parents are letting us live in their rent house free, so we can save money."

"I wish you could go to the community college with me."

"Me, too, but there's no way. June made such a mess of her life, marrying that man that beat her, and now she and her two kids are back, living off my parents. And of course there's Patty, always so full of herself. She'll be a freshman this fall. You can't believe what it's like in our house. I can't wait to get out of there."

Rhonda leaned back on the bench, stretching her long legs out, her feet nestled in the new green grass, and gazed up at the brilliant blue sky.

"I don't even care about going, but I have to do something, and my grades aren't good enough to get in A&M. I don't really know what I want to study, but my parents will pay for me to find out, as long as I live at home. They won't let me go to Brenham 'cause it's such a party school. Now that would be fun."

"I hear you can make good money in the medical field."

"I guess. Here comes Joe."

Carla sat up straight, then leaned over to whisper in Rhonda's ear.

"Don't make fun of his car."

They were both laughing, Carla's eyes sparkling, as Joe drove up in his battered but serviceable old Chevy.

"I had to drive all over looking for you," Joe complained.

"We had to hide out. We couldn't stand to be cooped up with old Haney a minute longer. And it's so beautiful out here under the trees."

"Besides, Carla doesn't even have to take the sociology final. And I can always BS it."

Both girls climbed into the worn front seat, Carla next to Joe slipping her hand onto his leg and caressing it.

"Just drop me off at Rhonda's."

Carla gave Joe's leg an extra squeeze and looked at his profile until he turned his eyes from the road toward her.

"I know you have to work late tonight."

Her eyes expressed a longing and a promise, and he thawed.

"Friday night," he said huskily.

Chapter 9

August, 1992, Graylor, Texas

"So what did you tell Leroy?" Rhonda was really curious. As soon as school was out, Carla had gone to Missouri to visit her aunt and help out with the children for two months, and Rhonda had heard nothing from her all that time. Now they were sitting in Rhonda's living room on the Duncan Phyfe sofa, admiring her bridesmaid's dress.

"Nothing. I sent him a copy of our wedding announcement anonymously."

"Carla!"

"Well, what could I say? It was just one of those things. How can you explain destiny to someone? He would never understand."

"I heard he went crazy after you went to Missouri. Said all kinds of wild things to your father. They had to call the police."

"Yes, it wasn't a fun time when I got back. Daddy had to get a restraining order against Leroy he was so afraid for me. I'm so glad Joe and I are moving to Wirz. I had to explain to Daddy how I ever got mixed up with such a psychopath, and all the time he knew nothing about it. It wasn't easy."

"I'm sure you managed."

"Rhonda!" Carla's eyes flashed.

"Okay, okay, just kidding. Still, I just don't understand why you gave up Leroy for Joe."

"You wouldn't understand. How can we control our destiny? There's just something that links me to Joe, an unbreakable bond that I can't explain. I couldn't explain it to Leroy or to you, not even to myself. It just is."

Rhonda looked at Carla admiringly. "That's so deep."

"But you know," she went on, "Leroy hasn't been the same. While you were gone, he tried to fight Joe, but Joe wouldn't fight. Leroy was screaming he was a coward and making such a scene Leroy's buddies had to drag him off. And now they say he gets drunk every weekend, and if it weren't for his mother, would have taken off for South America. And may do it anyway."

Carla looked solemn. "Well, I'm sorry. But I couldn't have made him happy on that farm. He should have known that."

"This is such a pretty color on you," Carla said, holding the deep rose gown up next to Rhonda. "I'm so excited. I know it's a small wedding, but you've always been my very best friend, my only really close friend. I don't need any other attendant."

"You will be so beautiful. I just hope Joe understands what a prize he's getting."

Chapter 10

Tuesday, August 19, 2003, Williamsville, Texas

By noon Deputy Sheriff Bill Cummins had contacted most of the landowners. He had picked up his hat and turned toward the door when the phone rang.

"Jeffrey won't mow the yard and he's rude to me."

"Now Mary Kay . . ."

"I came home from work to cook his lunch, and he won't even get out of bed." Mary Kay was sobbing.

"You let him stay out all hours, you don't have any rules . . ."

"But he's just a boy and it's summer. He ought to be able to spend time with his friends."

And likely to stay a boy, too, Bill thought, but said, "Well, what do you want me to do about it."

"You're his daddy. You need to see he does the right thing."

"Mary Kay, you wanted custody, with me just having him every other weekend."

"Yeah, and you running around every night, chasing every skirt in town. Fine example for a boy. And how many meals would you have cooked for him, how many doctors' appointments . . ."

"All right, all right. Let's focus on the problem at hand. Is Jeffrey going out for football this year? Practice starts in just a couple of weeks. Two-a-days should keep him busy and on track."

"I don't want him to. Too many boys die in the August heat. It's too dangerous."

"Mary Kay, you can't keep that boy tied to your apron strings. He's going to bust loose one way or another, and the way he's going, it's not going to be a good way."

Mary Kay was crying harder now.

"You're a deputy sheriff. Do something!"

Bill took a couple of deep breaths and gripped the desk hard.   Finally he said, "I'll try to talk to him this afternoon."

~ ~ ~

About 2:00 o'clock, Bill swung by what used to be his house in Graylor and knocked on the door. Jeffrey came to the door barefoot, yawning.

"Hi, son."

"Hi."

"Want to ride with me out to the government land? I need to check on the search."

"I'm hungry."

"Well, we could pick you up a burger on the way out. The Search and Rescue horse team is out there."

"Okay."

The two rode in silence while Jeffrey consumed his burger and fries.   Bill was at a loss as to how to start the conversation.

The sun beat down from a cloudless sky, reflecting off hoods of the infrequent cars they passed. The sky was a light blue, paling toward the horizon, as though whitened by the intensity of the sun.

Bill drove north on the state highway, a part of his mind observing the fields: a combine pausing in its journey up and down the rows to pour a stream of rusty red milo into the bed of a waiting truck; a tractor shredding the long rows of corn stubble, a cloud of dust following in its wake.

He turned right on the county road paralleling the San Sebastian River in the distance, the thick line of trees indicating its course. Maybe it was better just to see how things developed.

The search was temporarily halted during the intense afternoon heat. Bill pulled into the camp ground near the lake that shimmered in the distance. Horses tied in the shade of a few scrub elm and hackberry trees switched drowsily at flies, occasionally shifting from one hip to another.

Jeffrey looked with interest at the tethered horses. He had long since outgrown the pony of his childhood, and now that his parents were divorced, didn't go out to the farm much. He eased over to a stout palomino gelding and gently put his hand out. Soon he was stroking its nose. He loved the smell of horse sweat and leather.

Jim was sitting in the shade of a pecan tree, patching the two halves of a broken rein together when Bill walked up. He had punched two holes at the end of each piece of leather and was pushing a strand of latigo leather through one set of holes. Jim glanced up, but then looked back down and continued threading the latigo leather through the parallel set of holes. He evened the two ends of the leather string, then tied a tight square knot.

"I've got permission from most of the landowners."

Bill unrolled the big map he was carrying and stood there.

"Pull up a chair," Jim said, indicating a battered lawn chair folded and leaning against the side of his horse trailer. He made no move to stand up.

Bill unfolded the chair, placed it next to Jim's, and sat down heavily. The two men studied the map while Bill went over the particulars.

"These gates don't have locks, and the landowners said you're free to ride through and search their property. Haven't got ahold of the owner of the Wentrcek place yet. Man lives in Houston and leases it out." Bill put a big stubby finger on the map, indicating a place pretty far east where there was a big barn, but no house.

Jim nodded. "Looks promising. We'll follow these dirt roads to the river, fanning out to the sides. But if it was me, I'd go for some outbuilding or abandoned barn, like that one." His lean brown finger pointed to the Wentrcek place.

"I can track down who's leasing the place now and get

permission that way. Just takes a little doing."

Bill got heavily to his feet. Jim set aside the repaired reins and stood up, too. His lean, spare body and hawk-like face contrasted sharply with Bill's hefty body, broad square face, and protruding gut. The two men stood silent for a moment, Bill looking around the campsite, Jim waiting.

A little distance away, Jeffrey was still patting the palomino gelding and inhaling its aroma. For a moment, Bill saw the little Jeffrey in his cowboy boots and hat, proudly seated on his dappled gray pony, big smile on his face. Bill's throat tightened and he took a deep breath. Jim glanced sideways at the big man, then away.

The two men walked over to the horses and Jeffrey.

"Like that big boy?" Jim asked.

"Oh, yes. Is he yours?"

"Yeah, him and that big roan next to him. Good quiet horses, both of them."

There was a longing in the boy's eyes that both men noticed.

"You ride much?"

"Used to. Don't have a horse anymore."

"You want to try out the palomino? That is, if your dad's got the time."

"Oh, yes." Jeffrey looked questioningly at his father.

"Sure, son."

The two men stood awkwardly together while the boy and horse trotted away from the camp into the bright sunlight. The big gelding had an easy gait, his powerful haunches moving rhythmically above the dun grass. The boy sat easily in the saddle, his body synchronized with the motion of the horse.

Bill had a sudden idea, but didn't know how to broach it. Jim must have read his mind.

"You know, the boy's welcome to ride with us, if you don't mind him seeing what we find. Got the two horses, and I'd just as soon ride the roan."

"I'd appreciate that. The truth is, he needs to get a taste of the real world. I mean, he's a deputy sheriff's son, so he knows some things. But he mostly lives with his mother. And I can see how much he likes riding that horse of yours."

Jeffrey had urged the big gelding into a slow canter, a rocking-horse canter. He made an easy circle around the dusty dry tan field, then slowed the palomino to a walk as he approached the men, big smile on his face, bright sun backlighting the picture of horse and boy.

"Rides nice, don't he."

"Real nice."

"Son, Mr. Bowman here says you'd be welcome to ride with the men. Do you want to?"

"Yes!" Jeffrey's eyes lit up and he sat up straighter.

"It's hot dirty work, and there's rules you have to follow. There's no quitting in the middle of it just because you're tired and thirsty. But if you're willing to abide by the rules, I'd be proud to have you join us. You can ride the palomino. We start real early, while it's still a little cool."

"Dad, can we go get my tent so I can set it up here?"

"If that's okay with Mr. Bowman."

"Fine by me."

Chapter 11

October, 1993, Wirtz, Texas

The screen door banged behind Carla as she entered the kitchen of the small house in the small town of Wirtz carrying bags of groceries. She set them on the counter and looked around at the clean but dingy kitchen. The old refrigerator hummed. From outside came the thump, thump, thump of a basketball as the neighbor kid shot baskets, over and over and over. She was sick of it all. Sick of this neighborhood, sick of this old frame house, sick of her job clerking at the convenience store, sick of Joe.

She put the groceries away in her carefully organized cabinets and tidy refrigerator, and started supper. As she chopped up onions and bell pepper, the tension slowly seeped out of her body. She sautéed them, then added the hamburger meat. As it browned, she reviewed her options. If she had a chance to go to Concord Community College, you could believe she wouldn't flunk out like Rhonda. How stupid.

She put rice on to boil, then cut it back to simmer. There were plenty of jobs in the medical field. She didn't think she could stand emptying bedpans all day long, but surgery would be fascinating, especially if she were a trauma nurse. But it was a long road to get there, first an associate's degree, then a bachelor's, then a certification exam.

She rinsed and dried the iceberg lettuce, broke it up into small pieces and dropped them into the salad bowl. Only two years to become a med tech. And radiology would be interesting. She peeled and sliced a cucumber, then chopped up a couple of little green onions.

Outside, the thumping of the basketball ceased as the boy was called in to supper. A mockingbird settled onto the bough of an elm tree, visible from the kitchen window, to survey the world. A gray cat eased to the base of the elm, tail twitching, and looked stealthily upwards. The mockingbird soared, its tail feathers and unfurled wings flashing white.

Joe wasn't making enough money yet for her to quit her job, little as it paid. In fact, not until he got the two-year certificate would he be making decent money. Besides, she was getting really sick of him. She had thought he was ambitious, but here he was plodding along, taking a class or two at a time—paid for by his company. At that rate, no telling how long it would take. Give her a chance, and she would seize it.

She added Hamburger Helper and water to the skillet and stirred.

The mellow October light of late afternoon suddenly filled the little kitchen with a golden glow, illuminating the sink where Carla rinsed the cutting board and washed the knife. She swabbed the worn counter, now brightened by the sun, and swept the vegetable leavings into the cup of her hand and deposited them in the trash. The sun dropped lower, the light changed once again, and the drab colors returned. In recompense, a hint of coolness wafted in from the open window above the sink. A light breeze fluttered the white curtains.

Carla heard the loud old Chevy pull into the carport.

"Hey, honey," Joe said, coming in the kitchen door with a six pack under his arm.

Carla smiled. "Supper's almost ready."

Joe popped a beer and sat down. "Want one?"

"No, thanks. Don't you have class tonight?"

"It was cancelled. Which suits me fine. The Cowboys are playing tonight." He propped his feet up on another chair and took a long swig of his beer. "Mmm. Smells good."

Carla finished setting the small kitchen table, which was close enough to serve from the stove. She had covered the chipped and stained table top with a red and white checked, plasticized tablecloth that was easy to wipe off, but the spot of color simply emphasized the contrast with the worn kitchen counters and sad linoleum.

Joe got up to open another can of Bud, then sat down with a satisfied air while Carla served him a plate.

Afterwards, while Carla washed the dishes, Joe took more beer into the living room and turned up the TV.

"Don't you want to come watch, honey?"

"No, thanks."

In the small bedroom next to the kitchen, Carla sat down before the computer that rested on a battered wooden table. It had taken her a long time to save enough for the computer, but she was determined.

Online, she found the program for Concord's med tech associate's degree and the schedule of courses for the spring semester. She could pay for at least one class. Joe didn't have to know how she had been holding back a little money at a time from her measly paycheck.

She turned off the computer and got ready for bed. When she came out of the bathroom, she saw Joe asleep on the couch, the end table littered with beer cans. She turned off the lights in disgust and crawled into bed.

Chapter 12

Tuesday, August 19, 2003, Graylor, Texas

Mary Kay had just returned from work when Bill and Jeffrey drove up. She was a petite, trim woman with dark brown hair, brown eyes, and small, regular features.

Jeffrey jumped out of Bill's pickup and ran back to the garage for his camping equipment. Bill walked up to the front door of the brick house he had once lived in and knocked.

"Come on in."

Mary Kay had put a pot of coffee on, her usual routine after work. She moved quietly and efficiently about her well equipped kitchen. It was light and airy, and she had put a lot of thought into decorating it. A cup towel embroidered with yellow daffodils hung by the stainless steel kitchen sink, and sturdy oven gloves with a brown cross-hatch pattern hung by the stove. To the left of the back door, narrow walnut shelves displayed various curios: ceramic frogs, a pair of elves, a little statuette of Mary with a shepherd's crook standing by her lamb, a shiny black ceramic horse and an even smaller bronze one.

"Want a cup?"

"No, thanks." Bill was standing by the door from the hallway, just inside the kitchen. "Jeffrey wants to spend the night at the government land and ride with the men tomorrow."

"You're not going to let him!"

"Well, yes."

"You don't know those men. They could be child molesters, anything. Alone, by himself, with strange men, none of whom are from around here!"

"The Search and Rescue Team is a fine organization with a state-wide reputation. They find lost children and Alzheimer's patients. Jeffrey will be in good hands."

In the last few hours, Bill's opinion had completely changed, but he was unconscious of the process. He was unaware of any irony in his defense of Jim, the man he had been so suspicious of that very morning.

"And dead bodies! I don't want Jeffrey exposed to such things."

"He's not likely to see much. You know, I didn't realize how much horses meant to him. He's got his heart set on riding with the men tomorrow."

"No, he's not going."

"Then you're going to tell him, and I'm not going to back you. You make a mess of raising him, then come crying to me. But you block me at every turn. I'll keep quiet, but Jeffrey knows it's all right with me. You tell the boy no and you deal with it."

"It's not fair, you don't support . . ."

"What's not fair?"

"Oh, Jeffrey, honey. I need you to stay here with me tonight."

"What! But Dad, you said . . ."

"I think I'll have that cup of coffee after all," Bill said, walking to the stove and pouring himself a cup. He sat down at the kitchen table, stirred in two teaspoons of sugar, added a generous amount of cream, and leaned back in his chair. He took a deep, appreciative sip and looked up at mother and son. "You still make the best coffee, Mary Kay."

"Jeffrey, I don't want you out there in the wilderness with strange men."

"But Mom, it's okay."

Jeffrey turned toward his dad, but Bill was taking a deep interest in the curios displayed on the decorative shelves on the back kitchen wall.

"You stay here with me!"

"I'm not a baby. I'm fourteen years old. And Mom, you should see the horse Mr. Bowman is letting me ride."

Mary Kay looked helplessly at Bill, who was now

seriously contemplating his cup of coffee.

"How long do you think it would take you to finish mowing that lawn, son?"

"I can do it in forty-five minutes."

"Better get started, then."

Jeffrey rushed out the back door and soon they heard the roar of the mower starting up.

"Let him go, Mary Kay. He's going to hate you if you don't."

Mary Kay looked beaten.

"If anything happens to him . . ."

"He'll be fine."

Bill stood up and headed out the back door.

"I'll pick you up in an hour, son," Bill said as he walked through the back yard.

Already Jeffrey had made a pretty good dent in it. He paused with his hand on the mower.

"Yessir, I'll be ready."

Chapter 13

April, 1994, Wirtz, Texas

Carla raised the old wood frame window and sighed with pleasure. The soft night breeze entered carrying the scent of honeysuckle and the watermelon smell of new-mown grass. She had received the highest grade on her most recent exam in her first community college class. If only she could go full time. But no point in thinking about that. For now, it was a beautiful spring evening. She was glowing with youth and health, and the rising tide of spring was working its magic on her. Joe would be back from his class soon. Beforehand, she had made him an early dinner of his favorites —chicken fried steak, mashed potatoes and gravy, green bean casserole—and iced tea, which she had insisted on.

Carla slowly undressed and put on a filmy black negligee, Joe's favorite, but one she seldom wore. She let down her shoulder-length black hair that hung in ringlets and brushed it until it shone. She put a drop of perfume behind her ears and on the inner surface of her thighs.

When she heard Joe unlocking the back door, she slipped into the kitchen and leaned with her back against the refrigerator door.

"Honey," Joe said in surprise as he entered and saw her, the black hair and black negligee dramatic against the white refrigerator humming behind her. He came close. As he reached around her for the refrigerator door to get his customary beer, Carla leaned into his arm until it was half encircling her.

"I have a better idea," she said, pressing up against him.

He hesitated, the beer still present in his thoughts, but the soft warm body, half revealed by the diaphanous gown, now leaning into him, the faint mysterious perfume floating in the air—the humdrum married routine dropped away. Joe pulled her to him and caressed the smooth silky fabric covering the lush warm body. He throbbed with desire.

"Pretend it's the first night," Carla whispered, "and carry me to the bed."

Joe swept her up in his arms.

"You're so strong."

In the middle of the bed where he had deposited her, Carla turned on her side facing him while he struggled out of his clothes and slipped on a condom. Carla opened her arms to him, but she stopped him when he drew up her negligee and attempted to mount.

"Not yet."

She drew his head to her bosom. He kissed and nursed her breasts as she gave little cries of pleasure. He tried once more to move on top of her, but she gently pressed his face down lower. He kissed her stomach as she writhed to the beat of her desire.

He paused, and she pressed his head lower.

Suddenly he jerked away.

"I don't like that!"

In the dark, he couldn't see the flash of her black eyes and the scowl across her face.

Carla released his head and lay panting on her back. Joe crawled on top of her and began the staccato beat.

Chapter 14

Tuesday, August 19, 2003, Rural Central Texas
"Evening," Bill said as he and Jeffrey walked up to the fire pit where the men were gathered. The sun was low in the cloudless western sky. A faint orange, beginning to deepen, heralded the approaching night.

"Evening," Jim replied. "Men, this here is Deputy Sheriff Cummins' son. He's going to help in the search tomorrow. Name's Jeffrey."

There were murmurs of "Hey, Jeffrey," and a few nods.

"Better set your tent up, son, while there's still light."

"Any place," Jim said, in answer to Jeffrey's inquiring look.

Jeffrey chose a spot under a hackberry tree not far from where the horses were tied and was soon busy with the tent. He carefully set the poles and the double roof, tightened the ropes, then tapped down the stakes. Finished, he stood back and admired his handiwork.

After the momentary interruption of the new arrivals, the men around the fire resumed their conversation. The man who had appointed himself fire tender continued feeding sticks into the flame. A man popped a beer tab.

"You on duty, Sheriff?"

"Naw."

"Have a beer."

"Thanks," Bill said, catching it deftly as the man on the other side of the fire tossed it to him.

Jeffrey unrolled his sleeping bag inside his tent, looked around with satisfaction, then rejoined his dad and the other men. He dug around in his cooler and brought forth a string of red wieners wrapped in white butcher paper. His dad pointed to the improvised picnic table.

"Put it over there with the other food."

The roaring fire had settled down to glowing coals,

and the self-appointed cooks began setting meat patties and wieners on the grill. It was dark now, and the crickets and tree frogs serenaded. Fireflies winked outside the circle of firelight. Bill took a deep sip of his beer and wished he'd thought to bring a six pack. He looked at the flames highlighting men's faces, listened to the sounds of the woods, heard the banter of the men. He should have been taking Jeffrey camping.

"Why don't you join us?" Jim said. "Plenty of food."

He had told Linda he would be late. Anna would already be in bed. He looked at Jeffrey, on the edge of the circle.

"Yeah, thanks. Son, you got any cokes in that cooler?"

Jeffrey came over to his father and began to rummage around in the cooler.

"Hell, I got plenty," said the man on the other side of the fire, and tossed another beer to Bill, who caught it easily.

Bill walked some distance from the group, pulled out his cell phone.

"Go ahead and eat, honey. I'll grab something. . . . No, I've got to take care of something. . . . Well, I'm sorry, but I told you I would be late. . . . . You married a deputy sheriff. . . . . I'll see Anna in the morning. . . . . Oh, okay. . . . . Hi, sweetheart. Be good. I'll see you in the morning. Me, too. . . . Don't wait up for me, Linda. I'll be late. Okay. Bye."

Bill took a long drag from his beer and returned to the group. He put a hand on Jeffrey's shoulder. The boy didn't get enough of his time, he knew that. It was difficult, having a second family. Maybe if he had worked harder at it with Mary Kay . . . There were problems in any marriage . . . But then Anna's softly rounded face and big blue eyes rose before him and his heart melted. He couldn't wish that undone. A spurt of flame momentarily illuminated Jeffrey's face. He looked lost, as though yearning to be part of this fraternity, but unfamiliar with its rules. Bill knew he hadn't done right by his son. He wasn't there day by day to teach him. And Linda resisted any time away from her and Anna. Like tonight. He didn't know how they did it, but women had a way of sucking you into their orbit, so that gradually you just forgot about other things.

Bill shook himself and drained his beer. The man across the fire reached into his cooler.

"No, thanks, but I got to be going. Son," he said, turning to Jeffrey, "you listen to Mr. Bowman here. He's in charge of this search. If you need anything, you've got your cell phone?"

"Yessir."

~ ~ ~

It wasn't late when Bill reached his home in Williamsville. He hadn't stayed to eat and he was hungry. Linda barely glanced up from her TV program when he let himself in.

"Hi, honey."

"Hi."

Bill flipped the light on in the kitchen. It was spotless, everything put away, the coffee maker set for the next morning. He poked around in the refrigerator, made himself a cheese sandwich, wished he had another beer. Linda didn't believe in keeping beer in the refrigerator, said it would become a habit. She drank an occasional beer herself, but didn't much care for it. Bill thought about taking his sandwich into the living room. Instead, he sat at the kitchen table, opened a bag of potato chips, sipped at a coke, took a bite of his sandwich. He knew from experience, the less he said, the better. Linda would be over it in the morning. When Anna came running into their room and crawled into bed with them, shouting "Daddy, Daddy," life would resume its normal course. Linda would pad down the hall to the kitchen, push the coffee maker button, start bacon frying, pop frozen waffles into the toaster. A tall blonde who carried her weight well, Linda believed in starting the day off right. Anna would be shrieking with laughter as he tossed her up in the air. Then he would head down the hall for his first cup of coffee for the day. Soon Linda would be off to her job as a bookkeeper, Anna to daycare, Bill to his office in the courthouse annex, all the cheerful rituals of everyday life.

Out in the wilderness area, Jeffrey lay alone in his tent, his heart set on riding a palomino gelding.

Bill stood up suddenly. He washed his plate and mayonnaise knife, placed them in the drain, and headed off to bed.

~ ~ ~

Jeffrey lay in his tent, listening to the night sounds, sweating. The swelling chorus of crickets and tree frogs, just outside his tent, sounded loud. He wasn't used to going to bed this early or doing without air conditioning. One by one the men had retired for the night. Only one man had a tent like Jeffrey, a young man with an REI tent, though of course a man in his twenties seemed old to Jeffrey. When only Jim and Jeffrey were left around the fire, Jim had told him the history of the palomino gelding.

"Driving home a different way one day, I saw this skeleton of a horse in a bare pasture, head hanging. Couldn't stand it so I found out who owned him, made the guy an offer, and he was glad to sell. Some of these city folk get enthusiasms, then lose interest. If it's a boat, dry docked and deteriorating, doesn't hurt anything except maybe their pocketbook. A horse is a different matter."

"How long did it take him to get well?"

"Sooner than you'd think. A couple of months. Wasn't anything wrong with him except starvation. I had good grass and gave him extra feed. He turned out to be a fine horse. He'll do anything you ask."

"Wish I still had a horse."

"Well, time to turn in. We've got a long day ahead of us. Better check the horses one last time."

Jeffrey leaned up against the big palomino and patted his neck. Jim walked back with Jeffrey, saw him into his tent nearby, then headed for his own rig.

Now Jeffrey lay in his own sweat, hot and itchy. Finally, listening to the occasional stamp of a restless horse and the hoot of a distant owl, he fell into the deep sleep of the young.

Chapter 15

June, 1995, Wirtz, Texas

"Whatever happened to your friend, Rhonda?" June asked. She was slicing pickles and onions and arranging them on a tray in Carla's small kitchen.

"She's going to Concord College again. But this time she's actually doing the work. Sitting around the house for a semester doing nothing cured her."

"What's she majoring in?"

"Elementary education." Carla was mixing the dressing on the cole slaw while keeping an eye on the pinto beans simmering on the stove.

"I would love to be an elementary school teacher," June said wistfully. "That would be my dream job, working with little children. Having summers off to be with the boys."

She glanced out the kitchen window at her two sons, four and six, kicking a soccer ball around the back yard, not far from the men tending the grill. Bright sunlight etched the scene: the black and white soccer ball rolling across the close-cropped green grass, pursued by two vigorous little brown-headed boys; off to the side by the grill, the men standing relaxed, beers in hand.

June's dark brown eyes were thoughtful. Her features were unremarkable, but she was slim and neat, and when she smiled her plain face lit up with an inner warmth. She continued looking out the kitchen window at the men and her two little sons. The soccer ball, deflected from its intended course, rolled up to the grill. Joe stopped it with his foot. A little above the average height, lean and lanky, he had been a decent athlete, though not outstanding. He had the stringy muscles of the farm boy of his body type. He hauled back and kicked the ball hard, laughing as the two boys took off after it like a couple of untrained border collies chasing sheep.

"Joe is good with the boys. You're lucky to have him. I know he'll be a good daddy. Not like . . ."

"Don't even say his name. I don't know why you let that man treat you that way."

"You know I didn't want to be a burden on Momma and Daddy. They're barely getting by as it is. And what could I do?"

"So why did you leave him?"

"When he turned on Jason and Daniel. If it had been just me . . . But the night he slammed Jason against the wall, I waited until he had passed out. Then I bundled up the boys and walked to the convenience store and called Momma. That was it."

"Why didn't you just take the car?"

"He always kept the keys so I couldn't go anywhere without asking. And he would check the odometer before and after. And also time me."

"Let's talk about something else." Carla was afraid she would shout, "You're so stupid, you've always been so stupid!"

Outside Joe and a couple of his buddies from work burst out laughing. The one telling the story reached into the cooler for another beer, while another man took up the thread. The bright sun lit up the grill and illuminated the group of men whose easy camaraderie arose from shared experience and a common approach. Work should be hard and life fun.

"It's nice to get away for a while," June mused. "The boys are having such a good time hanging out with the men. Don't get me wrong, Momma and Daddy love their grandkids, but they're not as young as they used to be. And Patty is a handful. I sometimes think it's hard for her having older parents. She's in the band and I'll bet will be a majorette like you. She's pretty like you, too, but there the resemblance ends. She's so headstrong, so rebellious. In fact, a little wild when it comes to boys, and she talks back to

Daddy. Always getting grounded."

She's stupid, too, Carla was thinking. "What about her grades?"

"Oh, they're pretty good. Not as good as yours and mine, but only because she doesn't care as much. Daddy says you never gave him one bit of trouble all through high school. Just that mess with Leroy after you graduated—which he says he never did understand. To tell the truth, I never did either."

"Well, I guess I really don't either. I mean, I'd never been out of Graylor. I didn't know there were such troubled people in the world. I learned my lesson, though."

"Yes, Joe seems like such a steady, dependable person."

"He is that."

"Carla, honey," Joe called out, as if on cue, "the meat's ready."

"Bring it on in, sweetheart. Everything's on the table in here. And June made a wonderful potato salad, just the kind you like."

~ ~ ~

His buddies had left, and Joe had cleaned and put away the grill, tied up the plastic bag full of beer cans. Carla and June had put away the food and finished the dishes.

"Thank you for a wonderful evening," June said, picking up Daniel, who was beginning to whine.

"Here, let me carry him," Joe said, lifting Daniel out of June's arms and taking Jason by the hand. "C'mon, guys."

"I'm so happy for you," June whispered as she and Carla hugged goodbye.

"We'll do it again soon," Carla said.

"Honey," Joe said when they were alone in bed. He was rubbing her back. Carla felt good. She liked the way he massaged her back, gentle but firm. At least he was good at that.

"Mmmm."

"Let's make a baby."

"Not now, Joe.   You know we can't afford one yet. But we could practice what it takes."

Carla's lips curved in a soft smile. She pointed to the bedside table, and Joe obediently drew a pack of condoms from the drawer.

Gently Joe turned her over, caressed her a moment, then slid on top of her. Carla didn't protest. In her mind, the dark-eyed Jamaican with a sun-bronzed body was gliding into her. The white sugar sand spread out around them and the surf beat rhythmically.

Chapter 16

August, 1995, Cottonville, Texas

One thing about this dumb job, Carla thought as she looked up to see who was entering the convenience store, at least when it's slow I can get my school work done. She was wearing tan slacks and a maroon and tan striped knit top that fitted at her small waist. Standing quietly behind the counter, she looked both soft and self-possessed.

"Looks like we might get some rain," the old man said, holding out a twenty to pay for his pack of cigarettes. He was wearing worn jeans that hung loose on his spare body and a faded blue shirt.

"I sure hope so."

Carla gave him her sweetest smile, which is what the old man had mainly come in for. Her dark curly hair hung shoulder length, framing her pale face and dark eyes. She had just finished a chapter and needed a break. Besides, this old man was the store manager's uncle. She would need to adjust her hours so she could leave early on the days she had classes this fall, and although the manager was happy to work with her, it never hurt to have his favorite uncle say once again that she was the prettiest, sweetest little thing he 'bout ever saw.

"How'd your calves do Wednesday, Mr. Krueger?"

"Better than I expected." The old man stood a little taller. "Here, let me have one of those Snickers bars." He didn't much care for candy, but his grandson would eat it.

The door opened and the stranger Carla had seen filling his green Tahoe entered.

"Well, so long."

"Stay out of trouble now, Mr. Krueger." And Carla gave him her roguish smile, which was reflected on his lined and weather-beaten face as he turned and walked out, his step elastic and his shoulders back.

Carla turned to the young man paying for his gas and

gave him his change with a pleasant, business-like smile.

Alone once more, Carla stared out the big plate glass window at the state highway running past the tiny rural town. A little way past this Shell station on the other side of the road were the towering grain elevators. Just before them, a road at right angles crossed the railroad tracks and became Main Street on the south side of the highway and railway. What few businesses there were, were mostly located there: a hardware store, a tire place, a canned goods salvage store, a café.

Although Carla had grown up in the somewhat bigger town of Graylor eight miles west, she had quickly learned all the important farmers and business people here, such as they were. But never would she end up in a place like this. She had scrimped and saved all spring and summer to pay for the two classes she was enrolled in for the fall. Already she was reading the textbooks, which she had bought early.

Once more the door swooshed open. This time it was the manager, a slight young man of about twenty-eight.

"How's it going, Carla, a little slow?'

"Not too bad, Bob. How's that baby?"

Bob's eyes lit up. "Oh, great! He already weighs 15 pounds. He just drinks that bottle right down."

"You going to make a linebacker out of him?"

"Whatever he wants." Bob couldn't keep the grin off his face.

"That's the way. Say, Bob, I'm going to need to leave an hour earlier on Tuesdays and Thursdays when my classes start at the end of the month. Maybe I could make up the time on some other days."

Bob thought a moment. "You know, if you could stay an hour later on Mondays, Wednesdays, and also Fridays, I think that would work with that new clerk I'm hiring. Also, it would give you an extra hour a week."

"That would be great," Carla said, giving Bob her sweet smile.

Chapter 17

February, 1996, Wirtz, Texas

"This isn't right, Carla. I need a good supper when I get off work, and especially when I have to go off to class. A man can't work on an empty stomach. And you're never here."

"Now, Joe, you're a big boy. You can fix your own meals. I'm also working and taking as many classes as you are."

"Part-time. At a convenience store. And why do you have to take classes, anyway?"

"So I don't have to work at a convenience store the rest of my life."

"What you need to do is fix me a good supper and quit running around."

Carla's face darkened, but she turned away as though she were looking to see what was in the pantry and said nothing.

Joe stormed around, opened another can of beer, then sat down at the small kitchen table. Behind him the old refrigerator hummed. Outside children were playing a game of horse at a neighbor's basketball hoop, their taunts and laughter a distant background.

"You can reheat that leftover casserole," Carla said mildly. "Isn't there a game on TV tonight?"

She didn't wait for an answer, but gathered up her books and notebooks from her desk in the other room. Joe was sitting in front of the TV with yet another can of beer in his hand as Carla walked out the door.

I hate him, Carla thought. But as soon as she was behind the wheel, traveling west down the highway toward Concord, her spirits lifted. In twenty minutes she would be there.

The plowed fields, newly planted, were dark in the

evening light. A pale gold and silver sunset, scored by vertical jet trails, filled the horizon. As she drove, the clouds turned a bright copper gold that spread across the western sky. The cloud directly above the now invisible sun reflected a fiery orange as the wide wings of the sunset slowly turned pink. Gradually outlined in purplish gray, then turning dark and darker gray, the clouds merged into deep twilight. And it was over. Only a faint luminescence indicated the horizon as she parked in the college lot.

She had gone over her notes in her mind as she drove; it was all there in her memory, and she knew she would do well on the test. Afterwards, she would go out with Rhonda and her friends. She hoped that good-looking Frank Johnson would be there. One good thing—-the only good thing— about Joe's drinking was that he would be passed out by the time she returned. She didn't understand people's drinking. Rhonda liked her beer and wine, too, though she had settled down some. But she wasn't like Joe, either.

Carla was excited as she headed for her classroom. The campus was brand new and handsome. New subdivisions were springing up nearby, and just down the road was a huge outdoor mall, chain restaurants, a big movie theater. Carla liked feeling she was on the crest of the wave. Someday she would have her own new house in a new subdivision, everything fresh and clean. No more old frame houses in dinky little towns, no more cranky husband whose ambition had fled down a beer bottle.

Carla gathered up her books after class and looked down at the floor, hiding the gleam of triumph in her eyes.

"How'd you do?" the girl who sat in front of her asked.

"Okay, I guess."

"Did you study for it?"

"A little."

"I think I bombed it. So many questions were from that last chapter. I didn't read that one."

"You probably did okay," Carla said, but she was thinking, How stupid can you get. These little girls right out of high school thought they could pass the class without even reading the material or showing up to class half the time. She herself had read everything, underlining the important points to go back over several times. She took good notes and never missed a class. And it paid off. She had aced the test, she knew. That girl that sat in front of her would drop out before the semester was over.

"Hey, Carla!" Rhonda had a big smile on her face. "Let's go." She put her arm through Carla's and they walked briskly out the door.

"How'd you do?"

"Oh, these education courses are so easy. Nothing to them. Any idiot could pass. You just have to show up. How'd you do on your test?"

"Good."

"In that case, let's celebrate." Rhonda was laughing. "Let's take my car."

The bar in the shopping center was crowded. Community college students, employees from the nearby software manufacturer, local residents, mostly younger people in their twenties and thirties. Like the subdivisions and the shopping center itself, the bar was new. Everything was fresh and clean.

"Hey," Rhonda said, spotting a group of people she knew seated at a far table. Carla followed her, the two wending their way through the good-humored crowd. Rhonda was a tall, large-boned, fun-loving woman with a natural poise who attracted friends easily. Wearing a flowing blouse of muted purples and charcoals over a pair of designer jeans, she stood out in the crowd. In her faded jeans and close-fitting blue knit top, Carla was a petite contrast. She quickly sized up the crowd. Frank Johnson was with Rhonda's friends, Carla was glad to see.

"Here, I'll get some more chairs," that same Frank

said, offering his seat to Carla, who had maneuvered herself to Rhonda's right so she would be nearer Frank. He pulled up two more chairs and put himself in the one next to Carla.

"What would you like to drink?" Frank asked her as the tall waitress made her way to their table through the crowd.

"A Coke."

Frank looked surprised.

"That's it?"

Carla nodded, and Frank turned back to the waitress.

"A Coke and a Heineken."

Frank was in his mid-twenties, about medium height but muscular and trim. He radiated masculine energy. Like most of the young crowd, he wore jeans and a t-shirt, but Carla soon found out he sold real estate and was doing well. It was easy to get men to talk about themselves and their work; it was the subject most of them liked best.

Carla sipped her Coke and looked around. Rhonda was telling some story that made everyone laugh. Carla smiled, too. After a while, she touched Rhonda's arm.

"It's time to go."

Rhonda started to object, but stopped herself. It wasn't worth it to try to change Carla's mind. When she was ready to go, she was ready to go. Besides, Rhonda had to admit that Carla was a good influence on her. Granted, her classes were easy, but still she needed to show up for them. Left to herself, it was all too easy to fall back into the party routine. She wondered sometimes where Carla got it. You would never guess, if you didn't know her extremely well, how ambitious Carla was, absolutely single-minded. Rhonda admired that in her friend. It was so different from her own easy going nature. Maybe that's why they were friends, opposites attracting.

All the way down the highway from Concord back to Wirtz, through darkened fields and lighted-up strip malls, the exhilaration of the evening persisted, but when Carla pulled into the carport, her mood darkened.   As she had expected, Joe was sound asleep, and also as expected, beer cans littered the living room.   Carla slipped carefully into bed, remaining as far away on her side as she could in a regular double bed.

Chapter 18

Wednesday, August 20, 2003, Rural Central Texas

"Jeffrey, time to get up. Breakfast is ready, and we've got to get going."

At first Jeffrey covered his head and tried to blot out the sound. Then, suddenly realizing where he was, he shot up.

"Coming."

Jeffrey pulled on his jeans, t-shirt, and running shoes and was out of the tent in a flash, still rubbing his eyes. The smell of frying bacon drifted through the air. Everything looked different in the pale dawn light, the scraggly hackberry trees, the dun grass, the gray waters of the lake in the distance. The air, if not exactly cool, was fresh. Jeffrey couldn't remember when he had last been up this early.

"Grab you a plate," one of the men at the fire said.

"Hear you're going to ride the palomino," said another.

"Uh huh." Jeffrey was busy shoveling down bacon and pancakes.

Jim had saddled both horses, the roan and the palomino. He took a last sip of coffee and waited for Jeffrey to catch up with him, took a deep drag on his cigarette and released a thin stream of smoke. He and Susan had had no children. Somewhere on the West Coast, he had a son, fathered in his youth. Raised by his mother, the boy was estranged from him. Wouldn't return his phone calls—when he'd had his number. Heard he was working for one of those software companies.

It would be a hot day. Not a cloud in the sky, the air still.

"A couple of things you need to know," he said as Jeffrey walked up. "This is slow, tedious work, and you have to keep alert. Look for anything out of the ordinary: a piece

63

of clothing, anything shiny like a cigarette lighter or cell phone, any sign a vehicle has left, like tire tracks. And of course, a body. You got to keep scanning, in front of you, to either side, and even up above. Jack, the stocky guy over there in the red shirt, will give the commands. But if you see something, yell halt and stop. Everybody stays where they are, and that means you, too. Jack will look where you point to. Got that?"

"Yeah."

"It's like a grid, as best we can make it. Everybody has to do their part so nothing is missed."

Jim didn't think they would find anything on this run, but you never knew. He had a hunch about that barn way to the east, but had to wait until Cummins got permission to go on the property.

They loaded the roan and the palomino into the trailer, with its sleeping compartment in front. Jim watched how Jeffrey was with the horses, quiet and sure. Soon the caravan of pickups and trailers, eight in all, headed east on the county road, Jim leading the procession. On their right, plowed fields stretched south. On their left, mostly rolling pasture extended to the tree line that marked the edge of the government land along the San Sebastian River.

About a mile farther on, they passed a cluster of new brick houses on the left, each on about ten acres. A boat on a trailer sat near the rear of one. Two horses grazed in the fenced-in pasture of another. At the last, a kennel of Catahoula hounds sounded the alert as the line of pickups and trailers passed by.

The road veered slightly south, moving farther away from the river. A white two-storey farmhouse sat on a rise, a large pond between it and the road. Two big burr oaks shaded it from the western sun, and an ancient pecan stood on its eastern flank. Behind it the land dropped down to the river, now some distance from the road across a broad swath of pasture land, the coastal Bermuda grass still faintly green, the native grasses now dun colored.   The far line of trees marked the beginning of the government land.

Half a mile farther, Jim slowed and began to look for an aluminum gate with a "Hay for Sale" sign on it.

"There it is," Jeffrey said.   He jumped out of the cab to open the gate.   When all the rigs had passed into the hay field, the last man closed the gate, and the procession started up again.   A quarter of a mile down the field road, a second gate opened into the wilderness area.   Jim pulled off the dirt track and signaled to the rest to park in the hay field.

Trailer gates were opened, horses backed out to calls of "Easy, boy, hup, hup."   Gates clanged shut.   Bridles jangled, saddle leather creaked, and horses moved restlessly, some trying to take off as men mounted up.   Jeffrey swung up into the saddle while the palomino gelding stood rock solid still. Mounted on the roan, Jim addressed the group.

"Remember, if you see anything of interest, halt and shout, "Halt!" to stop the whole group.   Everyone remain in place until the sighting is checked out, including the one who calls it.   We're looking for any sign that anyone's been this way —in a vehicle or on foot.   Don't forget to look in all directions, including up.   Remember that time the body was found hanging from a tree.   We almost missed it.   Okay, let's go.   Jeffrey, you get the gate."

Jeffrey dismounted and opened the gate for the others to pass, the palomino following where he led and backing up out of the way of the gate.   The gelding was so well trained Jeffrey could have opened the gate from the saddle, but it was a difficult maneuver and Jim didn't say anything.

When all had entered the government land and Jeffrey had closed the gate, Jim had the ten riders form a wide line, each horse about fifteen feet from the next.   Each searcher was to look to the right from time to time to stay abreast of the adjacent rider.   Of course, as big trees or tangled thickets intervened, the line would become ragged.   At intervals Jack, the right-most rider and the leader for this search, would halt the group and realign them.   The rider following the road would have the easiest job.   Jim would follow along behind, observing everything, but free to make calls and keep in touch with the deputy sheriff.

The morning was pleasant, the air fresh, the temperature comfortable.   It was fun to be on the palomino, feeling the power of the big gelding underneath him, to know that on horseback he could hold his own with these men around him.   Jeffrey looked with interest at the woods surrounding them, his eyes scanning the underbrush, looking side to side and all around.   He felt strong and alert.

A cottontail leapt up in front of the dun mare two horses to his right.   She shied and wanted to bolt, startling the paint gelding on her left, but both riders calmed their horses and got back in line.   The rabbit darted away and disappeared into the underbrush.

A crow cawed a warning to others of his kind, a warning heard by all the secret life hidden from them: Intruders are coming!

Jeffrey bent low over his horse's neck to dodge a low-hanging branch.   Fifteen feet in front of him, an armadillo lumbered across a small glade, but the big gelding kept his slow steady pace, unperturbed.   A grasshopper whirred past and landed in the dry dusty grass.   A scant breeze ruffled the leaves of a pecan tree.

The air was warmer now.   The salty smell of horse sweat mingled with the moist smell of river bottom.   The paint gelding to his right stumbled in the underbrush, but regained his footing, while brush slapped at his rider.

Jeffrey couldn't imagine anything he'd rather be doing.

Jim's cell phone rang and he halted the roan.

"How's it going?"   Cummins' voice came through strong and clear.   When they dropped down the river bank, reception might not be so good.

"Good.   But nothing so far.   Jeffrey seems to be having the time of his life."

"Good, appreciate that. Guy renting the Wentrcek place is out of town, but his wife says he'll be back this afternoon. Should be able to check it out tomorrow."

"We'll have covered the rest by then."

Jim stuck the phone in his pocket and urged the big roan into a trot, slowing as he neared the others. They had reached the hiking trail paralleling the river, here some thirty yards from the river itself. Jack had called a halt. Riders sat loosely in the saddle and drank from their canteens. An old man on a gray gelding spat tobacco juice into the weeds beside him. A young man smoked a cigarette, then field dressed it: stubbed it out, then tore it into fragments before scattering the tiny bits.

"How you liking it?" the man on the paint gelding asked Jeffrey.

"Good." He didn't add that he wished he had a coke. He wasn't used to drinking water, especially not warm water. He was also getting hungry. It was just mid-morning, but it felt like he had been up a long time. All summer he had run with his friends at night, slept late, played video games in an air-conditioned house during the long afternoons. Now he was hot and prickly with sweat, tired and hungry. No one seemed to notice.

"Okay," Jim said. "We'll split into two groups, check along the river a little way in both directions. Just to be sure. I'll take the group headed east, Jack the one to the west. We'll ride out twenty minutes, then meet back here."

As Jim had figured, there was no sign anyone had been this way. Still, you had to be sure. Searching was a painstaking process, slow, deliberate, time-consuming, boring even until something—if anything—was found.

The riders regrouped, headed back to the trailers. When Jeffrey jumped down to open the first gate, his legs felt rubbery. He hadn't been on a horse in a long time, and he had been in the saddle for hours.

Jeffrey had thought they would return to camp now,

but Jim headed east on the county road. They passed a crossroads store on the left, and Jeffrey silently willed the pickup to stop. He could just taste a cold coke and a salty bag of potato chips. But Jim kept driving.

"We're looking for a small frame house on the left, with a red barn. Should be coming up soon."

Within a quarter of a mile, Jeffrey spotted the barn first, then the little house with a couple of hackberry trees in front. Jim slowed, then turned onto a dirt field road running between two corn fields, the corn harvested, the stalks shredded but not yet plowed under.

At the end of the dirt road, Jeffrey once again dismounted to open the gate to the wilderness area. The procedure was the same.

By noon, Jeffrey had had enough. He was hungry, hot, sweaty, and ready to go home to the air-conditioning. None of the men, though, seemed tired or irritable. And no one asked him how he was doing. He sucked it up, but he was through with this. It was boring now.

The big gelding plodded along and Jeffrey, no longer thinking about the search, was imagining his first taste of coke from his cooler back at the camp. Suddenly, the palomino shied violently, wheeled, and took off. Automatically, Jeffrey's legs had clamped the gelding's sides. He leaned low to avoid a branch that nearly knocked him from the saddle, then straightened up, got his balance, and pulled hard on the reins. The gelding, well trained, slid to a stop, in spite of his panic. It took everything Jeffrey had not to go flying onto his neck. Recovering his seat, he spoke reassuringly to the big horse, "Easy, boy, easy," and patted him firmly on the neck.

Blowing hard, the palomino trembled and pranced a few steps, half circled, then calmed. Jeffrey continued to pat him and talk to him. He could feel the tension in the horse gradually dissipate.

"That boy can ride!"

"Sure can."

"What spooked the horse?"

"I saw it. Big rattlesnake, maybe six feet."

"Never saw that big palomino of Jim's upset before. He's a lot of horse."

"Don't matter what horse it is, sooner or later something will get to them."

"Would've spooked me, too, if I'd seen it."

Jeffrey heard the chorus of voices and swelled with pride. He rode nonchalantly over to the group of men.

"What happened to the snake?"

"Slipped into the underbrush and disappeared. Scared as bad as that palomino."

Jim caught up with the men.

"Jeffrey here almost rode up on a rattlesnake. Got the horse under control, though."

"Good going, Jeffrey. We've covered this area pretty well. Let's break ranks and head on back."

Suddenly, Jeffrey wasn't tired anymore. He jumped down to open the gate, helped load up the horses. He sure was hungry, though.

Chapter 19

March, 1996, Concord, Texas

"Hey," Rhonda called out as Carla exited the classroom into the crowded hall. "Let's go get a drink."

"Oh, I can't. I've got stuff to do before I go home, and I have to be up early tomorrow. I'm filling in for another cashier in the morning."

"Maybe Wednesday then."

"I'll try, but you know how Joe is."

Carla smiled and waved as Rhonda walked out the door with a group of friends, then headed for the back parking lot. She had parked in a far corner away from the main entrance to the college and as far from the light as she could. She stowed her books in the back and sat in the dark interior of the car, waiting. A Toyota 4 Runner soon wheeled in next to her. She glanced around the parking lot. Everyone from the last class period had left, and only empty cars remained.

Carla slipped from behind the wheel, closed the door behind her, and darted into the black Four Runner through the passenger door that Frank, leaning over, had opened for her.

"Carla!" he whispered, reaching for her in the dark. He pulled her to him and bent down to kiss her. She turned her face up to him and returned the kiss passionately, but when he attempted to caress her breasts, pulled away.

"Not here."

"I know a place in the country, just a mile out. I have it listed, and I know no one is there. We'll be safe in the car."

He nodded toward the back, where he had pulled down the seat and made up a bed.

In the dark shadows underneath a large pecan tree next to the untenanted house, Carla lay gasping for breath.

"Oh, Frank," she said, still trembling with an

occasional aftershock.   This is what she had been missing these barren years with Joe. Oh, the difference between man and man! "But I have to go now."

She sped down the highway back to Wirtz through fields whose burgeoning growth remained unseen in the faint light of a pale half-moon, cut the motor as she turned into her drive, and silently rolled into the carport.   She slipped into the shower, briefly luxuriating in its warmth, then crawled into bed as far from Joe as she could get.   He stirred in his sleep and rolled over toward her, throwing one arm across her.   When she moved his arm off her, he awoke.

"Where have you been?" he asked groggily.

"Right here."

He reached for her breast, but she pushed his hand away.   He rolled closer to her and tried to pull her to him.

"No, Joe."   She tried to keep the disgust out of her voice.

"What's wrong with you?"

"I . . . I don't feel well.   I think I'm coming down with something."

Joe quickly rolled over with his back to her.

"Well, I certainly don't need that."

In the dark, Carla waited until she heard his breathing settle into the rhythm of deep sleep.   Then she smiled as she replayed the evening with Frank in her mind and drifted off into a dreamless sleep.

Chapter 20

May, 1996, Wirtz, Texas

Frank was so persistent, Carla thought. The pressure was getting to her, which was unusual for her. She hated Joe, hated Mrs. Dubacek, hated their dingy frame house, so reminiscent of the one she had grown up in. But she couldn't divorce Joe yet.

Carla sat at her desk, just a small worn table, really, but she had placed cheap plastic shelves on it and carefully organized her books and papers. In the center sat the computer. She had been checking her email, which she did regularly, with cool efficiency. Rhonda wanted to go out to celebrate after final exams, her message said. Everything came so easily to Rhonda, Carla thought, yet she seemed to drift through life. Just like choosing to major in education. Rhonda constantly sneered at the stupidity of education courses, but she had chosen that major because the courses were so easy and undemanding.

Carla didn't understand that kind of laziness. If only she could go to school full time, she would finish up her associate's quickly and get a good job. Then she could do whatever she wanted. It took all she made now, working at the convenience store part-time, just to pay for her classes and books and a few clothes. She and Joe were living rent free in the Dubacek house, and Joe's job paid for their living expenses. She couldn't leave yet, much as she wanted to.

She gazed out the window. In the front yard the leaves of the pecan tree, always the last to leaf out, were a delicate green. Morning sunlight streamed through the canopy of leaves, making a pattern of light and shadow on the clipped grass. Across the street, a row of crepe myrtles bloomed alongside the neighbor's sidewalk. A fluffy gray cat batted some of the fallen purple petals, then stalked up the steps to take her place on the most comfortable porch chair and look down on the world. From the far end of the block came the distant sound of a lawn mower starting up.

Joe was at the farm, helping his father this Saturday morning. What a loser he had turned out to be. Here his parents gave him a house to live in, his employer paid for his classes, yet he was throwing his chances away, drowning them in beer. So disgusting!

Frank, on the other hand, was already a successful man, driven to make even more money. A virile man, masterful and open in his dealings. She didn't want to lose him, but she didn't know how much longer she could hold him in a secret affair.

It was not in Carla's nature to worry. She had always simply done what she wanted. But now life had become complicated. How she hated living with Joe in this old house, hated his interfering mother. Carla was used to getting what she wanted, not suffering for it.

Outside, two squirrels raced around the bole of the pecan, one chasing the other in the perennial dance of spring. The scent of honeysuckle wafted through the open window, the sweet scent of longing and desire.

In her mind Carla could see the two men side by side. Frank so masculine and potent, so seriously ambitious. For her, a challenge and a reward. And Joe, babied by his mother his whole life, already showing the signs of alcoholism. With his weak constitution she could look forward to a long, slow decline. He was querulous, slack, soft yet demanding. What use was he to anyone? Why didn't he just die!

Chapter 21

June, 1996, Wirtz, Texas

Carla looked out the kitchen window. The early morning sun lit the tall grass in the backyard.

"Joe, honey, wake up. Breakfast is ready."

Joe stumbled out of bed into the bathroom. When he came into the kitchen, Carla was setting his plate of bacon and eggs on the table. He poured himself a cup of black coffee, sat down, and began to eat without saying anything. Already he had a slack look, his eyes puffy and his skin pale.

"As soon as you finish mowing the yard, I need you to straighten up the garage. Your parents will be here at 12:00."

Joe grunted and continued to eat his eggs in silence. Carla had finished her breakfast and was washing the dishes by the time Joe swabbed his plate with the last of the toast. He poured himself a final cup of coffee and looked out the window at the tall, unkempt grass.

"I'd better get after it," he said. He felt much better now.

When June arrived with the little boys at 11:00, Joe had mowed the yard and cleaned the garage, and the chicken was smoking in the cooker. He was icing down beer and soft drinks in the cooler.

"Jason, Daniel! What are you boys up to?"

The two ran full speed toward him, and he grabbed first one, then the other, and swung them into the air, the boys yelling and laughing.

"Carla's in the house. Go on in. I'll take care of these two."

The boys were giggling wildly as June, smiling to herself, walked into the kitchen. She set a bowl of potato salad and a big plate of cookies on the counter.

"Carla?"

"In here. I'm coming."

Carla had pulled her hair back into a ponytail, and loose black tendrils had escaped, framing her face. She wore jeans and a red knit shirt.

She is prettier than ever, June thought. Carla's pale complexion was suffused with a rosy tint and her eyes were bright.

"Oh, thanks," Carla said, noticing the dishes on the counter.

The two sisters set to work preparing for the meal, though both had done most of the work ahead of time, and it just remained to lay out the paper plates and plastic ware, line up the food on the counter for ease of serving, fill tea glasses with ice.

The crunch of gravel announced the arrival of a car, and Carla glanced out the window.

"Joe's parents."

"I don't think I've seen them since the wedding," June said, "but they look the same."

A large woman wearing black pants and a black and white blouse climbed the back steps laboriously, carrying two large pecan pies.

"You remember my sister June? Oh, thank you." And Carla set the two pies on the table.

"How are you, Mrs. Dubacek?"

"Yes, I remember June. You're back with your parents in Graylor, aren't you? Those your two little boys?"

"Yes, and Joe is so good with them. They're crazy about him."

The three women looked out the window where Joe's father had joined him next to the cooker. Mr. Dubacek wore jeans and a red-checked shirt. He walked with an arthritic limp, and his face was lined and weathered, but he had a smile on his face as he greeted his son and accepted a beer. The two little boys hung back and looked him over.

"So when are you and Joe going to give me a grand-baby?"

"As soon as Joe finishes his associate's degree."

"I hear you're going to school, too."

"Yes, I've been taking a few classes."

"In my day it was good enough for a woman to run a household and raise her children, but times change. One income isn't enough these days, they say. Anton and I did just fine, though."

"Honey, where's the platter for the meat?" Joe called out.

"Right here, sweetheart."

The kitchen table wasn't big enough for all seven of them, but recently Joe had built a picnic table under the pecan tree in the backyard. Carla had all the food lined up in the kitchen. The platter of barbecued chicken, June's potato salad, a Jello salad, a basket of hot rolls, and glasses of iced tea were on the counter, a pot of pinto beans on the stove. Desserts were on the kitchen table.

Out under the pecan tree, June had put Jason and Daniel to her left at the end of one side of the table. For the moment they sat quietly, digging into their food.

"Seems like it would be more convenient to have the food out here."

"Let me refill your plate, Mrs. Dubacek," June said before Carla could say anything.

"Well, a small slice of pie and a couple of those cookies would be nice."

"Would you like some more tea?" Carla was already reaching for the pitcher, which was on the picnic table.

"Yes."

"The corn looks real good, so far." Anton Dubacek took another sip of his beer and continued. "'Course, we could use a good rain about now."

"Might get some the first of the week. At least that's what the weatherman says."

Joe opened another beer and looked questioningly at his father.

"No, no, I'm fine."

"These are real good," Mrs. Dubacek said, biting into a lemon square. She looked appraisingly at June.

"Thank you. It's my aunt's recipe. Jason, stop that. If you and Daniel are finished, you can go play."

"Yes, ma'am," Jason said, slyly pinching Daniel, who yelped. June frowned and Daniel started to say something but changed his mind. The two boys ran off and began tossing a football around.

"Those are fine little boys," Mrs. Dubacek said, then looked pointedly at Carla.

~ ~ ~

"I'm so tired," Carla said as Joe pulled her to him and set down his beer to fumble at her blouse.

"You're always tired."

"I love having your mom and dad over, but it is a lot of work, and I haven't finished cleaning the kitchen."

"It looks fine to me."

"No, I have to mop the floor. Little kids are fun, but they do make a mess. You go on in and watch television. I'll be in when I finish."

After she mopped the kitchen floor, Carla carefully removed the magnets holding snapshots and schedules from the refrigerator door.

"You want another beer, honey?"

Joe barely looked up from the TV as she handed him a cold beer.

Carla looked critically at the old white refrigerator, then sprayed it with a new cleaner she had bought recently and carefully wiped off every trace of dirt. She replaced all the magnets and the items they held, then stood back. It looked better, but still, it was the same old refrigerator.

She peeked around the corner into the living room. Joe was sprawled back on the couch, his mouth slightly open and a little spittle of drool running down one corner. Carla tiptoed into the bedroom and silently pulled on her gown and slipped into bed.

Chapter 22

July, 1996, Wirtz, Texas

"Damn it, Carla, where are my clean jeans?"

"Don't speak to me like that, Joe," Carla said calmly but firmly. "They're folded on top of the dryer."

"I can't ever find anything around here, and you're never home. I'm so late now I might as well skip class."

Joe didn't look good. A dark stubble covered his face, his skin looked blotchy, and his abdomen was distended. He threw himself onto the couch, almost spilling his open beer. He cursed softly to himself, then picked up the remote and began to flip through channels.

Carla continued setting the table for one, at intervals stirring a pot of beans. She spooned a helping of slaw onto a plate next to some reheated sausages.

"Your supper's ready, Joe. Just leave the beans on the stove, and I'll put them up when I get back."

"Where are you going?"

"You know I have class tonight and a study session afterwards."

"I'm tired of you always being gone."

"You wouldn't notice if you went to your own class."

Carla headed for campus early so she could go over her notes one more time. Fields of corn lay on either side of the highway, the dry leaves of the mature corn rustling in a light breeze. An occasional stand of cotton, the green bolls still tightly closed, alternated with the fields of corn. Closer to Concord, subdivisions encroached on the rich, fertile land. Usually observant of the world around her, Carla was consumed by her thoughts.

It was becoming harder to study at home, with Joe so irritable and demanding. He was going to fail his classes, she knew, at least one of them, maybe both. His drinking disgusted her. He disgusted her. If only she could get rid of him. If only she had the money to go to school full-time.

As soon as she pulled into the campus parking lot, the feeling lifted. She was excited. She was doing well in her classes, and already she had pre-registered for two fall classes. The only thing she hadn't figured out yet was how to keep seeing Frank after this summer semester ended.

She had promised to join Rhonda and friends, including Frank, at the nearby bar, and had arranged with Frank to leave separately and meet afterwards.

"Let's go dancing, and then you can stay at my place."

"You know I can't, Frank."

"I don't see why you don't get rid of that husband. Why stay with him when he makes you so unhappy?"

"You don't understand. He's ill. I can't just abandon him when he's in such awful shape. When he gets better, I'll file for divorce. I promise."

"I admire you for that, but I can't take much more of this. I like to live my life out in the open, do what I want."

"I'll make it up to you. . . . I know how," Carla added, giving him a meaningful look and a roguish smile.

Frank laughed and pulled her to him. "That you do."

Chapter 23

Wednesday, August 20, 2003, Rural Central Texas
        Jeffrey drank two cokes with his sandwiches back at
the campground, and when the caffeine hit him he got
restless.   He had unsaddled, watered and curried both the
roan and palomino, had given them hay, and now there was
nothing left to do. The heat was oppressive. Some of the
men had driven into town. One had disappeared down the
trail with his fishing gear. The young man with the REI tent
was sitting under an elm tree reading a book, apparently
oblivious to the heat. Jeffrey was hot, restless, and bored.
        In the distance the shimmering lake looked inviting.
Jeffrey headed down the path and soon emerged from the
scattered trees into the full glare of the mid-afternoon sun.
He was bareheaded and squinched up his eyes against the
fierceness of the sun. The heat pressed down on him like a
heavy hand.
        It was farther to the water than he had thought.
Sweat rolled down his face and stung his eyes. Not a hint of a
breeze stirred the air. He felt gritty and prickly and a little
light-headed. He gritted his teeth and kept walking.
        The bank sloped steeply near the edge of the lake, and
Jeffrey picked his footing carefully, alert for snakes.
        He found a small rocky outcropping and dropped his
clothes there. Stripped down to his briefs, he plunged into
the water.
        It felt wonderful.   He swam a few strokes, then
flipped on his back. He kicked and splashed and flipped back
over. He stretched out and swam hard for a little distance,
then ducked under the water and glided below the surface,
pretending to be a fish. He could see little in the murky
water and soon came up for air.
        He treaded water and looked around. He was on the
south side of the lake and close enough to the dam for there

to be some depth to the water. It was not an impressive lake. Thousands of acres of rich farmland and native pasture had been covered by the shallow lake, and ancient pecan trees lay on its bottom. But the reservoir provided water for several little towns, and developers hoped to carve up the surrounding rich black fertile land into cookie-cutter subdivisions.

Jeffrey flipped onto his back and squinted up at the pale blue sky, the vast and cloudless dome. A buzzard circled lazily high above. The summer sound of the cicadas was muffled by the water encircling his head and filling his ears.

He could be the last person on earth, the only survivor of a deadly virus. He closed his eyes, moved his hands and feet just enough to keep from sinking, and felt the hot sun on his face. He imagined casting a line into the lake for his supper, his hook baited with grasshoppers, or wasp larvae pried from the large papery nests, or big fat earthworms harvested from the moist riverbank. He saw himself slipping through the woods, gun in hand, stalking feral hogs. He would build a big fire and over the glowing coals roast wild pig. On higher ground he would erect a shelter of logs, digging deep into the earth underneath it for a cellar. He would skin the squirrels he shot, smoke the meat to make jerky, save the hides. Long winter evenings could be spent shelling pecans and bull nettle nuts he had collected in the fall. In the spring he would feast on sweet dewberries and tart wild plum, in summer on tangy mustang grapes and red prickly pear fruit. Maybe he could learn how to grind up dried mesquite beans for flour.

His face was hot and he flipped over face down and swam a few strokes. Suddenly, he felt alone and bored. The lake was wide and empty. The sun bore down on its slate-grey surface, and the whir of the cicadas rose and fell, lonesome in the distance.

He swam quickly to shore, pulled his clothes on over his wet body and wet briefs, and hiked back to camp.

Jim was back from town, the REI guy had put his book aside, the fisherman was gutting a string of catfish.

"Saw your dad," Jim said. "Said he'd be out later on."

~ ~ ~

The sun was low in the west, its rays not so fierce, but the heat still lay like a heavy blanket over all when Bill drove up, made his salutations.

"Son, you need to go back to your mother's. She's got supper for you."

Jeffrey didn't know whether to be glad or resentful. His mother was a good cook, and he missed the air conditioning. He could use a break from the heat, and it seemed like he was hungry all the time now. On the other hand, he didn't want to look like a baby, and he liked being with the men. Jim had been teaching him some useful knots.

"Aw, Dad."

"Your mother needs to see you're okay. I can bring you out first thing in the morning if you still want to ride."

"Oh yeah, I do." Jeffrey felt a surge of pride, remembering his adventure with the horse and the rattlesnake.

"You can leave your tent and things till tomorrow."

Jim watched them drive off and thought about the son he had never really known. Alice had disappeared with the boy, and he hadn't been able to track them down. Or maybe he hadn't tried hard enough.

Jeffrey was a good kid, but spoiled. He wanted to be a man, but he was soft, overindulged. He wondered if Alice had made the same mistakes with their son. Probably different ones. She had been a flower child the last he had known her, more apt to let the kid fend for himself than wait on him hand and foot. Well, enough of that. He hadn't stepped up to the plate, either.

Tomorrow they would check out the old barn farther

east.   Bill had gotten tentative permission, he said, but still had to meet up with the renter to assure him he'd be compensated if the horses damaged anything.   Some people were just suspicious by nature, reluctant to meet you halfway. Still, they would get there sometime the next day. Jim had a strong feeling.   He had learned to pay attention to those feelings.

Why, though, had he had no premonition about Susan? Well, sometimes you did, and sometimes you didn't. And he had still been upset by their quarrel of the night before and was not in an open peaceful state when he left for work that morning.

Jim checked on the horses. Jeffrey had cared for them well. The boy had that going for him. You never knew about a youngster like that, which way he would turn. The lure of the wrong crowd, the adrenaline rush and the easy self-indulgence, were strong. He needed firm male guidance.

The western sky blazed orange and red, streaking a ripple of clouds just above the horizon, when Jim took his place by the fire with the rest of the men.

Chapter 24

August, 1996, Wirtz, Texas

It was hot, oppressive August heat, and the humidity was high, but Carla didn't want to turn on the old window unit air conditioner until she absolutely had to. She felt sticky and irritable. But her mind was racing. Last night she had overheard Mr. Dubacek telling Joe that he had made a change to the life insurance policy he had taken out years ago on Joe, naming Carla the beneficiary instead of himself and Charlene.

Fifty thousand dollars, he had said. Not all that much, but it would allow her to go to school full-time, finish quickly, get the job she wanted.

She sat down at her desk, intently focused. How? What would be the best way? His drinking was already becoming obvious. In fact, Mrs. Dubacek was now blaming her. If Carla were the wife she ought to be, then Joe would not drink so heavily, Charlene Dubacek's reasoning went.

So how could this work? Joe regularly passed out now. A pillow might do it, though Joe was still strong enough to fight free if the survival reflex kicked in. Too, suffocation left signs, hemorrhaging around the eyes, if anyone were suspicious. However, old George Lockwood pretty much took things as they came. He had been Justice of the Peace so long he wasn't excited by the job any more—-if he ever had been. A dead body was a dead body. Joe's eyes were often bloodshot from heavy drinking. If the cause seemed obvious—acute alcohol poisoning—Lockwood wasn't going to exert himself.

Still, it was better to be safe. If Charlene Dubacek had the slightest suspicions, she would turn the county upside down until she got answers.

Heavy drinkers, particularly binge drinkers, sometimes aspirated their own vomit and were found dead the next morning.   But how could you make that happen? There would have to be the actual substance in the lungs.

Carla remembered an old Law & Order episode in which the killer had put frog poison in DMSO, then put the mixture in shaving cream or body lotion.   The poison was absorbed through the skin.   But that was too exotic and contrived, and of course the killer had been caught—-the point of the program. There had to be something simpler and more direct.

Carla glanced out the window.   The grass needed cutting.   Unusual rain had fallen in late August, and Joe hadn't kept up with the mowing.   Across the street, the hospice woman had parked her car and was walking up the steps to the McClearys' door.   Mr. McCleary was taking a long time to die. Mrs. McCleary had been at his bedside for months as the cancer progressed.   Why didn't he just end it instead of lingering?

The subject had come up in the student lounge the other day.   Taking a break from her studies, Carla had sat down in an empty chair with her cup of coffee.   "If I were terminal and suffering, I wouldn't put up with it," a young woman had said. The man sitting across from her brought up Dr. Kevorkian, and the discussion turned lively.   "You don't have to depend on a doctor like Kevorkian; there's always the Hemlock Society," said someone.

Of course, thought Carla.   The Hemlock Society. Immediately she began to search online and soon began taking notes. Nitrogen, she read, hardly leaves a trace, since it is already present in air.   Furthermore, inhaling nitrogen doesn't cause the body to panic, because it is not lack of oxygen but a build-up of carbon dioxide that induces panic. If the suicide had a friend who could remove the equipment afterwards, then the death might not be discovered to be a suicide.

Carla paused and looked out the window, her mind racing.   She didn't see sunlight illuminating the tall grass or the neighbor's black dog wandering down the street or a gray sedan parking in front of the McCleary residence. She saw deliverance.

She turned back to her computer. Several people a year die accidentally from nitrogen inhalation, she read, because nitrogen is odorless and tasteless. Perhaps a tank is not properly sealed. A lab tech may become unconscious without warning, fall to the floor, where the heavier nitrogen is concentrated, and die. Death occurs within minutes.

Carla sat up straighter, her dark eyes intently focusing. She would have to prepare for this, step by step. Purchasing a canister of nitrogen and a hose at any welding shop or paintball store, making a suicide bag with a drawstring for the neck, would be simple. But sudden death couldn't come out of nowhere. Joe would have to be sicker, his health dangerously fragile. Although alcoholic, with a weak constitution, he was primarily a beer alcoholic. In the ordinary course of things, it might take years for him to die.

Perhaps she could speed up his deterioration. In the shopping center across the street from Concord Community College was a liquor store frequented by all the students, though Carla had never been in it. She didn't know anything about hard liquor.

Carla turned back to the computer and looked up mixed drinks.

Across the street, the door of the gray sedan slammed shut, and an elderly man assisted by a middle-aged woman headed up the sidewalk to the McClearys' front door. The black dog sniffed at the bole of a pecan tree and lifted its back right leg.

Chapter 25

August, 1996, Wirtz, Texas

Carla heard the old Chevy pull into the carport just as she was setting the oven timer for the hot rolls. A pot roast and vegetables, the roasting pan covered with foil, sat on top of the old gas range. She looked around the kitchen with its worn linoleum and rasping refrigerator, pleased with her work. A good supper, even if it wasn't Joe's favorite.

He entered the kitchen without speaking and headed for the refrigerator.

"Wait, honey. You know how I can't stand the taste of beer. Let's try something new."

On the counter was a bottle of vodka, two glasses with ice, and a pitcher of orange juice. Joe stopped, hesitated, and before he could reach the refrigerator and grab a cold beer, Carla was at the counter pouring a generous helping of vodka in each glass.

"What's on TV tonight? Supper is ready whenever we want it. Maybe we could relax with a drink first. I know I've been stressed out a lot lately. I'm sorry if I've been irritable. Maybe this will help." And she smiled prettily up at him while she topped off the vodka with orange juice and handed him a glass.

Joe was so surprised he downed a big swallow without saying anything, while Carla sipped daintily at hers. It was a stiff drink, and he felt the alcohol course through his system, warm and strong. It felt good.

"Why don't you go see what's on TV and I'll mix us another drink."

Joe tossed off the rest of the drink and silently handed the glass to Carla. As soon as he had left the kitchen, Carla quickly emptied her drink into the sink and refilled her glass with ice and orange juice. Then she made him an even stronger drink.

She was wearing a sleeveless white top, fitted at her small waist, with a blue flower pattern at the neck, and white clam diggers with the same blue flowers around the hems. She smiled at Joe as she entered the living room and handed him the drink, but he wasn't paying attention.

Joe was flipping through the channels, his empty glass on the coffee table, when the timer in the kitchen went off.

"That's the rolls, honey. Are you ready for supper?"

"I guess."

Joe felt good, but not really high, in spite of all the alcohol. He filled his plate at the kitchen stove and sat down.

Carla stood thinking, her empty plate in her hand.

"Would you like to switch to something besides orange juice? I have coke and sprite and V8."

"I'll take coke, though rum would go better with it."

Carla made a mental note.

Carla ate heartily, while Joe just picked at his food. He mixed himself another drink.

"Now, honey, you don't want to overdo it."

"Don't tell me what to do. Don't start that again. I deserve a little comfort in life, not some nagging wife."

"But Joe . . ."

"Enough! This my house, and I'll do whatever I want in it."

Joe stumbled a little and sloshed the vodka as he poured more into his glass.

Carla kept her back to him to hide her face as she cleared the table and put away the food. He might take care of it himself, she thought, as he staggered into the living room carrying the vodka bottle. She put the last plate in the drainer and swabbed down the ancient counters. But she wouldn't wait too long.

Chapter 26

September, 1996, Central Texas

June stood on the gravel driveway of the small frame house she had grown up in, waving goodbye to the boys, who weren't looking back at all to see her. She smiled and turned toward the house. It was so thoughtful of Carla to suggest taking the boys with her. She led a busy life herself, with little time to spare, but she understood what a small break could mean for June. The boys adored Joe and were excited about going to the farm.

Mama was in the kitchen baking a cake to take down the street to a neighbor who had just lost her husband. Daddy was in his big overstuffed armchair in the small living room, reading the paper. Patty hadn't gotten up yet. The house was unusually serene for a Saturday morning. June retreated to the bedroom she had once shared with Carla, set up the old ironing board and began preparing her clothes for the coming week.

In the back seat of the old Chevy, Jason was gazing out the window at the farmland the highway bisected. Most of the fields were empty now, but in one that stretched south from the railroad tracks paralleling the highway, the white cotton, overflowing the opened bolls of the poisoned brown stalks, silently awaited the stripper.

Daniel was drumming his heels against the back seat.

"Can we go down to the creek, Aunt Carla?"

"You'll have to ask Uncle Joe about that."

Daniel was heartened by the answer. Uncle Joe was sure to take them.

Jason jumped out of the car and manfully swung open the gate in the lane leading down to the barn, then carefully closed it behind the car. Both boys leapt out once Carla had parked near the barn.

Joe and his father were putting away a roll of barbed

wire, some six-foot steel fence posts, and the heavy driver in a shed next to the barn.

"Uncle Joe, Uncle Joe!" both boys shouted as they ran full speed toward him. He grabbed each in turn and swung him high into the air.

Both men were sweaty, and Joe's right cheek was streaked with grime where he had wiped the sweat away. His complexion was pasty, but he looked better than he had earlier that morning when Carla had fixed his breakfast.

"Can we go to the creek, Uncle Joe?"

"Sure. C'mon."

The boys took off running toward the back of the property where the creek wandered through scrub elm and hackberries and underneath overhanging willows.   Joe followed more slowly.

Carla gazed after them until they were almost out of sight, then turned toward Anton Dubacek. Her dark eyes filled, and for a moment she didn't speak, just looked solemnly at her father-in-law.

"I'm so worried about Joe. I don't know what to do."

Anton waited, not sure what to say. She looked so sad, so fragile.

"It's his drinking. He's just ruining his health. And if I say anything, he gets so angry. I just don't know what to do. Maybe if you talked to him . . ."

Anton knew very well his son was drinking too much. He could see it in his face. And in his lack of stamina. The boy was weakened. He'd had a hard time that morning, obviously hung over, though he seemed to do better after he had sweated out the toxins.   Anton was no stranger to hangovers, back in his younger days. Everyone drank beer, and youngsters often overdid it in their wild days. But this was different. Carla was right, Joe's health was affected. It was time for the boy to take hold, be a man. He was married now, had a promising job and was going to school to move up. Anton felt sorry for Carla, and a little ashamed. The poor little thing was trying so hard herself, ran her house well, held down a part-time job, even took a class or two on the side to better herself. She was doing her part.

He stared off across the pasture, noted the cows lying down for their late-morning rest in the sparse shade of a few scraggly hackberry trees. A red-tailed hawk swooped silently past, scanning for rabbits and field mice. From down at the creek, exuberant shouts, Daniel's voice topping Jason's, greeted the discovery of a turtle.

"I'll see what I can do."

Chapter 27

Wednesday, August 20, 2003, Graylor, Texas

Heading west, Bill had a brilliant view of the sunset through the pickup windshield, the hues of pink and red stratus clouds covering half the sky and changing minute by minute.

"How was the search?"

"Okay." And then Jeffrey was telling his father all about the palomino's sidewise leap and attempt to bolt, how he brought the gelding under control, how one of the men had seen the six-foot rattler. His pride and excitement shone through.

Bill smiled.

"Maybe you shouldn't tell your mother that story."

He and Jeffrey exchanged a complicit look.

The color had faded from the sky, the clouds graying, and twilight was deepening as they reached the house in Graylor. Bill drove around back and he and Jeffrey entered through the kitchen. Mary Kay was just taking hot home-made biscuits out of the oven. On the stove was a platter of fried chicken. Already on the table were bowls of mashed potatoes, green beans, creamed corn, a plate of sliced tomatoes, and a boat of cream gravy. A pitcher of sweetened ice tea stood ready to be poured into glasses full of ice.

"I fixed your favorite meal. . . Oh, Jeffrey, honey, you're all sunburned. Let me put something on it. Bill, I fixed plenty. Pull up a chair."

Bill started to decline, then saw Jeffrey's look. He could eat a little. Linda would never know. And Mary Kay was a fine cook, everything from scratch.

"I've got some lotion in the medicine cabinet, won't take me a second to get it."

"Mama, I'm so hungry."

It came out plaintive, almost as though he were a little

boy again. Mary Kay stopped in her tracks.

"Of course, honey. You just sit down and fix you a plate."

She put the platter of chicken in the center of the table, put the hot biscuits in a basket.

"Will you pour the tea, Bill?"

Without knowing exactly how it happened, Bill found himself seated with his son and ex-wife, almost as a family. Jeffrey was digging in as though he hadn't eaten in a month. Bill was sopping a fluffy, tender biscuit in rich cream gravy.

"You always could beat the nation cooking, Mary Kay."

Mary Kay flushed and smiled. Jeffrey was too busy to pay attention.

"Well, I've got to be going." Bill pushed himself away from the table. He had already eaten too much, though he felt like he could have taken another helping of everything.

"Dad, you're going to get me first thing in the morning?"

"Sure."

"What!" Mary Kay glared at Bill. "Jeffrey, honey, you're already sunburned. You need to stay in out of the sun."

"I'll put on sun block, I promise."

"I won't have . . ."

Jeffrey looked at Bill.

"Mary Kay, Jeffrey's real good with the horses. That's what he likes so much. You remember how he was with that dappled gray pony. Remember him in that cowboy hat and boots, looking so proud."

Why did they always gang up against her? Mary Kay was beaten, but bitter.

"Oh, all right."

"Be ready, son. I have to meet with the renter, so I'll be here by eight. Thanks for the meal, Mary Kay."

And Bill was out the door before anyone could say anything else.

Chapter 28

September, 1996, Wirtz, Texas

Carla hummed to herself as she removed the pot of rice from its burner and fluffed it once with a fork, then took the lid off the iron skillet and with the fork tested the liver covered with onions and cream gravy.   Turnip greens simmered on another burner, and the cast iron skillet of cornbread in the oven was almost done.   Carla liked the bottom crispy and the center of the cornbread moist, which could be achieved by heating oil in the skillet to just the right temperature before pouring in the batter and placing it in a hot oven.

She looked cool and comfortable in loose pink cotton pants and a white t-shirt with a wreath of pink roses across the front.   Her dark hair, framing her pale complexion, looked even darker against the white shirt.   As she moved swiftly and efficiently around the kitchen, carefully placing the silverware and plates on the small breakfast table that served for all the meals, just a hint of rose suffused her pale cheeks.

On the counter stood rum and vodka bottles, a big plastic bottle of coke, a pitcher of orange juice, two glasses, and a bucket of ice.

When she heard the old Chevy rumble into the carport, Carla added ice to the two glasses and filled one with orange juice.

"Hi, honey. Did you have a hard day?"

Joe didn't look good. His distended abdomen swelled underneath his loose shirt, and there was a yellowish tinge to his tanned face.

"Yeah. I'm not going to class tonight."

"I'm sorry. Maybe a drink would pick you up. Do you want rum and coke or a screwdriver like I'm having?"

"Rum and coke."

Carla fixed the drink.

"Here, honey."

Joe tossed it off, and the taut lines in his face relaxed. He mixed another stiff one.

Carla lifted the hot skillet of cornbread from the oven and set it on a hot pad. With a kitchen knife she scored the cornbread into slices. On the table, a dish of butter had been softening.

"Everything's ready."

Joe filled his plate from the stove, wrinkling his nose at the smothered liver. He didn't absolutely hate it, but it wasn't his favorite dish. He finished his drink and mixed a third to take to the table. He drank steadily but ate little.

"Honey, you need to eat your liver and onions. It's good for you. I fixed it 'specially for you, knowing you haven't been feeling well lately."

"Just leave me alone."

Joe was getting to the belligerent stage.

"But honey . . ."

"Just shut up and leave me alone!"

Joe stood up, knocking over his chair, and stumbled to the counter where he poured his glass almost full of rum and sloshed a little coke on top. He stalked out of the kitchen. In a moment Carla heard the TV blaring.

She smiled, buttered another slice of cornbread, and dipped it in the gravy on her plate.

Chapter 29

December, 1996, Wirtz, Texas
    In the bedroom of the small house, Joe lay on his back snoring loudly, his breathing labored. Outside, a north wind swirled leaves that still lay on the brown grass. An occasional gust rattled the windowpane.
    Young as he was, Joe seemed about to drink himself to death. Already the Dubaceks were thinking about rehab centers—or at least their friends were. Carla had overheard Charlene fuming about the nerve of her best friend suggesting they get help for Joe. All Joe needed, she had said to Anton, was a wife who truly supported him. She, Charlene, might take to drink herself if she had to go home to someone like Carla. She never had liked her. She wasn't good for Joe. Anton didn't say anything. He was worried about his son. But he believed a man ought to have the gumption to take control of his own life. And he couldn't get the picture of Carla, large dark eyes brimming with unshed tears, out of his mind. She looked so fragile. Why couldn't his son get hold of himself?
    Carla stood listening to Joe's ragged breathing. It was best to go ahead. If the Dubaceks did finally decide to intervene, Joe might be pulled back from the brink. She could see Joe lapsing and relapsing, in and out of dry-out centers. It could go on for years.
    The wind grew stronger, moaning around the corners of the house. A little cold air edged in where the window frame was slightly off kilter.
    Tonight, after Joe's first drink, she had switched a rum bottle filled with Everclear for the one full of rum. His tolerance for alcohol had increased, at least it took more for him to feel intoxicated, while at the same time his liver was deteriorating. He very well might not make it through the night, but if he did, he was sure to be hospitalized. She

couldn't take the chance.

She tiptoed out of the bedroom. From a big plastic storage bin in the pantry, Carla removed a nitrogen canister and a large plastic bag. With deft hands she assembled the "exit bag" described in a Hemlock publication.

Joe still lay on his back as she entered the bedroom quietly, the soughing of the wind and his labored breathing the only sounds disturbing the silence. She set the nitrogen canister on a chair drawn up to the bed and inserted its hose into a hole she had made in the bottom of the heavy plastic bag. Carefully she sealed it with duct tape, taking her time to secure it.

The next part would be tricky.

She thought a moment, then lifted Joe's head off the pillow just far enough that she could slide the plastic bag over his head and down his neck. She tightened the Velcro she had affixed around the bag's open end, careful to seal the bag around Joe's neck without causing him discomfort.

He sighed in his sleep and flung one arm out.

"Easy, honey," Carla said soothingly as she grabbed his arm and caressed it. Quickly, she turned the valve on the canister hose. The hiss of the releasing gas was barely audible.

The articles she had read said death would occur within minutes. Some said seven, others twenty minutes. It probably wouldn't take long in Joe's state, but she would make extra sure. She looked at her watch: twenty minutes after midnight.

She sat back and watched.

The wind picked up and the small house seemed to tremble. Though solidly built, it was old and seemed frail in the face of the forces arrayed against it. The fingers of the wind plucked at the windowpanes. The house creaked and the panes rattled.

Carla waited.

A sudden gust and the bare limb of a pecan tree scraped against a corner of the roof. A trimming job Joe had left undone. Well, he would never get to it now.

Joe's breathing continued, rasping but regular. Then a tremor began, and his whole body was suddenly convulsing.

Carla leapt to her feet and grabbed the canister, holding it close to the plastic bag to make sure the hose didn't pull loose.

After a bit, the convulsions ceased and the body lay still. It didn't look like it was still breathing.

Carla waited. Seven minutes of oxygen deprivation causes death of the cerebral cortex, she had read. She waited some more, watching carefully for any indication of movement. She looked at her watch: 12:32.

Carla picked up Joe's wrist and felt for a pulse. Nothing.

Still she waited.

The wind slacked off and the gusts ceased. In the sudden stillness, a distant dog bark sounded.

At 12:45, Carla shut off the valve. She thought for a moment. How much nitrogen was still in the bag? Carla tugged at the wooden window frame by the bed until the window was wide open, then retrieved a pedestal fan from the pantry and dragged it to the near side of the bed so that it blew toward the open window. Then she ripped the Velcro apart, slid the bag over Joe's head, and quickly left the room, closing the door behind her.

She cut the Velcro in even lengths, rolled them up and put them in her sewing drawer. She tore up the plastic bag and deposited the pieces in the trash. Then she returned the canister to the plastic bin in the pantry. She would dispose of it tomorrow.

Back in the chilled bedroom she closed the window and stood thinking. What would be the best way to do it? The longer she waited, the harder it would be to detect an unusual level of nitrogen in the body, in the highly unlikely event that anyone should demand an autopsy. Carla looked down at Joe's distended abdomen, his enlarged liver visible to the medical eye. The cause of death seemed quite clear. The most likely scenario would be for her to wake up and discover this horrendous event.

In the bathroom, Carla brushed her teeth, rubbed night cream into her soft skin, and slipped on her gown. She brushed her hair until the waves and curls shone. Then she returned to the bedroom, climbed into bed, and paused a moment. Propped up on one elbow, she contemplated the still body beside her. A subtle change had come over the face, the features sharpened, the color gone, the ineffable essence of life vanished. Pleased, she curled up on her side of the bed with a satisfied sigh, her dark hair spilling over the white pillow in dark ringlets. She fell into a light but restorative sleep, and awoke before it was light.

~ ~ ~

The phone rang many times before Anton Dubacek answered it. At first he couldn't make out what she was saying because of the hysterical sobs. Then the vise tightened around his heart.

Chapter 30

January, 1997, Concord, Texas

"I did everything I could," Carla sobbed. She sat next to Frank on the sofa in his living room on the first floor of the townhouse, staring at the flickering flames in the fireplace. She turned toward him, her dark eyes brimming with tears.

"I'm sure you did." Frank reached out and took her in his arms until she had cried herself out. She felt soft and vulnerable, and the blue flame of the gas log made the room cozy and warm.

"He was so young to die."

"Every few years some young man at the university dies of acute alcohol poisoning." Frank didn't have much patience for what he saw as weakness or stupidity.

"No one knows how terrible it was to live with his drinking, not even you. I couldn't tell you. It was too horrible. Still, I kept hoping that he would get back on his feet enough so that I could leave him. He was just destroying his health."

Frank was tired of this. No doubt it had been hard on Carla, but it was over now. He had no sympathy for a man who wasn't a man. He couldn't pretend to feel something he didn't feel. Still, women were different. They often made excuses for pitiable creatures. He couldn't help thinking about his mother and his younger brother. He was still angry at Jimmy for being so stupid and reckless. His mother had never gotten over his death.

He looked at Carla, the dark tendrils clinging to her soft round cheeks, her dark eyes seeming even larger after her tears.

"It's over, now," he said, gently caressing her cheek. Carla looked trustingly at him, and he bent to kiss her, softly at first.

"Oh, Frank."

~ ~ ~

Frank was an early riser, but the other half of the bed was empty when he awoke, and the smell of coffee drifted up from downstairs. He leaped out of bed and jumped into the shower. He hummed to himself as he dressed, then ran lightly down the stairs.

A plate of hot blueberry muffins sat on the counter. Carla set her empty coffee cup down.

"I've got to go now. Enjoy your breakfast."

She waved her hand toward the muffins and started toward the door.

"Wait."

She paused for Frank to come up to kiss her goodbye, and then she was gone.

Frank felt off balance. Women clung to him. He was usually the one racing out the door. Carla was different from every other woman he had known. And not just because she was the most exciting, creative sex partner he had ever had. He sipped his coffee and nibbled a muffin. Those were good, too. Frank smiled to himself and strode out the door, into the cold morning air, to begin his day.

Chapter 31

May, 1997, Concord, Texas

Late afternoon the May sun was still hot.   Frank and Carla sat on his back patio in the shade of a live oak, sipping iced tea.   Carla looked cool in white Capris with a loose ice blue and white top of soft thin cotton knit.   White sandals revealed her pearly pink painted toenails.   With the insurance money, she was able to dress better.   Frank noted the difference without really thinking about it.

"Shall we pop around the corner to that little Mexican place for dinner?   Something quick.   I've got to prepare for an early day tomorrow."

"Thanks, Frank, but I have to be going."

Carla set her glass down on the patio table and stood up.   She had dropped by after leaving campus for the day. She was spending most of her time on campus now, not only because of the number of classes she was taking, but also because she preferred to study there.   The new campus in a brand new area was much more pleasant than that dingy frame house she couldn't wait to leave.   Also, she didn't have to run the air conditioner all day if she was on campus.   The old window unit was inefficient and expensive to run.

Frank was nonplussed.   He admired Carla's single-minded focus on her studies, he said to himself, but without putting it into words, he felt he should be the object of her intense focus.

Carla smiled prettily up at him.   She was ravishing and self-possessed, yet at times so vulnerable.   He never knew what to expect.   At first he hadn't wanted her to spend the night, but now he did.   He pulled her to him and gently stroked the dark ringlets.   He bent to kiss her and she felt soft and yielding, but when he began to caress her breasts, she pulled away.

"Not this evening," she said softly, yet firmly.

"Tomorrow?"

"Perhaps."

"Look, I'm closing a deal tomorrow. Let's celebrate by going to dinner at that new restaurant on the lake."

Up to now, she had refused to go to any high profile place, claiming she just wasn't ready yet, so soon after Joe's death. He was hoping she could put it all behind her now. He could see why she hadn't wanted to be seen with him right after her husband was put in the ground, but now after all these months he was eager to live his life out in the open again. Enough of going to obscure places where they wouldn't run into anyone who knew Carla, like that fun-loving friend of hers, Rhonda.

"All right," Carla said, knowing what Frank was thinking. "I'll go with Rhonda to the pub after class tomorrow night, and you ask me out, as though it was for the first time. And it will be the first time you've asked me out for a regular date. We can ease into it."

~ ~ ~

"Rhonda," Carla said in the hall the next night after class, "I'm ready to be around people now. I need to be with people." She choked up on the last words, and Rhonda put her arm around her.

"It's been so hard for you, I know. But it will be good for you to get out. You've got to get back to living your life. Joe would want you to."

Carla teared up at the mention of Joe's name, and empathetic tears sprang to Rhonda's eyes. She held Carla tighter and didn't say anything.

The bar was packed and noisy as Rhonda swept through the crowd of laughing young people to her favorite table in back, with Carla trailing behind. Frank was in the middle of the group. Carla didn't look at him as she sat next to Rhonda, a little apart.

Eventually, as people left and chairs opened up, Frank moved over next to Carla.

"There's a good band at the Broken Spoke tonight. Would you like to go dancing?"

"I don't think so."

"Well, how about dinner? Everyone has to eat."

Carla looked helplessly at Rhonda.

"Do it, Carla. You need to start getting out now."

"All right, Frank, but I don't know how much fun I'll be."

Carla looked down at the table. Rhonda reached over and squeezed her hand.

"You'll be fine."

Chapter 32

June, 1997, Wirtz, Texas

Carla was thrilled. All her hard work had paid off. In her hands she held her associate's degree. She studied it a little longer, then carefully filed it away in the two-drawer filing cabinet, secondhand but still respectable, next to her desk. She looked out the window of the small frame house and noticed the cars parked across the street in front of the McCleary residence. Mr. McCleary had finally died, shortly before Joe's death, and now less than a year after her husband's death, Mrs. McCleary had succumbed. Over coffee in the student lounge one day, the nursing students had spoken of how with long-married couples, one often followed the other to the grave within a year. An interesting fact, but it made no sense to Carla. Death wasn't catching. What connected one death to the other?

Carla rarely allowed herself to waste time in idle musings, but now was a time to celebrate both getting her associate's degree and getting out of this shabby old house. Already she had been hired by Concord Radiology Lab. Carla enjoyed the work at Concord Radiology, the pay was decent, and her sense of independence thrilling. And soon she would be living with Frank. Although she had been spending many nights at the town house, she had had to work hard to make Frank think it was his idea for her to move in. Frank's town house was new and everything about it modern, especially the kitchen and its appliances. So much more soothing and pleasant than this junky old frame house, though it certainly wasn't the height of her ambition. In her mind, Carla had a ladder of goals. She had achieved the first and hardest step, and there was no stopping her now. She smiled to herself a moment. She would savor each success. Then she gathered up her purse from its accustomed place and walked briskly out the door.

The sun shone in an almost cloudless sky as Carla drove to Concord, where she was meeting Rhonda for lunch. The corn was green and sturdy, the milo beginning to head out, the stalks of cotton not quite their full height. A hawk perched on a fence post surveyed a pasture enclosed by the fence. As the car came abreast of him, the hawk left his fence post and soared high above the short thick Bermuda grass, a fading green now. Beneath him four good-sized calves—two Brangus, a Charolais cross, and the last a reddish brown one —in single file crossed a draw that traversed the field in a wandering diagonal. They followed a well worn cattle path that led up a slight rise toward a couple of hackberry trees.

But soon subdivisions and strip malls appeared, car lots and gas stations, the fertile black loam hidden under concrete and asphalt.

Carla looked with interest at the newest subdivisions rising up near the college, abutting the strip centers. She found the raw newness exciting. Frank's townhouse was all very well, but someday she would have a house in a brand new subdivision, with the most modern appliances and all new furniture carefully chosen by her.

The coffee shop in the big shopping center across from the community college was a favorite student hang-out. A few newly planted trees attempted to shade its patio, where Rhonda had secured a table. She beamed as Carla approached.

"Congratulations, Carla! I'm so proud of you. What will you and Frank do to celebrate?"

Rhonda was wearing Calvin Klein jeans and a loose-fitting purple top that went well with her dark burnished hair. She was tall and large-boned, but never awkward. She looked happy and relaxed, seated in a patio chair with an expensive sandal dangling from one foot. A cup of half-drunk herbal tea sat in front of her.

Carla smiled as she seated herself at the round white table. In her pale blue blouse fitted at the waist and flared over white slacks, she was a petite contrast to her friend.

"He's going to take me to a really nice restaurant, that new Argentine one."

"Oh, all that meat.   But I've heard it's really good. You're happy, aren't you, Carla?"

"Yes . . . but it's not the same."

"I know," Rhonda said, squeezing her arm. "Joe was so young. It's shocking. But you're young, too, and you need to live. Don't be hard on yourself."

"I try not to be.   Work helps.   I really like it. Radiology is interesting."

"It takes all kinds." Rhonda was laughing. "Me, I'll be stuck with a bunch of little kids. But then they're fun, too."

The sun was shining on the little patio where they had met for a sandwich, catching the highlights in Rhonda's hair and suffusing their faces with warmth. Bold grackles hustled for fallen bread crumbs near their feet. At a table nearby, a young woman stared intently at her laptop, an empty coffee cup abandoned next to it.   Farther away, a young man slouched in his chair, his feet propped on another, reading a worn paperback copy of The Stranger. In a far corner of the patio, a couple held hands across the table and spoke quietly, their cups of coffee forgotten.

"I still have a year to go. How will I do it without you to keep me in line?" Rhonda looked affectionately at Carla.

"You know you don't need me. You're doing so well. I'm proud of you."

"Well, any fool could pass these education classes. Who couldn't cut out and paste like a second grader? But it's true I've gotten more into it. Next semester I'll be student teaching. I'm so excited."

"You and Fred will have to come to dinner with Frank and me. I think I'm going to move in with him soon."

"That's wonderful! I'm happy for you."

"It's a big step, but he's just about convinced me."

Carla would do anything to get away from the Dubaceks, especially Mrs. Dubacek. What a domineering woman. But she had needed to live for free in that horrible rent house of theirs while she finished school. After taxes, the insurance money had been barely enough. She was so tired of scrimping and doing without. But now she was making a decent salary of her own. She got a warm glow thinking about it. Yes, she was going to live in Frank's town house—and about time he asked her—but someday she would buy her own house with her own money, and it would be all hers. Already she knew that she would work her way up. Concord Radiology would even pay for classes she could take to better herself. She couldn't imagine being stuck all day in a roomful of kids, like Rhonda. But to Rhonda, that was the easy way out. How stupid. But then Rhonda had never had any ambition.

"Here, I'll get this," Rhonda said, reaching for the check, and when Carla started to protest, added, "You know what a big allowance Daddy gives me, more than I really need."

Everything always comes so easy to Rhonda, Carla thought, but she looked up at Rhonda and smiled. "Thank you. You're such a good friend."

Chapter 33

June, 1997, Wirtz, Texas

Carla heard the car pull into the drive and glanced out the kitchen window of the little frame house. Mrs. Dubacek hauled herself out of the Chevrolet sedan and started up the steps with a decisive if laborious tread. Carla met her at the door.

"Won't you come in?"

It irked Charlene Dubacek no end to be invited into her own rent house, but she had to pause to catch her breath. The kitchen was spotless. No room for leverage there.

"Would you like a cup of coffee? I'm just making a fresh pot."

And in fact, the coffee maker was just sputtering to a stop and the aroma of freshly brewed coffee filled the small kitchen. There was no sign of cookies or other sweets, however.

"No thanks."

Mrs. Dubacek peered around the small house and stalked into the living room, which was neat and clean. But from there she could see clothes piled on the bed in the bedroom.

"Sort of messy, isn't it?"

"Yes, I've been going through my clothes, deciding which ones to take and which to give away."

"In my day we kept our clothes until we wore them out. Didn't always have to have something new. Just glad to have anything at all." Then it struck her. "Take them? Where do you think you're going?"

"I've found a place close to my work."

"You were just going to leave? Not tell me? What's the matter, this place not good enough for you?"

Of course it isn't, Carla thought, but she looked solemnly at Mrs. Dubacek.

"It's not just that the drive is hard, but I need to get away from all the memories. Everywhere I look in this house, I see . . . ."

"You've managed to live with them quite well for some time now. Don't think I don't know you were just waiting until you could finish school. If Anton hadn't insisted . . . . You never cared about Joe. You were probably just glad you got the insurance money. Another thing Anton did. If it had been left up to me——"

"Enough! You can insult me all you want, but don't you dare say anything about Joe. That's sacred to me. Now if you're through inspecting the house, I'll escort you to the door."

Somehow Charlene Dubacek found herself outside and stomping down the steps of her own rent house, with that hussy inside and probably laughing at her. Well, she was through with her. She couldn't stand the sight of her. She didn't care what Carla said, if she'd been any kind of wife to him, poor Joe wouldn't have taken to drink like that. Men just weren't as strong as women. You had to take care of them. Like Anton, now. What a softy he was, changing the insurance policy, letting that hussy keep on living there rent free. It made Charlene's blood boil every time she thought about it. She was well rid of her.

She had wanted the confrontation, but somehow it hadn't ended the way she had planned.

Charlene drove home and stormed into her own house still seething.

Chapter 34

June, 1997, Concord, Texas

Carla traveled lightly. All she took to Frank's town house were her clothes; computer, textbooks, and files; and a few kitchen items, like her cast iron skillet, favorite set of mixing bowls and measuring cups. Her wardrobe was slim. A careful observer of the world around her, she had paid special attention to the attire of women at the restaurants where Frank took her. She had discarded most of her earlier clothes, keeping only the ones necessary for work and her recent purchases, which she intended to add to.

"That's all?"

Frank was surprised when he unloaded the car for her. She had refused his offer to help her move out of the Dubacek house, claiming she had neighborhood boys eager to work. In reality, Carla never wanted him to see where she lived. Although Frank himself had spent his early life in Wirtz, he had long since moved on to a very different life. Carla had a way of adapting to men's expectations. The Dubacek house, Wirtz itself, did not fit her now cool sophisticated image.

Carla inspected the kitchen critically, opening up cabinets and looking into drawers, as though she had never been in it before. She looked behind the stove and ran her fingers across the top of the refrigerator.

"Frank, you need to fire your housekeeper."

Frank looked surprised. He had hired a woman to come in once a week, the house had looked fine to him when he dashed in and out on his way to some appointment, and he had assumed that was all there was to it.

"I know a good cleaning service that will do a better job for probably the same amount."

It was nothing to Carla that the women who worked for such services lacked health insurance, were ill paid, often mistreated, and subject to abrupt dismissal. She knew that such services were also not up to her standards, but they would do the basic heavy work and she could do the rest. Most importantly, she preferred the anonymity of a cleaning service.

"Okay."

"I'll take care of everything."

Carla seemed different to Frank. He couldn't put his finger on it. She had had her hair styled that morning and wore a deceptively simple outfit she had bought at Chico's (on sale as she bought everything). The lines of the pale gray slacks and the paisley patterned blouse that went with them were elegant even on her petite body. Without realizing she had changed, he admired her new look.

He had almost regretted his decision to ask her to move in with him, but she had seemed so elusive and he hadn't wanted to give her up. He liked having her on his arm. Men looked at her everywhere they went. But now she looked like she belonged in his town house. As for the housekeeping, he was happy to have her take over.

Chapter 35

August, 1997, Concord, Texas

"Frank, honey, there's something I need to tell you."

Carla stood at the kitchen sink, washing up her coffee cup. She half turned toward Frank.

"What? I've got to meet a client." Frank looked at his watch and then impatiently at Carla.

"I think I'm pregnant."

"What!"

"I know. We were so careful."

Shock, disbelief, anger, pride paraded across Frank's face in quick succession.

"Go on. Don't be late to your appointment. I just wanted you to know as soon as I did."

"We'll talk tonight. I have to go now."

Frank, always so decisive, strode out the door, but on his face lingered an expression almost of bewilderment.

He'll want to get married now, Carla thought. By the time he gets home tonight, he'll be excited and proud—almost as if it was his idea. She laughed to herself. Frank was a complex and strong-willed man, but he was no match for her.

"How did you find out?" Frank asked, sweeping Carla into his arms as soon as he walked in the door that evening.

"I went to the doctor yesterday, and they called today. Are you happy?"

"It was a shock, but I've always wanted to be a father. I wanted to wait longer, but yes, I'm excited. I'm making enough money now. You can stay home with the baby."

Carla looked away to hide her expression.

"I had better start supper—especially now that I'm eating for two."

"And you don't even drink alcohol. Not like that friend of yours. The baby will have a good start."

Yes, Carla thought, he's talking himself into it. Men were so easy.

She hummed to herself as she tossed the field greens with a balsamic vinaigrette. The new potatoes boiling on the stovetop were just done, and she drained them carefully. She closely monitored the ribeyes under the broiler. Frank liked his rare, so she had started hers sooner so that it would be well done by the time his was ready. The small toaster oven dinged, and she removed the hot rolls. Softened butter was already on the table. Earlier, she had made a cheesecake with a raspberry glaze; it really was beautiful, she thought. Men were different in their tastes, but they all reacted the same when you fixed their favorite meal.

Carla had carefully set the table in the dining room before Frank's arrival. Now she lit the candles. The soft light made the room seem warm and cozy.

"Supper's ready."

Frank took it all in.

"I should have brought flowers. I will, tomorrow."

"Hmm," said Frank, taking Carla in his arms after dinner and gently caressing her. "I suppose this is wasted effort."

"We could pretend we were going for twins."

The darkness hid Carla's look of triumph as Frank slid into her, but she made no attempt to stifle her moans of pleasure as Frank plunged deeper into her.

Chapter 36

Thursday, August 21, 2003, Graylor, Texas

It was 8:30 by the time Bill pulled up in front of the house. Mary Kay had already left for work. It was quiet. Bill rang the doorbell, waited, rang it again and again. Then he pounded on the door and shouted Jeffrey's name.

Jeffrey was still in his pajamas, his hair tousled, looking grumpy, when he opened the door.

"If you want to go, you better be ready in two seconds flat. And get you a hat and some sun block."

Jeffrey wheeled and ran back inside.

Bill leaned against the door of his pickup and waited.

In a remarkably short time, Jeffrey came running out, clutching a hat in one hand and sun block in the other. He hadn't combed his hair.

Bill started up the pickup without saying a word.

"Mama didn't wake me up."

"You think that's her job? To get you up for something you want to do? That she doesn't want you to do?"

Jeffrey was silent.

Bill drove.

Several miles down the road he said, "Son, you're responsible for yourself. Not your mama. Not anyone else."

After a while Bill slowed.

"We're looking for a brick house on the right. Big tractor barn, a couple of silos."

Within half a mile, Jeffrey had spotted the place. Sam Spacek, the man leasing the Wentrcek farm, was on the gravel yard in front of the big tractor barn, working on a shredder.

"Morning. I'm Bill Cummins. Talked to you on the phone. My son Jeffrey."

Mr. Spacek held out a hand to Cummins, nodded to Jeffrey. A black and white dog, medium sized, sniffed Jeffrey's leg. Jeffrey held out his hand to be sniffed too, was accepted, patted the dog.

"Looks like another hot one." Bill looked up at the cloudless sky.

"Yep. No rain in the forecast. Hard on the horses, ain't it?"

"Yeah, but they quit during the hottest part of the day. Should be finished with the Wentrcek place by noon."

When the ritual was finished, father and son drove back to Graylor, continued north past town, past the county road heading east, and pulled into the Oatville Store. Bill waited in the pickup, with the motor running and the air conditioner on, while Jeffrey ran in. Slight wispy clouds barely streaked the deep blue sky.

A black F 250 pulling a trailer load of calves passed the store, headed south down the highway to the auction barn two miles distant. A red Honda zipped past. Then Laura, a widow who lived three miles to the north, pulled in to the gas pumps. Today her arthritis was acting up, and wearing a shapeless brown dress and her sensible brown shoes, she leaned on an aluminum orthopedic cane. She filled her dark blue Corolla with gas before going into the store to catch up on the local gossip with Shirley. Bill nodded and touched his hat as she walked past his pickup. Old man Moravsky, once a farmer, now a lone widower, drove a battered old Dodge slowly into the parking lot and stepped spryly out of the car. He was wearing overalls that had seen better days, and his long white beard was stained with tobacco juice. His thinning hair was long unwashed and a little askew. He smiled and waved to Bill, then headed into the store for his first beer of the day.

Jeffrey came out clutching his coke and packet of peanuts, and Bill drove back south to the county road and headed east. It was almost ten when they reached the camp site.

"Talked to the renter, Sam Spacek. It's okay."

"We're loaded and ready to go," Jim said.

Bill turned to Jeffrey.

"Mr. Bowman will contact me if he finds anything and I'll come straight away. Otherwise, you can call me when you're finished for the day."

Bill and Jim exchanged a look. Bill headed for his pickup, and Jim gathered his men.

Chapter 37

October, 1997, Concord, Texas

"Will you be my maid of honor again?"

Carla and Rhonda were sitting on the beige leather couch of Rhonda's apartment in Concord, not far from the education complex that housed both Concord Community College and a secondary campus of the state teachers' college, where Rhonda was finishing up her degree. An entertainment center with a 32 inch TV, a VCR, and shelves of tapes faced the couch. The big living room window looked out on rolling, as yet undeveloped farm land. Everything was new, with almost a raw feel. Carla liked it.

"Of course, but you're making me feel so old. Here you are marrying a second time and I have yet to marry at all."

"If I could choose, there wouldn't be a second one."

Carla faltered on the last words, and Rhonda looked stricken.

"Oh, Carla, I'm so sorry. You know I didn't mean . . . How insensitive of me."

"It's all right. Frank will be a good husband. And I'm excited about the baby. It's just . . . sometimes I feel I haven't fulfilled my destiny."

"I remember all you used to say about you and Joe. But I guess God's plan was different. I mean, I'm not real religious or anything. But sometimes I do think things happen for a reason, although we don't understand it. Even though Joe will always be in your heart, I think you and Frank will be happy."

"Thank you. I know you understand. You're a true friend."

Rhonda's eyes filled with tears and she clutched Carla's hand.

They sat silently for a moment, and then both reached

for the Kleenex box on the coffee table at the same time, bumping hands. They looked at each other and began to laugh, the light-hearted laugh of the young, a tear still wet on Rhonda's cheek.

"Jason will be ring bearer. Would your little niece be flower girl? It's funny, we're all girls, but June only has boys."

"Of course. Rita will be so cute. She's adorable."

Carla stood up slowly. She didn't look all that big, but she felt big. And she couldn't believe how tired she felt at the end of the day. Work was hard, even though she loved it. She just didn't have much left for Frank afterwards. He had been disappointed when they found out the baby was a girl. "That's okay, Frank. We can have a boy next time," she had said. But there wasn't going to be a next time. As soon as this baby was born, she would take care of that. One was enough.

"What about you and Fred?"

"Fred who," Rhonda said and rolled her eyes. "He's such a loser. I don't know why I ever got mixed up with him anyway."

"You thought he was a lot of fun at first."

"Yeah, he was. And he's good-looking. But he'll never amount to anything. Not like Frank. I'm so happy for you."

Carla sighed. "Your turn will come."

Chapter 38

June, 1998, Concord, Texas

"Oh, Carla, she's so beautiful!" June could hardly keep her hands off the baby. "I love my boys to death, but I've always wanted a little girl, too. And now I have this precious niece."

At three months, Jenny was a beautiful baby. She was what is called a "good" baby, meaning she had a well-developed digestive system, and as long as she was dry and fed, was pleased with the world. It would be some time before she started to teethe.

"I know you miss Joe sometimes, but Frank is as crazy about this baby as any man could possibly be. It was terrible what you had to go through. But you've been rewarded. You are so incredibly lucky."

"Yes," Carla agreed, but she was thinking, Luck? You make your own luck. Could anybody be as stupid as June?

Carla looked at her sister holding the baby. Jenny was beautiful. She was proud when people admired her baby. Granted, there was luck there, though Carla was inclined to think that it was only natural that she should have a beautiful baby. Poor June. It was perhaps bad luck that June should be so plain. Not that she was bad-looking. She was slender, a little taller than Carla, always well kept, and she carried herself well. But with Patty and Carla herself as sisters, she faded into the background. Still, June apparently wouldn't know what to do with her beauty if she had any. She was so stupid.

It was a beautiful late Sunday morning in early June, and the two women were sitting upstairs in the nursery in Frank's town house. Sunlight streamed through the east window, lighting up the coffee cups sitting on a gaily painted child's table. Outside, the two little boys, Jason and Daniel, were tossing a football back and forth.

Frank, who had just returned from showing a house, walked into the room and took Jenny from June's arms.

"How's my beautiful girl?"

He cuddled and kissed her, gently stroked her soft little cheek, gazed at her adoringly, before finally letting June have her back.

"I've got another showing at two.   It's 45 minutes away, so I need lunch by 12:00."

"It'll be ready, sweetheart."

Now, three months after the baby's birth, Carla was back to her old self, full of energy, doing whatever she felt like.   She took a last sip of coffee and watched as Frank strode out the door.   Although he was just average-sized, he was athletic and fit, with not a spare ounce.   He ate well, jogged regularly, occasionally worked out at the gym.   As a realtor, he was always on the go.   When he walked into a room, he radiated masculine energy.

"I've never seen a man so silly about a baby," June said after he had left.   She was smiling to herself and to the baby. "Isn't that right, sweet pea?"   Turning to Carla she added, "But he's awfully serious, isn't he?   Sometimes I'm almost afraid of him."

"You just have to know how to manage him.   He likes things done a certain way, and he's very organized, but so am I.   You know how much I like to cook.   If you feed men well, they're generally happy."

June laughed.

"You were always so level-headed.   That's what Daddy used to say.   And we were lucky to have Momma.   She taught us both well.   Patty, too, is a good cook.   She's not so flighty as she was, but she and Daddy still get into it sometimes.   I think you were his favorite."

"Well, you were Momma's."

"I don't know.   I was the oldest, and she put a lot of responsibility on me.   But then she had to, with two even younger.   Always having to scrimp and save.   Making all our clothes. She even took in sewing sometimes. You should come see Momma and Daddy more often. I know they miss you. They haven't seen the baby in over a month."

"I try. But you know I work. And I have to keep Frank happy. Plus it's like packing for an expedition just to take a baby twenty miles."

It was fun to show off the baby from time to time, but after a while it got boring. Momma and Daddy were old and in a rut. Plus Patty was a pain in the butt, always so full of herself. Entered the house like a hurricane. Now that June had a job at the telephone company, she was helping out at home. In fact, Momma and Daddy were dependent on her. Well, June had always been stupid, letting someone else suck up her life. Imagine all of them—Momma, Daddy, Patty, June, Jason and Daniel—all crammed into that small house. Carla shuddered. She didn't know how they could stand it.

"I'd better get lunch on the table. You can play with the baby and keep me company."

"Nothing I'd like better. But I can help, too."

June held the baby cradled in her left arm while she set out silverware and paper plates. Carla heated up homemade chicken and noodle soup she had made the day before and set out a plate of tuna fish salad sandwiches she had made earlier that morning. The two sisters worked quickly and efficiently until everything was ready a little before 12:00.

"You boys come wash up."

Jason and Daniel entered noisily, but soon settled down, so that when Carla called Frank in, they were seated quietly at the table.

"Hey, boys. You hungry?"

"Yessir," they said almost in unison, and Frank laughed.

Jenny began to fret, and Carla handed June the bottle she had been warming.

"You want to feed her?"

"Oh, yes."

As soon as the boys had torn through their sandwiches and soup, they asked if they could be excused.

"Can I hold the baby?" Jason asked, holding his arms up.

"Me, let me hold her," Daniel said.

June glanced over at Frank.

"When you get a little older. Now go out and play while you can, because we have to leave soon."

No one else said anything. The boys started to protest, but June looked at them sternly and Frank suddenly stood up and took the baby himself.

"I'll put her down for her nap," he said.

Carla and June put away the food, cleaned the kitchen.

"He's so good with that baby. Not every man is."

June gathered up her purse and called the boys.

"Come see us soon. Momma and Daddy are getting up there. And Patty will be a senior and gone before we know it."

Every little bit helps, Carla thought, but she said, "Oh, you know I will. I miss everybody. But you see how it is here. Frank works so hard. I have to take care of him. But I will come soon. Give them my love."

The baby was asleep, Frank was gone, and the house was still. Carla poured herself a cup of coffee and sat down on the couch with the state college fall schedule. Already she had worked out a plan to complete a four-year nursing degree. Starting in the fall, she would take two night courses, then more in the spring if she felt she could handle it. She hoped Concord Radiology would pay for the courses, even though she would quit there as soon as she got a job as a trauma nurse. But they didn't have to know that. And Frank could keep the baby.

Chapter 39

August, 2001, Concord, Texas
"We are all so proud of you, Carla—the first in our family to get a college degree!"

The two sisters were sitting across from each other at the kitchen table in Frank's townhouse. Outside, sunlight filtered through the small hard leaves of the live oak shading the patio, an errant beam falling on a bright red cardinal poised on the concrete edge of the patio.

"Once you put your mind to something, you never quit."

"Thank you, June. It's your turn, now."

"I know. You've inspired me. I've signed up for two classes this fall. Someday I'll live my dream of teaching fourth grade."

"I know you will, and those children will be so lucky," Carla said, but she was thinking, Why is June so stupid? Always putting herself last, never going for what she wants.

Their father had died suddenly of a heart attack, the year before, and their mother now lived on social security and what June contributed to the household, which was almost everything she made. Patty was finally out of the house, living with an aunt in East Texas and going to junior college, working part time.

"The boys are old enough they're not a burden on Momma now. I don't mind being gone two evenings a week. I'm really excited, to tell you the truth."

"You'll do well. School's fun. But you'll be shocked at these young kids who think all they have to do is show up. And they don't even do that half the time." June would be an outstanding student. Both sisters were organized and worked hard. But she couldn't believe June. She could have her degree by now, or be close to it, if she had gone for what she had wanted. I guess Momma can take care of the boys, Carla thought, with June supporting her all this time. What was June thinking?

"Aunt June, Aunt June!"

Jenny came running into the kitchen where her mother and aunt were drinking coffee. She was a pretty child whose straight blonde hair framed a soft round face with hazel eyes.

"Look what I drawed."

"Oh, that's nice. Is that your momma and daddy?"

The two stick figures looked indistinguishable, but June had made a good guess.

"Yes, and that's our house. And a tree. Daddy's taking me to the park after lunch."

"And after your nap," Carla added.

Jenny wisely chose to ignore this unwanted addition and began to play with the buttons on June's blouse.

"Would you like to come to Grammy's tomorrow?" June asked.

"Grandma's taking me to church tomorrow."

Carla's face darkened but she said nothing.

"Then maybe you can come to Grammy's next Sunday and go to church with us. And play with Jason and Daniel."

Jennifer looked questioningly at Carla, who nodded decisively and said yes.

June put her arm around Jenny.

"Maybe Jenny could spend Saturday night and watch a movie with the boys."

"Oh, please, Momma."

"I think that might just work out. Thank you, June."

Frank and I need a night on the town, Carla was thinking as she and June embraced goodbye; he's getting way too irritable. The real estate market was not good these days, and Frank had a tendency to take out his frustrations on those around him. And that mother of his was unbearable. Who did she think she was, trying to take over Jenny, immerse her in that weird church she belonged to? Carla's family was

Southern Baptist and church had been part of her life growing up. Although she wasn't much interested in spending her Sundays that way now, she thought it was a good thing for Jenny to go to a good solid church.

She and Jenny waved as June drove off.

"Come on, honey, let's go fix Daddy's lunch."

"Daddy, Daddy!" Jenny cried, running to meet Frank as he came in the front door. He swept her up in his arms.

"How's my beautiful girl?"

"I'm going to church with Grammy. And watch a movie with Jason and Danny."

Frank looked at Carla and scowled.

"That's next weekend, sweetheart," Carla said, bending down to check the casserole in the oven, her back to both of them. "Tomorrow you're going to church with Grandma."

"Be my horsey, Daddy."

"It's time for lunch now, sweetheart," Carla said, taking the casserole out of the oven. "Go wash your hands."

While sounds of laughter and running water issued from the bathroom, Carla took the salad from the refrigerator and placed it on the carefully set table. Her dark eyes flashed, but her face had softened by the time Frank and Jenny returned, hiding the determination underneath.

Chapter 40

November, 2002, Concord, Texas

Almost every time Carla entered the ER, she felt a little frisson of excitement. The cold air, the antiseptic smell, the bustle, the anticipation—one never knew what would happen, one of the things she liked best about the job. The hours could be difficult, the days changing by the week, and Carla liked that less. But she was adaptable, and her strong organizational skills enabled her to keep everything running smoothly at home as well as at work. What she liked least of all was a shift during which nothing much happened. Fortunately, there weren't too many of those.

She was on the 1:00 p.m. to 1:00 a.m. shift now, which was often slow in the afternoon, but picked up in the evening hours, especially late at night. Carla liked having full days off, when she could get everything done and still pick Jenny up from daycare. Some days she kept Jenny home and let her help in the kitchen. Sometimes they went to Graylor to visit Grammy, June, and the boys, or perhaps went shopping together. She kept a calendar of her work schedule and coordinated it with Frank, so he could pick Jenny up on days when she couldn't. Fortunately, he adored his daughter and as a realtor could schedule his own hours.

A call came in and suddenly the atmosphere in the ER changed: forty-six-year-old man thrown from his motorcycle at high speed. Helmet intact. Fully conscious. Severe injuries to arms and legs. Doctor needed immediately.

Within minutes the medics rolled the man in. The hand had been torn off the right arm, exposing the muscles and tendons, and the right foot had been crushed. The left hand was also badly mangled and the left leg injured as well.

The doctor took a deep breath. They would be lucky to save the man's life.

Carla was already taking blood pressure and checking

the pulse, while the doctor checked for a pulse in the mangled right foot. He shook his head. The only limb that could possibly be saved was the left leg and foot. The open wounds of the extremities, full of dirt and grit, would have to be fully cleaned before surgery.

Carla looked with interest at the tangle of exposed tendon and muscle in what was left of the right forearm. She set to work to thoroughly and carefully clean the bloody mass. Intently focused, she barely heard another nurse quietly vomiting into a barf bag in the corner of the room.

As he prepared for surgery, the doctor noted with admiration Carla's cool professionalism.

The injured man appeared strong, with good vitals considering, and the CT scan showed no internal bleeding. A couple of fractured ribs, but the spine intact, no collapsed lung. Blood flow to the left leg and foot looked okay, though a bad fracture of the ankle. Triple amputations—right arm just below the elbow, right leg at the knee, left hand.

Carla watched with fascination as the saw ground into flesh at high speed, spraying bits of bloody flesh and shards of hard bone like sawdust, and as the drill bit into bone for the placement of screws in the one possibly salvageable leg. Afterwards, the three bloody stumps were wrapped round and round like mummies.

The doctor felt good about his work and afterwards complimented the team.

"This was a real challenge, and we can expect to have nightmares for a few nights. I know I will. But you have done a fine job (and here he couldn't help glancing at Carla, who cast her eyes down modestly) and given this man a chance to survive. The next few days will tell the story."

The team had hardly taken a breather when the next call came: bad wreck, child involved. Carla set her coffee cup down.

Medics rushed three stretchers in, prioritized. The driver, the father, though in shock, had no apparent serious injuries.   The mother, lying weakly on the stretcher, was bleeding from cuts to the head and face. Semi-hysterical, she kept crying, "My baby, my baby!" as one of the medics patted her arm and told her everything would be all right.   The toddler, a handsome boy with beautiful brown eyes and thick dark brown hair, his head at a slightly odd angle, was the first priority. He lay still, with wide open eyes, barely breathing, surrounded by the ER team. No sensation in the legs or feet. Likewise, none in the arms and hands. The nurse standing at the foot of the stretcher looked down at the lovely boy, her eyes filling with tears.

Carla listened with interest as the doctor summed up the case: although the neck was not broken, the CT scan revealed serious damage and displacement. The prognosis was not good, he said. The child would not likely regain function. He would have to be on a respirator, and the risk of infection was high.

Before her shift was over, a man had been brought in with a severe cut to the leg, a chainsaw accident, and an older woman had fallen and broken her hip. At midnight, the medics rolled in a man with a large knife stuck in his chest, the handle and part of the blade sticking straight up and pulsating. The man was conscious, but in shock.

After her shift had ended, Carla drove through the city, still partially awake at this hour, and into her sleeping neighborhood. What an interesting and unusual shift it had been, she thought, as she reviewed the afternoon and evening. All the different ways the human body could be injured or compromised. She enjoyed the exercise of her skills and the respect she could see in the doctors' eyes. Sometimes people survived and sometimes they didn't, but the injuries in all their variety were fascinating.

The November night was still with a pleasant chill in the air. A full moon illuminated the neighborhood, lighting up the lawn and causing the trees to cast faint shadows. A few brown leaves scattered across the walk crunched underfoot.   She let herself into the townhouse and silently climbed the carpeted stairs.

Frank lay sleeping quietly, the bed comfortably warmed by his body, as Carla slipped in beside him, uninterested in waking him.   The events of the night passed before her: the triple amputee, the gory chainsaw cut, the quivering knife in the man's chest, the paralyzed child.   She curled up in the warm bed and floated off into a deep and dreamless sleep.

Chapter 41

December, 2002, Concord, Texas

When Jenny woke up that morning and looked out her bedroom window, the sky seemed to be filled with dark birds. As she watched, they wheeled, circled, and landed in a flock in the back yard. The ground was covered with black chattering birds busily pecking at the earth.

Jenny raced downstairs into the kitchen. Her mother was busy at the stove, her back to her daddy, who was scowling.

"Daddy, Daddy, the back yard is full of birds, lots and lots."

Even as she spoke, there was a loud whirring noise as the birds rose in unison and blackened the sky.

Frank held his arms out to her.

"Those are blackbirds, sweetheart. It's winter time."

"But, Daddy, why so many?"

"I don't know," Frank said, as she snuggled into his arms, "but it happens every year. They fly in big flocks and all feed together. Some are redwing blackbirds, and if you look real closely, you can see a bright spot of red on their wings."

Unbidden, the image rose before him: against a gray winter sky, a great mass of blackbirds wheeling in unison, dropping to earth and covering the dark plowed rows of the quiescent fields, then suddenly whooshing upwards, while he and Jimmy stared in wonder. The sudden stab of pain hit him for the first time in many years—the loss of his little brother and all they had shared. He held Jenny tighter.

"I'm hungry," Jenny said, wriggling loose.

"Your oatmeal's ready." Carla was already setting the bowl at Jenny's place, along with a little pitcher of milk and the bear-shaped plastic bottle of honey.

Frank rose from the table.

"We'll talk about where to spend Christmas later."

"All right," Carla said mildly.

As soon as the front door closed behind Frank, Carla turned to Jenny.

"How would you like to go see Grammy, Aunt June, and the boys this morning?"

"Oh, yes. Could I spend the night, too?"

"Well, I'll have to call and see. I know Grammy would like to take you to church in the morning."

"I could wear my new blue sweater set."

Carla smiled, picked up the telephone, and arranged everything

Jenny sat happily beside Carla, clutching her overnight bag containing the blue sweater set as they drove east toward Graylor, the highway bisecting the vacant fields. The bright but distant sun shone down on the colorless landscape: gray fields, dun pastures, bare trees. Half a dozen brown calves clustered around a half-eaten round bale of pale hay in a small, over-grazed pasture. Two of the calves locked heads, shoving each other, trying to establish dominance. Jenny gazed out the window, taking in everything. She was wearing a pink jogging suit with a little brown bear on the front of the top and little brown bear footprints at the bottom of the pants legs, her favorite play clothes. She had packed a little jacket, but would probably not need it, for the temperature would rise to the sixties by afternoon. Sweater weather, Carla thought, remembering her own childhood and the thrill she felt when a cool spell finally interrupted the long heat of summer.

She was glad Jenny was spending the weekend in Graylor. She was tired of Frank, tired of his domineering, tired of his insistence that Jenny spend time with his mother and not her family. He was getting to be more trouble than he was worth. He would be angry when he discovered where Jenny was, but his lunch would be ready when he got home at noon, and then she'd be off to work. He'd get over it. Someday she wouldn't need Frank at all. He had no idea how much she made, how much she had socked away. The pride of the man made it easy: he believed a man should support his family, and that whatever a woman did was just pocket money. Carla smiled to herself.

Chapter 42

January, 2003, Concord, Texas

Carla was excited. Frank was away for the weekend at a realtors' convention, and Jenny was spending the night with his mother and going to her church in the morning. Although she disliked Lucille Johnson and Lucille Johnson's fervent church, she was glad to be free to go out with her colleagues.

"Do you like to dance?" one of the nurses had asked.

"Oh, yes, but I haven't in a long time."

Carla never talked about her personal life at work, except for arranging her schedule around her child. Somehow the impression had been left that she was a single mother. Carla liked it that way.

Now the four of them were on their way to a small dance hall in a nearby town whose main street was only two blocks long. The only businesses left were a large barbecue place and, around the corner, the honky-tonk, once a saloon, whose Old West swinging doors were still the entrance.

They sped down the highway through bare, darkened fields and eventually turned onto a winding county road. They passed an occasional crumbling frame house, uninhabited, dimly caught by the side illumination of the headlights. More substantial and grander houses, set back from the road, remained unseen. At a crossroads, they passed a hamburger joint. Pickups and a few cars crowded the small parking lot in front of the weathered wooden store. Across the road was a filling station, now closed and darkened, and to the north of it, a few houses trailed along the west side of the road, quickly succeeded by open farmland. A single brick home sat on the east side, catty-cornered to the store. To the south, open pastureland descended toward a large creek no longer visible in the darkness.

"Joe's Place is doing a good business tonight," one of

the nurses remarked.

"Did you know that Mr. Novacek had a second heart attack? They brought him in on my shift last week. He made it, but I don't know for how long," said another.

"Well, Ma has been running the place for some years now. His health hasn't been good since the first one."

They turned right on a state highway, passing now through pasture land alternating with cropland. The stars were clearly visible in the cloudless night sky, the air pleasantly chill on this still evening.

From the highway they turned left and drove through the small collection of houses that passed for a town. All was dark along the two-block main street except for the barbecue place, and around the corner, the honky-tonk.

The four women had arrived early. Passing through the swinging saloon doors, they quickly secured the last vacant table. Like all the women there—and the men, too—the nurses wore jeans. Carla was wearing a white shirt embroidered with a blue and green curlicue pattern, tucked into her jeans. A leather belt with a little silver buckle encircled her small waist.

Soon the band, already set up, began with "Whiskey River."

"Yee Hah!" shouted the crowd in one great roar at the opening notes. The band responded enthusiastically, the first couples stepped out onto the floor, and the evening was on its way.

Carla sized up the crowd as she sipped her coke. Nothing much of interest. Still, she loved to dance.

A few single men approached their table, the first asking Carla to dance, the others settling for the other nurses, though some men preferred a big buxom woman, a nice handful, and others were just happy to have a partner.

Many of the men, as well as the women, were surprisingly good dancers, fluid in their movements, decisive in leading their partners through intricate movements to the two step or an occasional waltz. Young people, middle-aged people, and older couples who had long since passed their fiftieth wedding anniversary, shared the dance floor.

Carla thrilled to the beat of the music, the exuberance of the crowd. Light on her feet, she intuited a man's movements almost before he knew himself. She never lacked for a partner.

As the evening wore on, the room turned hazy with cigarette smoke, hot with the heat of many exerting bodies, and Carla had had her fill. Her colleagues, however, had settled in with their beers, and a couple of men had taken up residence at their table.

Carla's dance partner twirled her around just as the swinging doors swung open and a large man entered. About six feet four, with broad shoulders, he was powerful and work-hardened. His expression was good humored, but he glanced around the room with a penetrating gaze, a gaze that landed on Carla just as her partner swung her around in a double twirl. Carla almost dropped her partner's hand, but recovered herself and gave the stranger a bewitching smile on the second turn.

He stood stock still as the dancers swirled around him, then followed Carla as her partner escorted her to the table, and immediately asked her to dance.

He marveled at her petite beauty. He was a good dancer himself, but in his arms she seemed light as milkweed down floating on a summer breeze. She felt his every move, and it was as if they had been dance partners for many years.

"Let me buy you a beer," he said, seating himself in an empty chair at her table, so that one of the nurses had to find another when she returned.

"No, thank you, but a ginger ale would be nice." She smiled sweetly at him. "What is your name?"

"Ray. And you?"

"Carla."

Ray would have driven to the next town for ginger ale

had the bar not had some. He returned to the table and couldn't stop staring at Carla, the dark waves framing her pale face, now slightly flushed from the dance, the dark eyes seeming to draw him into their depths. She sipped her ginger ale and exerted her power.

They danced almost every dance, Ray reluctant to let go of her. As it grew late, Ray suggested he drive her home.

"No," she said firmly, "but I will give you my phone number."

She gave him her cell number and turned back to the other nurses.

"Let's go home."

The others were ready. It had been a successful evening for some, and a lot of fun for all. As they gathered their purses and headed for the door, Carla turned and gave Ray her most dazzling smile. He might as well have gazed on Medusa, for he was rooted to the spot.

Just before the swinging doors closed behind her, Carla glanced back and gave him her roguish smile. He leapt to his feet, but the band had started up and by the time he fought his way through the dancers, the women were driving off.

Carla laughed to herself in the back seat of the car.

Chapter 43

March, 2003, Concord, Texas

The front door slammed shut. Frank was later than usual. His compact athlete's body was as tense as a coiled spring, but his words slurred slightly as he spoke.

"Where's Jenny?"

Carla turned from the counter where she had been emptying the dishwasher and putting away the clean dishes. She wore gray slacks and a soft blue sweater, her hair in a French twist, with a rebellious curl or two escaping around her pale face. Her dark eyes looked even bigger with her hair upswept.

"With June and the boys, for supper and a movie. Don't you remember?"

"I don't like her spending so much time with those rough boys."

"They're her cousins, Frank, and they think the world of her."

"Well, I don't like it." Frank looked around at the clean and empty kitchen and stepped forward. "Where's my supper?"

"We were supposed to go out to eat. An hour ago."

Carla had her back to the counter and stared at Frank. Frank lurched toward her.

"I don't want to go out. I want my supper at home, right now."

He took a few more steps toward her, scowling.

"Fix it yourself. I'm going out."

As Carla walked briskly past him, her heels clattering on the tile floor, Frank grabbed her arm and jerked her backward.

"Where do you think you're going?"

He swayed a little and tightened his grip, his tone belligerent and menacing.

"Get your hands off me!"

She turned and looked him full in the face.

Frank caught his breath.

"Hateful.   You should see your face.   Hateful. Hideous!"

"Let go of my arm." Her voice was low but steely.

Frank's fingers were bruising her arm, already leaving red marks.   With her free hand, Carla tried to shove him away.

As though a spell were broken, Frank suddenly punched her in the face, connecting with the bone just under her left eye. He staggered a little, almost losing his balance, and in that instant Carla was at the kitchen counter. She whirled around with a butcher knife in her hand.

Speechless, Frank looked into her eyes and shuddered —he couldn't help himself.

"Get out! . . . I said, 'Get out!'"

"Take it easy." Frank held out his hands and slowly backed away.

"Get out now!"

"I'm going, I'm going. I'll come back when you've had a chance to calm down."

He was completely sober now.

Carla stood rigid, butcher knife in her hand, and said nothing.

As soon as the door closed behind Frank, Carla ran upstairs and started packing, her hands shaking from the adrenaline overload. She pulled out her cell phone.

"June, can you keep Jenny for a few days?"

"Sure, but what's the matter?"

"Don't ask me now. I'll tell you later. Wait 'til you hear from me. Just make up anything to tell Jenny."

"Okay, but . . . "

"I'll be all right. You know I can take care of myself. I just need time."

"Be careful, dear. Don't worry about anything. I'll

take care of Jenny. But call me. I'll worry until I hear from you."

"I'm safe. I'll call you tomorrow."

Carla carried suitcases and boxes out to her car until she had all of her clothes and all of Jenny's clothes and her favorite toys. Then she drove off.

~ ~ ~

Carla entered the empty new house in the subdivision. Everything smelled fresh and new, and the empty rooms echoed. She set down suitcases in what would be her bedroom, then returned to the car for more. What would eventually be the front lawn was recently sodded raw earth.

A high March wind rattled a For Sale sign in the yard across the street and cut through her thin blue sweater as she traveled back and forth between the car and house.

She hadn't planned to make her move so soon, but Frank had left her no choice. Her eyes burned, the adrenaline still coursed throughout her body, and her thoughts were dark. He would pay for this. She touched the darkening bruise on her left cheek and seethed.

After she had completely unloaded the car, she drove to Walmart and bought two thick pieces of bed-sized foam rubber, some pillows, and linens. Her next stop was H.E.B. When she returned with her purchases, she paused to survey the interior of the house, imagining how each room would look when she had furnished it just the way she wanted. The front door opened on a hallway that bisected the house. To the right was the living room, to the left her bedroom with its own bathroom. Then two more small bedrooms, with a bathroom between them. One would be Jenny's bedroom, which she would decorate with an animal motif, little bears in particular. The other small room would be her study. Already she could visualize the placement of her desk, her filing cabinet, a small bookshelf. A large open dining/kitchen area completed the right side of the house. Fortunately, the kitchen—her first love—was already complete. She admired the dark granite counter tops, the well-made cabinets, the state-of-the-art stove, the refrigerator/freezer combination, the free-standing butcher block. She soothed herself, stocking the refrigerator and cabinet shelves, putting aside the events of the night.

After she placed the foam rubber pieces, one in her bedroom, one in Jenny's, she returned to the kitchen to make herself a ham and cheese sandwich and a glass of tea.

The downturn in real estate had been a boon for her. She had gotten this brand-new, three-bedroom house, in a subdivision not completely built out, for a very low down payment, and she knew she could make the monthly payments. It might not be easy at first, especially since she still had to furnish most of the house, but she could do it. Damn Frank! Why did he have to force her hand so soon? He was so stupid. Falling apart just because business wasn't good. Men were so stupid.

Well, it was a good thing they were. It was so easy. Frank had no idea that she had been putting aside most of her salary, that she had bought her own house! For a moment she luxuriated in the sheer thrill of it. She had done this herself. This was her house, and everything in it would be just as she chose.

She wondered if she should call Ray. No, not yet. She had way too much to do. Let him worry about her a little while, anyway.

Carla wrinkled her nose at the new smell of the sheets as she spread them over the foam rubber. It felt strange, alone in the empty house, making up a bed on the floor. Outside, the rise and fall of the wind sounded muffled and distant. She opened up her cell phone. Ten o'clock. The adrenaline had ebbed away, leaving her tired and weary. She would sleep well. A good thing, for she would be up early—so much to do. Carla smiled with satisfaction as she rolled onto her side and fell fast asleep.

Chapter 44

March, 2003, Graylor, Texas

"Oh, Carla," June said, looking at the ugly purple bruise on her face, "I can't believe the same thing happened to you."

They were sitting in June's bedroom in the old frame house they had grown up in. A new cream colored duvet with a subtle light brown pattern and brown and tan matching pillows covered the bed. A small desk and lamp sat in one corner, and a worn antique love seat, on which the sisters sat, flanked the wall, the furniture the result of long hours spent in secondhand stores and flea markets. The room was a little crowded, but the overall effect was charming.

Carla looked up stone-faced, and the hardness in her expression startled June. Carla could see the shock in her face. With an effort, she softened her expression. She looked down at the floor and said in a low voice, "The same thing will not happen to me. He will never touch me again. He won't have the chance."

"But think about Jenny. He loves that child."

"I am thinking about Jenny. Do you think I want her to grow up believing it's all right for a man to hit her? For someone who claims to love her to beat her? Besides . . . ."

Carla paused, as though she were searching for the right words, words that wouldn't come to her, then continued with a rush.

"Besides, Jenny will have a good life. I'll see to that."

"Oh, I know you will. Will you come live with us? Now that Patty is gone, we can make room. Momma would be thrilled to have her only granddaughter here. Jason and Daniel would be so excited. They would be like big brothers to her. And it would be so nice to have my sister back—

144

almost like when we were kids.”

Carla looked down to hide the disgust in her eyes.

“That’s so sweet of you. But Jenny has her friends, she’s happy with her school—and it’s a very good school. Besides, the commute would kill me. I love my job, but it’s so demanding. And the salary is enough for Jenny and me to make it on.”

June looked at her sister admiringly.

“You have been through such hard times, but you always land on your feet. I know you work hard, but God has been with you. I can’t call it luck. Your luck has been terrible. First your teenage crush on that unstable guy we never even heard of, crazy Leroy. Then Joe, the love of your life, dying so young. That good man. I don’t know how you survived, how you pulled yourself together to finish school. You are so strong. And now this. Oh, Carla, I do feel for you.”

June reached out and Carla let herself fall into her arms. June held her without saying anything until finally Carla pulled away, a single tear running down her cheek.

“It helps to know you’re always there for me.”

June’s eyes filled and she brushed away the tears.

“Here comes Grammy.” Jenny’s high voice came from the side yard. “You’d better get that football out of her roses.”

June and Carla looked at each other and smiled.

“We’d better get ourselves in hand, too, before “Grammy” gets here,” June said, standing up and smoothing down her skirt. Then she and Carla walked into the kitchen arm in arm.

Chapter 45

May, 2003, Graylor, Texas

June was puzzled. Why wouldn't Carla let her come to Concord to see her and Jenny? Why wouldn't she at least let Jenny spend the weekend with them?

June paused and wrung out her mop. Outside, she heard loud laughter and the rough screeching sound of bikes sliding to an abrupt stop on the gravel drive.

"You boys stay outside. I'm mopping the kitchen floor."

"We just came to ask if we could go to Benny's house to shoot baskets," Jason called out.

"And stay for lunch," Danny added.

"Did Mrs. Markham ask you?"

"Yes," Jason answered.

"Okay, but remember you have to help Grammy in the garden later this afternoon."

"Yes, ma'am, we'll be back in time."

June paused until she could no longer hear the clatter of the bikes or the loud voices of her sons. She slid the mop back and forth, thinking about that last conversation with Carla.

"I'm just not ready," Carla had said. "Jenny and I have to get our lives settled. You know I have to do things my own way."

Well, that last was certainly true, June thought. As a child Carla had always wanted her way. But then, didn't all children? June thought of her two willful boys and smiled. Carla had grown out of it, matured. Unlike Patty, who couldn't stop fighting with Daddy—until Daddy had died. That had been so hard on Patty. She had cried and cried. Never could she make it up to him now. That was one reason, June thought, that Patty had fled to their aunt—to get away from the memories.

Carla had seemed so hard—momentarily—but that look on her face still haunted June. In some ways, she felt she didn't really know her sister. Like keeping them all at arm's length, now, when you'd think you would need your family the most. But Carla kept everything inside. Patty, now, was an open book. Whatever Patty felt, everyone knew—whether they wanted to or not. June had to smile when she remembered all Patty's teenage dramas. But it had been exhausting at the time.

June took a last swipe across the faded linoleum of the old kitchen floor before emptying the bucket at the foot of the hackberry tree in the back yard. White cottony cumulus clouds piled up on top of each other in a deep blue sky, slowly metamorphosing from castles to whales to oddly shaped elephants. The air was still and the warmth of the sun like a downy wrap. Honey bees haunted the honeysuckle growing on the wire fence dividing the back yard from the neighbor's yard.

Mid-morning, yet soon it would be hot. June put away the mop and bucket on the back porch and went into her room. Its well organized neatness comforted her. A van Gogh sunflowers print now hung above the love seat. She added little touches of beauty as she discovered and could afford them, and the subtle transformation of the room seemed to reflect the opening up of her own life. She paused just inside the doorway.

Carla seemed soft. She had wrapped Daddy around her little finger, never given him a moment's worry. But there was a hard streak inside her, a disturbing hardness. Well, that was how she had survived. Terrible things had happened to her.

June sighed and sat down at her desk. It would all work out. She opened up her textbook on curriculum development and was soon deep in concentration.

Chapter 46

June, 2003, Concord, Texas

Carla was tired but exhilarated. Her shift was over, and now she had three days off. The most interesting case on this shift had been a gunshot wound. A six-year-old playing with his father's pistol had shot his four-year-old brother in the head. The bullet had just penetrated the child's skull, and removing it had been a delicate and dangerous operation. The boy survived the operation, but the prognosis was uncertain. Carla was fascinated by the surgeon's skill and knowledge. She enjoyed trauma nursing. The work was complex, the pace often fast, and she throve on the challenge. She didn't understand people complaining of stress and burn-out. Other nurses often spoke of the emotional toll dealing with horrific trauma took. Carla wasn't sure what they were talking about. Perhaps it was another way of saying they couldn't organize their time well and adjust. Long periods when nothing happened during her shift, Carla would relax with a cup of coffee or sometimes even take a quick cat-nap, all of which fully revived her. People were just too stupid to catch the rhythm of the job and take care of themselves, she guessed.

Carla especially enjoyed the high salary trauma nursing provided. She looked around her living room with its brand new furniture, the 32 inch TV, the picture window with its heavy curtains. She sighed with pleasure and lay down on the cream-colored leather sofa, a show room piece she had gotten discounted even off the sale price.

Jenny was visiting a friend in the neighborhood, and the house was quiet. A nice nap would fully restore her, and then she would drive Jenny to Graylor to spend the night with Grammy, Aunt June and the boys. Jenny could go to church with them the next morning, and that would make everyone happy. And she and Ray could have a night all to themselves. It was okay if Jenny mentioned Ray now. It had been long enough, and besides, Jenny had no idea how long she had been seeing Ray. Soon she would start letting Ray spend more time at the house.

Carla curled on her side on the cool leather of the sofa and drifted off to sleep, dark ringlets framing the soft smooth face.

Chapter 47

July, 2003, Graylor, Texas

"Momma, June."

Carla's mother reached out and grabbed her, holding her for a long time.

"I've missed you and Jenny." Then holding her at arm's length, "You look good, though you could put on a few pounds. Are you eating right? And Jenny, come give Grammy a big hug."

June released Jenny and she ran to her grandmother, whose dark eyes lit up as she put her arms around her only granddaughter. Her soft wrinkled face softened even more as she gazed at Jenny.

"Where are Jason and Danny?"

"They'll be here soon, sweetheart. They knew you were coming. June made oatmeal cookies. Want one?"

"And Momma made a pot of coffee," June said, as the three women and Jenny headed for the kitchen. "Here, take some cookies out to the boys. I hear them now," she added, as the squeal of brakes and the crunch of gravel, accompanied by loud laughter, announced the arrival of Jason and Danny.

"Now tell me all about everything. You look like you've lost weight. I know it's been hard. Are you eating like you should?"

"Yes, Momma, you know I am. You taught us right. It's just that I work long hours and sometimes I'm too tired to eat much. But I love the work. It's so interesting. And it makes me feel good to help others."

Her mother reached over and squeezed Carla's hand. "And how are you getting along?"

"It's okay, Momma. I just don't think about him anymore."

"But he's Jenny's daddy."

"Yes, but . . . ." Carla looked down at the table and

paused a long time, her shoulders slumped, as if carrying a burden she couldn't express.   After a while, she sat up straighter and looked into her mother's eyes.

"I'm seeing someone, Momma. I don't know if it'll go anywhere. We've gone to dinner once or twice. Jenny has met him. I was just so lonely."

"Well, dear, take it slow."

"I will, Momma."

"You don't want to do anything foolish on the rebound. And you've got to think about Jenny."

"Oh, I do, Momma, I do. That's almost all I think about. That and my work—and I have to work to provide a good life for Jenny."

The back door slammed and feet pounded on the worn linoleum as three breathless children crowded into the kitchen.

"Can I go to the park with Jason and Danny, please Momma?"

"If it's okay with your Aunt June."

"Sure. But you boys take care of Jenny."

"Of course, Momma," Jason said, drawing himself up and looking insulted.

"I know you boys will look after her," Carla said, smiling at her nephews. "I have to go now, Momma. Be good, Jenny. Thank you, June."

Carla drove exactly the speed limit back to Concord, but her thoughts were flying. Ray was taking her to Cattle and Land Company for dinner, and afterwards they had the whole night alone together in her house. She smiled when she saw Ray's truck parked in her driveway. It was good that he had to wait a little for her.

Chapter 48

July, 2003, Concord, Texas

Jenny was playing on the wooden play center. From the kitchen window Carla could see almost the whole of the backyard, divided from the adjacent yards by a wooden privacy fence, just like all the yards in the subdivision.

"Look, honey, I just don't know what to do. He's a monster."

Carla looked soulfully at Ray, now her live-in boyfriend. Her large brown eyes filled with tears.

He was a big man, sinewy and strong. The short sleeves of his soft red cotton shirt revealed strongly muscled biceps and forearms. He wrapped his arms around Carla, feeling the swell of her soft voluptuous breasts. He had never met a woman like her, so vulnerable, so in need of a man's protection, yet a tiger in bed. He got chills just thinking about it. No woman before had ever turned him on like that. He couldn't get enough of it.

"I mean," Carla continued, "I'm afraid to let Jenny even be with her dad. If he got shared custody . . ."

Carla shuddered and moved closer in to Ray. Already he had an erection. He bent down to kiss her tenderly and she melted into him.

Outside they could hear the rhythmic thump of the swing as Jenny swung back and forth, back and forth, the legs of the swing, though anchored, lifting with each thrust and thumping on the downward swing.

Ray cradled Carla's bottom in his hands and pulled her closer. She thrust up against him and he felt his penis, rock hard, straining to get free.

"Tonight, honey," Carla said, and pulled firmly away. She moved briskly about the kitchen, getting out the cutting board, taking meat from the refrigerator. She was a good cook.

How lucky can I be? Ray thought, aching to touch her, but knowing that Carla always meant what she said: not now, the child could come in any minute. But tonight . . . He grew weak-kneed just thinking about it. He never knew what to expect.   Would she come out of the bathroom wearing black stiletto heels, black lacy bra, black lacy panties with no crotch, as she had done on one memorable occasion? Once, she had gotten down on all fours naked, barked like a dog, pretended to bite and play with a ball, and he had mounted her from behind. Another time, he lay on his back and she tied each arm and leg to a different bedpost. He had been reluctant at first, yet she had insisted. But the way she moved on top of him, totally in control . . . it was a completely new experience. He had thought he was going to explode.

He had always been a good lover, sensitive to his partner's needs and able to last a long time. He thought he had had a great and varied sex life, taking charge and making his lover happy. Now he saw that with all his other partners it had been the same old thing over and over. Carla had taken him to a whole new dimension. He couldn't believe what she could make him feel.

He had to stop thinking about this or he wouldn't be able to control himself. And he had to. When Carla said, "Not now," she meant it. Only once had she cut him off, and he was not about to suffer a repeat. He could wait until tonight—and it would be even better.

"Need some help, sweetheart?"

"No, thanks," Carla said, her motions swift and efficient as she sliced up fruit—fruit salad was one of Jenny's favorite dishes.

He bent over to kiss the top of her head, then went outside to play with Jenny.

Chapter 49

July, 2003, Wirtz, Texas

Lucille Johnson strode about her kitchen, washing up from the noon meal and thinking. She placed rinsed dishes in the new dishwasher and put away leftovers, in Tupperware boxes, in the large refrigerator. Plenty for supper without cooking again. An intermittent rattling sound showed the ice maker was hard at work. Otherwise the big refrigerator stood silent. Outside the window above her kitchen sink, just at the edge of its scope, to the right of the pecan tree and the birdbath, she could see buzzards circling above a distant field. A neighbor's dog barked excitedly.

She had never liked Carla, and now she was furious. Jenny was her very own granddaughter, and she hadn't seen her in two months. Carla was a sneaky thing—butter wouldn't melt in her mouth. She had never trusted her. And now she was proved right.

She looked out once more across the open fields, the corn eared out and the milo heads turning rust colored, ready for harvest soon. Her house was on the north edge of a subdivision on the north side of Wirtz, and from her kitchen window she could watch the eternal cycle: planting, cultivating, harvesting. Sometimes she missed the old frame house in the country, all the memories of married life and raising her children, but she didn't miss the cold drafts of winter or the heat of summer. She was too old for all that, and she liked the warm even heat in the winter time and the refreshing coolness in summer. She liked it a lot.

Frank was a good son, so successful. She looked around with pride at this house he had gotten her. Solid brick, three bedrooms, two baths. More than she could ever use, but nice to have.

That hussy had snagged him, and now that times were tough had abandoned him. Not that she was sorry to see her go, far from it, but she had another think coming if she thought she was going to separate Lucille Johnson from her own granddaughter.

Lucille wiped once again the already clean counter, then rinsed the sponge in hot water, squeezed it dry, and placed it in its little plastic tray behind the sink. She dried her work-worn hands on her brown and white apron, leaving the hand-stitched cup towel with its pattern of roses to hang in a neat fold from its holder. She glanced out the window above the kitchen sink again. The buzzards in the distance had disappeared. In the foreground, two sparrows perched on the edge of the bird bath. Each in turn splashed in the water, drops pearling on its feathers in the noontime sunlight.

Frank hadn't been himself lately. You'd think he'd be glad to see her go, but no, he missed her. Women like that knew how to get a hold on a man. Lucille frowned darkly as she imagined just what that hold was. Worse, Frank was feeling guilty. Well, a woman like Carla needed some sense slapped into her. She had shown her true colors by running out on Frank when times got tough. Frank might be down now, but she knew her boy. He wouldn't let a woman walk all over him like that. Already she was shacking up with another man. Lucille's lips curled down in scorn.

Frank loved Jenny. But Carla would hardly let him see her, just for an afternoon here and there. And this a daddy devoted to his child, a good father. But just wait. The right judge might not think that exposing a young child to some strange man in the house was such a good idea.

Well, Frank was a fighter. He ought to have custody of that child. Lucille's face softened as she thought of caring for that precious little girl. She had never had a daughter, and with Jimmy dying so young, Jenny was her only grandchild. For a moment, that night arose with startling clarity: the deputy standing on the front porch, the outside light illuminating the softly falling rain. "I'm sorry, ma'am, there's been a terrible accident."

Lucille gripped the edge of the sink and leaned forward, bracing against the pain. After a while she straightened up. "The Lord is my shepherd," she began and recited the whole psalm. Then she went into the living room and sat in the easy chair in front of the TV, but she didn't turn it on. Instead, she picked up the stocking cap she was knitting for Jenny. That nice young woman, a new member of the church, had brought her the most ingenious, but simple thing. You just wrapped and knotted the yarn around wooden knobs, and everything came out even. It was so easy. What would they come up with next? She even brought a pamphlet that showed pictures of what was popular now. All the girls wanted these stocking caps, it seemed.

As Lucille began to knit, the frown lines in her face relaxed, and she imagined teaching Jenny. What fun they would have.

Chapter 50

August, 2003, Concord, Texas

Frank picked up the pace. He ran smoothly with an athletic grace. It seemed effortless, but he began pushing himself faster and faster, racing to keep up with his thoughts. The hike and bike trail stretched out on the level plain before him beneath an unrelenting sun.

He had been married to Carla for nearly six years, but only in this year of separation did he feel he was finally beginning to know her. Had he loved her? Well, he sure didn't now. He had wanted to possess her, yes. What man wouldn't? She was the most exciting woman in bed he had ever known.

His rage and jealousy had been almost unbearable when he found out about Ray. When he finally tracked Carla down . . . . He couldn't believe Carla had bought a house on her own—and him a realtor—and he didn't even know it! But in the confrontation with Ray, Frank had backed down. Ray was a big man. Not the jogging type, but a hard-muscled outdoorsman. Carla had him wrapped around her little finger. She stood sheltered to one side while Ray warned him off.

"You will never hit this little lady again. You'll have to go through me first."

Ray was six feet four, with a broad chest and work-hardened hands; his voice was angry and contemptuous.

Frank stared at the rough man looming in the doorway, then turned and walked away.

No, he thought, he would never have hit Carla again —quite apart from Ray. He would never forget the look in Carla's eyes as she held the butcher knife toward him. It was like looking into the dark abyss. The hair prickled on the back of his neck just remembering.

Grudgingly, without his acknowledging it to himself,

he felt respect for her. No, he would not have dared to hit her again. Carla seemed so soft on the outside, but inside she was as hard and cold as steel.

From the level plain, the trail descended sharply to the creek, curved to the right, and followed the meanderings of the stream. Frank slowed his pace and ran carefully, nimbly picking his way through the rocks.

She had seemed so pliant, catering to his tastes, but ultimately she always did exactly as she wanted. Even the marriage. Looking back now, he realized she had probably gotten pregnant on purpose. Well, Jenny was the best thing that had ever happened to him. He could never regret that.

Frank's face momentarily softened, then hardened. No way was she going to keep him away from his daughter. He knew he could get shared custody. Not only did he deserve it, but he had the best divorce lawyer in Concord. His mother, he knew, wanted him to get full custody, wanted to help raise Jenny herself. But that wasn't going to happen. To begin with, Carla was a good mother. He had to hand her that. He couldn't prove she was seeing Ray before they separated, and besides, these days no one cared—except for his mother. Carla had a good job and provided a stable life for their child. No judge would take Jenny away from her. Besides, he had to admit it wouldn't be good for Jenny to be separated from her mother. Mom is just thinking about how much she loves Jenny, Frank thought. She's not thinking that Jenny loves her mom, too. Frank's mother would be a good influence on Jenny, and he would see that she spent a lot of time with her grandmother, but even Frank didn't want Jenny to be too deeply immersed in Wirtz. He wanted the very best for his daughter: the best schools, the greatest opportunities. In her pursuit of a career, Carla was a good role model.

Frank would give Carla her due, but Jenny was his daughter. He would, by God, have her half the time. Carla might be clever, but she was no match for him and his lawyer.

Up ahead, the trail split, the left fork continuing along

the creek bank.   Frank ascended the right fork, emerging alongside the street just blocks from his town house.   He slowed to a walk and breathed deeply.   He felt good now, relaxed and confident, his trim body glowing with health. Tomorrow he would confer with his lawyer.   He wished he didn't ever have to see Carla again, but that wasn't important. Soon he would have Jenny back on a regular basis.   He would give her such a good life.

Chapter 51

Friday, August, 15, 2003, Concord, Texas

"I want my daddy!"

"I know you do, sweetheart, but you know Mommy and Daddy don't live together anymore."

"But why?"

"When you're older, you'll understand. There are just some things that children don't know. You'll grow up some day."

"But I want my daddy now!"

Jenny stood in the middle of the kitchen, her straight blonde hair framing her thin oval face and greenish blue eyes. Her slender body was clenched with emotion, and her eyes were filling.

Carla thought a moment. In some ways Jenny was a little like her Aunt Patty. Her emotions were powerful, and she didn't care who knew how she felt.

"I know, sweetheart, it's hard. But you know that the hearing is coming up and the judge will decide everything. We just have to wait. Now I have to cook supper. Would you help Mommy? Maybe we could make that chocolate cake you like for dessert."

Jenny hesitated, tears in her eyes. "Okay," she said finally.

Carla pulled out the step stool that enabled Jenny to stand tall enough to work comfortably on the kitchen counter. She measured out the flour and handed Jenny the sifter. She was teaching her how to cook from scratch. Once you knew the basics, Carla thought, then you could build on that to cook any dish. So many young people today didn't know how to do anything, but her daughter would have the confidence that comes from expertise.

Jenny happily sifted the flour over and over, six times. Little clouds of flour drifted down and settled on the dark granite counter.

"Now what, Mommy?"

Carla plugged in the mixer and showed Jenny how to cream the butter and sugar. Jenny stood staring dreamily down at the whirring beaters, watching the bowl go round and round.

Carla rinsed and dried lettuce, tore it into pieces for the salad, peeled cucumbers and sliced tomatoes. She moved easily between her tasks and Jenny's. When the cake layers were in the oven, Carla let Jenny wash the bowl and beaters— after Jenny had licked them to her satisfaction.

The warm soapy water felt good. Jenny carefully washed everything and placed beaters, bowl, cups, and spoons in the drain, paying close attention so as not to break anything.

"What a good little cook!" Carla said, smiling at Jenny. "Do you want to watch your new DVD while the layers cook? I'll let you know when it's time to take them out."

Jenny hopped happily off the stool and ran into the living room. As for all children these days, thought Carla, electronic devices were no mystery to Jenny.

Potatoes were baking in the oven, and a huge sirloin steak, enough for all three of them, was resting on the counter. Carla filled a set of small bowls on a tray with the potato fixings: sour cream, butter, bacon bits, chopped green onion. By the time Ray came in, Jenny, with Carla's assistance, had iced the chocolate cake, and the steak was cooking under the broiler.

"Jenny made the cake. Isn't it pretty?"

"Did you do that all by yourself, Jenny?"

"Mommy helped me."

"I showed you what to do, but you did almost all of it by yourself. So now you know how to do it. You'll be a good cook."

"And know the way to a man's heart," Ray said. "I

can't wait to eat a slice."

After supper, when Jenny was safely tucked into bed, Carla turned to Ray. They were sitting on the white leather couch in the living room in front of the TV, but it was turned off.

"She was asking after him again. We have to do it."

"But the hearing is Monday. Let's at least wait to see what happens."

"Frank has hired the best lawyer in Concord, and he also knows the judge personally. There's no way he'll be kept from Jenny. I know he'll get shared custody. It's so horrible. We have to stop him. Look at Jenny, look at that innocent child. Can you even imagine his putting his hands . . ."

Carla began to sob hysterically. Ray put his arms around her and pulled her to him.

"It's okay, it's okay."

"No, it's not okay! I won't stand by and see my daughter destroyed. How can you say that? You don't even care."

She jerked away from him and stood up. She began to pace up and down.

"No, that's not what I mean. It's just . . ."

Carla turned and glared at him.

"Just what?" She stood rigid, every muscle taut. Her eyes burned. "You have no more feeling than a stone. You don't even care about Jenny. Think about that child. You know what he's done to her, what he will do. What kind of man are you? I thought you loved me. I thought you would protect me and my child. If I were a big strong man, I wouldn't be afraid of him. I would tear him to pieces with my bare hands. I would rip out his guts and feed them to the buzzards."

Ray was electrified.

"Carla! You should have nothing but sons!"

So petite, so vulnerable, yet looking as though through sheer force of will alone she could do anything. Ray thought his heart would tear in two.

"God knows I love you. I'll do it. He'll never hurt Jenny again."

Ray enveloped Carla in his big arms, and she melted into him. He bent to kiss her, his emotions overwhelming him. "Carla, Carla."

He lifted her up easily and started for the bedroom.

"Ray."

"Hmm?"

"I can't. Put me down."

Ray carefully set her on her feet and stood there trembling.

"All I can see are images of . . . of . . . Oh, Jenny, Jenny. Oh, please, Ray. Erase those images. Erase him. Not till then can I . . . Oh, I just can't."

Ray eased Carla back onto the couch and held her close to him.

"All I can see is his face . . . looking at her . . . his eyes . . ." Carla sobbed until she was hiccuping ". . . following her . . . wanting her."

Ray leapt to his feet.

"Tomorrow. I'll do it tomorrow. Tell me how."

Carla nodded, as though unable to speak. Finally she said, "Please, bring me a blanket and let me stay here."

Ray gently covered her with a blanket and turned off the light. He strode to the bedroom with a grim, determined look on his face, and took a long, long hot shower before finally falling into bed.

Alone in the dark, Carla curled over on her side and smiled.

Chapter 52

Saturday, August 16, 2003, Graylor, Texas

The phone rang mid-morning. There were several rings before June looked up from her desk, almost disoriented from the force of her previous concentration. Then she remembered Momma was out in the garden and answered.

"Carla? You sound so stuffy. Are you sick?"

"Yes. Working too hard, I guess. But I don't have to go in today. I was wondering if Jenny could spend the night with you all, go to church in the morning. Ray could bring her this afternoon."

June looked down at her desk, at the paper she was writing.

"Of course."

She would just have to rearrange her day. The boys could take Jenny to the park and she could get in a couple of hours' work then.

"You know we'd love to see her. Momma will be thrilled to have her go to church with us. Don't you worry about anything, just take care of yourself."

"Oh, thank you, June. I don't know what I would do without you."

"Nonsense. That's what family is for."

After she hung up the phone, June went back to her desk. She thought a minute, then began to make notes. She didn't even hear the back door open and close, and not until her mother called her did she look up from her writing.

"Lunch is ready, June. I've made ham sandwiches and heated up that leftover vegetable soup. Here come the boys now. You boys go wash up."

"Oh, thanks. I'm so excited about this paper, Momma. There is so much research now about the different ways children learn. It's fascinating. And this fall I'll begin my student teaching."

"I'm glad for you, dear. You've worked so hard. You deserve to finally get the work you've always wanted. You'll be the best fourth grade teacher ever."

After lunch, Momma went back to her room to nap, while June washed the dishes and cleaned the kitchen. She was showing her age, June thought, her hands occupied in the soapy water. Momma still worked in her garden and stayed busy with her church; her cakes and pies were still sought after for every fund raiser. She did a lot of the cooking for them, too, especially now that June was taking more classes, trying to finish her degree. But she did tire more easily.

June heard the crunch of car tires on gravel.

"Jenny's here," Danny called out. He and Jason were tossing a football in the front yard, waiting for Jenny's arrival. June had promised pizza and a movie—-they could pick it out (within certain limits, of course)—-if they would entertain Jenny for the rest of the afternoon.

June rushed out.

"Hi, sweetheart. Grammy's still taking her nap, but she'll be up later. Hi, Ray. Thank you for bringing her."

"Sure. How you doing? Hey, boys."

Ray looked pale, distracted. His eyes were hollow, and though he tried to smile, he didn't succeed very well.

"Won't you come in? I've got a pot of coffee on."

"No, thank you. I've got to get on back."

"Carla's okay, isn't she?" June was beginning to feel worried.

"Yeah, just wore out. A good sleep ought to fix her up."

"Well, tell her to take care of herself. We'll have a good time, won't we, sugar?" June smiled down at Jenny, giving her an extra squeeze.

"Come on, Jenny. We're going to the park," Jason said, feeling there had been enough standing around. "I'll push you on the swing like you like."

"Go ahead," June said, as Jenny looked at her

questioningly.

"We're going to have pizza and a movie afterward," Danny added.

June smiled and looked up at Ray to catch his eye, but he was staring off into the distance. She had never seen him like this.

"I got to be going," he said abruptly and got in the car.

June stood looking down the street long after the car had gone. Then she shook her head and went into the house. Momma was just coming out of her bedroom. Her face was softly wrinkled and her housedress a drab gray, but she was neat and tidy and still reasonably strong.

"Coffee's made. Want me to fix you a cup?"

"That would be real nice."

After her nap, Momma liked to read the Bible and drink a cup of coffee. She would sit in her rocking chair in the front room, reading and occasionally looking out at the street. It was her quiet time. Now she sat in her rocker with its old comfortable brown cushions and looked out over the small front yard, the grass dry and turning tan in the August heat. The big tabby cat from next door was dozing under one of the rose bushes flanking the sidewalk near the street. The faded green Ford sedan belonging to Mr. and Mrs. Baker up the street passed by, Mr. Baker driving and petite Mrs. Baker barely visible in the passenger seat. Momma wondered where the elderly couple were going. It was the hottest part of the day, too hot for running errands, one would think.

"Jenny's here. The boys have taken her to the park. I bribed them with pizza and a movie tonight. I've got to get this paper done."

June handed her mother a cup of coffee, fixed just the way she liked it, black with sugar, and took her own, just black, back into her bedroom. She sat down at her desk and took a sip of coffee. She couldn't get Ray's face out of her mind. It haunted her. Well, maybe he had quarreled with

Carla. She took another sip of coffee, then turned resolutely
back to her paper.

Chapter 53

Saturday, August 16, 2003, Concord, Texas

At midnight it was quiet in Carla's subdivision, most families in bed or perhaps watching a late-night movie back in the den. Clouds muffled the stars and drifted across a quarter moon, alternately revealing and concealing it. Carla's street was finished out, but just two streets over bare plats stood waiting in the darkness.

Ray backed out into the street in Carla's Camry and headed in the direction of Frank's town house. He knew the general area, but would have to get explicit directions from Carla. He had to grip the steering wheel hard to keep his hands from shaking. The closer they got, the more he wanted to be somewhere else.

Carla looked over at him and began to talk in a low voice, so quiet he had to strain at first to hear her.

"Ray, I never told you how he forced me . . . how he hurt me . . . how he tore at me with his hands . . . his fingers."

In spite of himself, Ray had an erection. Powerful, unidentified emotions swept over him.

"And then he would whisper dirty things . . . about Jenny . . . make me listen . . ."

Ray felt sick. He didn't want to hear this.

Then he looked over at Carla, shrinking into the seat, so small, so soft, so helpless. Dark ringlets had escaped from her pony tail and clung to her pale cheek. She looked hardly bigger than a child.

A surge of anger shook him. The bastard. The smooth little bastard. Adrenalin shot through his body until he felt if he didn't do something soon he would explode.

"Here. Turn right. At the end of the next block, turn left. It's the third one on the right. . . . Park right here, where he can see the car. You hide in those bushes. I don't think he'll try to do anything to me, but you can get to him quickly from there."

Ray grabbed the tire iron and quietly closed his car door. Just before he slipped into the bushes, Carla put her little hand on his big one and whispered huskily into his ear.

"Remember Jenny. Don't let him do to her what he did to me."

Ray entered the bushes stealthily, every sense alert, gripping the tire iron. He quieted his breathing and slipped naturally into the hunter's mode: waiting, listening, watching.

Carla rang the doorbell over and over until the outside light came on and the door opened.

"Carla?"

"It's Jenny, Frank. You've got to come."

"Where? What's wrong?"

"Here. In the car."

Frank started down the sidewalk, but Carla was in the way. He tried to get past her.

"Don't touch me, Frank!" Carla screamed.

Frank stood looking at her with a bewildered expression. He never saw the big man charge out of the bushes, and when he turned slightly at the sound of footsteps, it was too late. The tall man loomed above him and the tire iron descended from its high arc, crushing his skull.

Ray stood over him, breathing heavily, gripping the tire iron, but the man laid out on the sidewalk would never move again.

"Quick, Ray, put him in the trunk."

Carla had the trunk open. It was lined with heavy plastic.

On automatic, Ray picked up the body, still warm but not breathing, blood that had spurted now oozing out of the gaping hole where brains mixed with crushed bone. He placed the body in the trunk, closed the lid, then stood there dazed.

"Come on, Ray. We have to go."

Carla waited till Ray had gotten in the car, moving

like a sleepwalker, then closed the door on her side.

"Go to the highway and head east, past Wirtz, then north at Graylor. You remember what I told you. When we get north of Graylor, I'll give you directions from there."

Both were silent for a long while. Ray drove automatically, not speaking, not thinking, hardly knowing what he did. Carla looked down, hiding the blazing triumph in her eyes. Her body was rigid with excitement. She gripped the door rest hard and tried to slow her breathing and relax her body.

"Ray, honey," she said once they were out on the highway, "you need to slow down. We don't want to attract any attention."

Ray eased off on the accelerator without speaking. He couldn't talk. He had been racing away from what he had done, feeling that if he just drove faster and faster he could speed away from the crime, leave it behind him forever. Now it seemed that time had slowed down and that over and over he could see himself swinging the tire iron, hear the sickening thump like a busted watermelon, feel the hot blood geysering across him. He longed to floorboard the accelerator, to outrun the images.

"Up here, Ray. Turn right on that county road."

Ray slowed automatically, flipped the blinker, carefully turned right on the county road and drove straight ahead, waiting, without realizing he was waiting, for further instructions.

It was darker in the country than in the city, though occasional security lights near farm houses marred the night. The road wound through the countryside, slicing through farmland. To the left, trees defining its banks, a darker line in the darkness, flowed the San Sebastian River.

"Turn left here, honey. That little dirt road."

On either side of the dirt road, fields spread out in the distance. A jackrabbit, dazed by the glare of the headlights, zigzagged crazily across the plowed earth until he vanished in the enveloping darkness.

"Keep going. Follow this little track to the right."

The headlights glimmered on a picket fence half tumbled down, briefly caressed the leaves of an ancient pomegranate tree, and slid across an unkempt rose bush. Then a large barn loomed before the car.

"Stop here. Turn off the lights."

Ray obeyed automatically. Carla was out of the car and opening the trunk before he had lumbered out of his seat. She was holding a flashlight that shone on the bloody thing lying in the trunk.

"Quick. Pick him up."

Ray stood staring at the grotesque body, now becoming a rigid corpse, blood congealing around the crushed bone and brains, the mouth strained in a rictus of death. His mind was blank, and his powerful limbs heavy and paralytic.

"Wrap him in the plastic, Ray. We can't leave him in my car."

Slowly Ray began to move, as though a huge piece of machinery, its mighty motor finally revved up and its gears engaged, shuddered into motion. He wrapped the heavy plastic around the body and hauled it out of the trunk.

"Follow me."

Carla walked swiftly into the barn, shining the light before her, and with sure steps reached the dark interior.

"Here. Put him down here and slide the plastic out from under him. Don't touch him, just the plastic."

Ray did as he was told, automatically but carefully. Following Carla's directions, he folded up the bloody plastic and placed it in a bag she held out to him.

"Now take off your clothes, all of them, and put them in the sack."

Ray looked at her in surprise. His mind didn't seem to be functioning.

"I have clean ones for you, boots too."

Slowly he began unbuttoning his shirt.   Carla discreetly turned the beam away from him.   In the darkness without his clothes, he felt naked, naked in a way he had never felt before. He wanted to cover himself, like an untried girl. And he felt as helpless as one.

Carla stuffed the bloody clothes, including his boots, into the bag with the bloody plastic.   She handed him his clothing, one item at a time, and he slowly dressed. When he had stepped into his last boot, Carla headed for the open barn door. He slowly followed.

"Ray, honey, you need to pull yourself together for one last thing.   Follow this road past the barn as far as it goes."

Ray drove carefully down the dirt track until just before it dropped down the bank toward the San Sebastian River.

"Stop here, honey. I don't think we should drive all the way down. We might not be able to get back up."

Ray did as he was told, lugging the bag of plastic and bloody clothes down the steep riverbank onto a gravel bar.

"There," Carla said, pointing to a level area of rocks about four feet from the dark waters of the San Sebastian murmuring in the shallows. Automatically, Ray dropped the bag onto the rocks. Carla unscrewed the cap from a can of kerosene and thoroughly soaked the bag and its contents, then flicked a lighted match into its center and stood back as the flames roared into life.

One corner of Ray's mind noted the skill and efficiency with which Carla worked. She leaned in close to him as they stood watching the fire consume the bloody evidence. The plastic melted and curled and blackened. The clothes took longer, though they had been thoroughly drenched.   And the boots, though blackened and distorted, remained. Carla found a long stick, inserted it into the center of what was left of one boot, and half lifted, half dragged it down the gravel bar until she could fling it with the stick into deep water. She repeated the process with the other boot, then threw the stick into the water, where it slowly bobbed downstream.

She put her little hand into Ray's big one. "Let's go," she said softly.

~ ~ ~

Ray pulled into the garage of the Concord house, his face pale and strained. At the kitchen table, he sat staring off into space as Carla moved quietly and efficiently. She looked over at him and thought a moment. Then she passed before his line of vision, paused, and started to sway.

"Ray," she called out weakly.

His eyes refocused. He leapt up and raced around the table just in time to catch her as she sank toward the floor.

"Ray. Oh, Ray." Carla tried to speak more, but her sobs grew in intensity until she was semi-hysterical.

"Oh, baby, baby." Ray cradled her in his big arms, rocking her gently as her tears streamed down his chest. Then he carried her to the white couch in the living room and held her tight.

"Jenny . . . Jenny . . . You've saved . . . my baby . . . Nothing bad . . . will ever happen . . . to her . . . again," Carla sobbed out brokenly, clutching Ray around the neck.

He gently caressed her until her sobs subsided.

"It was terrible," he said simply.

"But not as . . . as . . . as . . ." Carla began to hiccup, and her body went rigid in Ray's arms.

"Easy, easy. It's okay now."

Ray gentled her as he would a wild-eyed fearful colt, his voice soft and soothing.

Carla finally relaxed in his arms and her breath came more evenly.

"Ray," she said, looking deep into his eyes, "I owe you everything."

Ray gazed back steadily, taking in the pale tear-stained face with large eyes framed by dark ringlets, the petite body so light in his arms, and shouldered his burden manfully.

"Ray, Ray. I've never known anyone like you. You are the only real man I've ever known."

Carla snuggled in closer, her warm breath pulsing gently against the hollow of his neck. Ray bent down and gently kissed the soft full lips. Carla was receptive but completely passive. He kissed again, lingering a little longer. Then suddenly a surge of emotion hit him and although he stayed gentle, it was all he could do to restrain the fierce passion which almost overwhelmed him. He picked Carla up as though she were a rag doll and carried her into the bedroom. She returned his kisses, but passively, letting him pull her clothes off, the only sign of her response the quickness of her breathing. As he entered her, she began to call out his name, softly at first, her body moving sinuously. But as he thrashed and plunged wildly, like a charging stallion, all restraint gone, Carla let herself go. She bucked beneath him, dug her nails into his back, and screamed with pleasure as he roared like a mad bull and collapsed on top of her.

~ ~ ~

Ray awoke to the Sunday morning light streaming through the bedroom window. He sat up and looked over at Carla curled like a kitten on the bed beside him. Her dark hair lay tangled half across the white pillow case, half curled down concealing her face. Her breast rose and fell with the gentle even rhythm of her breathing.

For a moment his mind was blank. Then he almost groaned aloud as it all came rushing back. Surely it was a dream, a nightmare. Yesterday couldn't have happened.

Ray eased out of bed, slipped into his clothes, and walked into the kitchen to make coffee. He sat staring into his coffee cup and the endless day stretched out before him.

"Morning, honey." Carla was one of those women who look fetching even as they stagger out of bed. The dark curls in all their disarray framed her face prettily. A pale blue wrapper belted around her waist emphasized the slightness of her build, yet Ray could see the swell of her full breasts.

"Morning."

Carla placed her little hand on his shoulder and automatically he put his arm around her small waist. After a moment she gently disentangled herself and walked to the counter to pour a cup of coffee.

Ray said nothing more, just gazed at the table, at his large hands dwarfing the coffee cup.

Carla drank half her coffee, then got up to begin breakfast. She moved lightly about the kitchen and soon bacon was sizzling, eggs scrambled, toast made.

"I'd better finish that shed today," he said at last. Ray leased a lot of land to run cattle on, but he had also inherited a small farm. Keeping everything on it in repair was a lot of work, but work he enjoyed.

"I'll get Jenny this afternoon. Maybe we could take her swimming."

Ray didn't know how to answer. Carla acted as though nothing had happened, as though this was an ordinary day like any other. "I killed a man!" his mind was screaming at him. "I'll have to live with this the rest of my life." Yet what was she supposed to do? he thought. He certainly didn't want to talk about it. Maybe it was best to ignore it, pretend it never happened.

"I got to get going," he said, getting up abruptly. Ray grabbed his hat and fled the house.

Carla hummed to herself as she cleaned the kitchen. When she was finished, she surveyed the immaculate appliances, the neat cabinets, the shining floor, with a satisfied air. She showered and dressed, then sat down at her desk to pay bills and plan her week.

Chapter 54

Sunday, August 17, 2003, Wirtz, Texas

A bright red cardinal landed on the edge of the bird bath beneath the pecan tree outside Lucille Johnson's kitchen window. It stepped into the shallow water, cocking its head first one way, then the other. As it splashed, sunlight reflected off the droplets on its fast fluttering wings. Then suddenly it flew off.

Lucille stared unseeing out the kitchen window, leaning against the sink. One worn hand rested on the counter, fingering a damp cloth.

Where was Frank? He hadn't come or called, didn't answer his home or cell phone. It wasn't like him at all.

A blue jay had taken the place of the cardinal. A shaft of sunlight filtering through the leaves of the pecan tree illuminated the blue of its neck. Then it, too, flew off, disappearing into the foliage.

Lucille was aware of nothing but a growing panic and a dull ache in her breast. Church was over by now. Frank had promised to pick her up in Wirtz, then drive to the church in Graylor. He knew she missed Jenny and was worried about the custody hearing coming up the very next day.

Dear God, don't let anything have happened to him.

She gripped the edge of the sink and stared out the window, past the birdbath underneath the pecan tree, over the yellowing grass, and across the mosaic of the distant fields.

Unconsciously she wiped the clean counter over and over.

She dropped the rag, turned and picked up the phone.

"Bill? Bill, I hate to bother you, but it's Frank. He was supposed to have come hours ago. He doesn't answer his phones. You know that's not like him."

Bill Cummins heard the panic in her voice. He remembered rain dripping from the eaves as he stood in the dark on her front porch knocking and knocking, a young man then, his first official notification of a death. It didn't get any easier with the years.

"I'll get right on it, Mrs. Johnson. Don't worry."

Chapter 55

Sunday afternoon, August 17, 2003, Graylor, Texas

"Carla's here, Momma," June said, looking out the front. The old lady set down her coffee cup and peered out the window.

"I declare it is Carla."

June stepped to the door, and after Carla had entered and all the greetings made, Momma said, "Now let me look at you. You look good, all rested, but a little thin."

"Yes, Momma, I feel so much better. June, thank you so much. I feel like a new woman."

"I was glad to do it. We've had so much fun with Jenny."

"She's a right well-behaved child," Momma said. "I was proud to have her in church."

"I've got a fresh pot of coffee," June said. Carla followed her into the kitchen with Momma's empty cup, which she refilled and sugared while June poured two cups the way the sisters liked it, just black.

"Here, Momma," Carla said.

"Why, thank you."

"It's not often I get to do these little things for you. I miss you two."

"I know you work hard, honey, but I sure wish we could see more of you."

"Me, too, but I have to provide a life for Jenny. It's all on my shoulders."

Momma nodded sympathetically. It was hard for her to imagine a woman having to go out to earn a living all on her own, with no help. Cooking, cleaning, sewing for three girls, barely getting by on her husband's salary—-it had been all she could do. Carla, though, was strong willed, for all her thinness and small body. If any woman could do it, Carla could. Of her three girls, Carla was the one she understood

178

the least. June had been her right hand. And Patty—what a handful. Always something with her. But Carla? Well, still waters run deep.

"How's Ray?" June was asking.　"He didn't seem himself yesterday."

"He's fine.　He's got some financial troubles that worry him, but he won't talk about it. You know how men are."

"I thought he seemed distracted when he brought Jenny." June hesitated a moment. "He's good to you?"

"Oh, yes."　Carla looked down and played with her coffee cup to hide the fierce emotion that arose.　No man would ever lay a hand on her again.　"The price of cattle is down and the price of hay up, so Ray gets worried.　But he never brings his troubles home."

She looked up and smiled sweetly.

Carla is so pretty, June thought, noticing her clear pale complexion with just the hint of rosiness when she was animated.　This morning Carla's hair hung loose to her shoulders, the dark curls slightly unruly.　She was wearing jeans and a slim white embroidered blouse that fitted at her small waist.　She looks almost like a girl, not a woman with a demanding, stressful job and a child to raise single-handedly, June thought.　Her looks belied her strength.　Well, Carla had always been different.　June admired her ability to get on with life in spite of tragedies, even though sometimes that strength seemed to come from a source that was vaguely disturbing, though June couldn't say why.　But God made us all different for a reason. It was up to her just to accept.

The back door slammed, and Jason and Danny, followed by Jenny, hurtled into the house like a herd of stampeding cattle.

"I declare, boys are different from girls," Momma said.

"They sure are," Carla said with an arch look, and Momma chuckled.

"They're good boys, but my goodness, they make a lot

of racket. They sure do help me in the garden, though."

"Look what we found," Danny shouted as the three children burst into the room. He pointed toward Jason.

"Say hello to your Aunt Carla first."

"Hi, Aunt Carla," both boys said in unison.

"Mommy," Jenny said, running to her mother's side. Carla put her arm around her daughter. "Look what Jason has."

Jason opened his two cupped hands to reveal a small green grass snake.

"And Jenny wasn't even scared," Danny said, trying to regain his audience.

"You boys take that snake outside right now," June said.

"We want to make a home for it," Jenny said.

"I'm going to build a box for it, with a place for water and grass," Jason said, looking important.

"We can put it in a coffee can now," Danny offered.

June went to the kitchen for a clean coffee can, as the quickest way to get the snake out of the house.

"More coffee, Momma?"

"No thank you, dear. I've had enough."

"I've got to go now, Momma, but I'll try to bring Jenny back real soon."

"You do that sweetie. I miss having little girls around. And Jenny is such a sweetheart."

June was laughing as she re-entered the room. "I think Jason is planning some kind of snake Hilton. You should see those three drawing up plans."

"Jenny has such a good time with the boys. Thank you, June. I feel so rested. I'm ready to go back to work tomorrow and take on the world."

"We loved having Jenny. The boys adore her. And you come back soon, too."

"Jenny," Carla called out the back door, "come get your things."

"But Mommy . . ."

"I know you'd like to come back another day."

Jenny started to say something more but looked at her mother's face and turned toward the boys.

"Bye, Jason. Bye, Danny. Bye, Snake."

She ran into the house and grabbed her duffle bag, which was already neatly packed.

As Carla drove off down the street, June and Momma settled back down in their chairs. Out in the back yard, the boys were hammering and sawing.

"I thought Carla looked real good," Momma said.

"She did. Not only rested, but something else. Like she was real pleased with herself."

"Well, she ought to be. Imagine being a trauma nurse. I don't know much about it, but I watch these TV shows. It can't be easy, gunshot victims, all that blood, life and death. So much pressure. And she's a good mother. Jenny is such a joy. I've been lucky with my girls."

"Well, there's Patty."

Momma laughed. "You just wait. She'll finally grow up and surprise us all."

Chapter 56

Sunday, August 17, 2003, Rural Central Texas

Ray had parked his pickup in the shade of an elm, but even so the sweat was running down his face and his light blue cotton shirt was soaked. He was using the tailgate for a sawhorse as he cut boards he had carefully measured to length. Boards at one end of the north side of the cow shed had started to rot, and he was replacing that section. The work required concentration, and Ray was focused on what he was doing.

A cicada whirred, the rise and fall of its drone the very sound of summer. A few cumulus clouds, like puffs of cotton, floated high above in an otherwise cloudless sky. Ray carried the stack of cut boards to the back of the shed, and as he left the shade, the sun beat fiercely down on the large straw Stetson protecting his face. He set the first board in place, pulled a nail from the pouch at his waist and placed it against the board. He drew back the hammer for the first swing, and suddenly the images were in his face: the arc of the tire iron, the sickening thud as it crushed flesh and bone, the blood . . . the blood . . . the oozing brains . . . the final twitch of the legs.

Ray dropped the hammer and staggered backwards, away from the sight. But it followed him, as though it were a palpable presence, visible in the air before him. He tripped on a tree root and sat down heavily. He stared at his boots, the toes pointing skywards, and he started to sob, hoarse wracking cries that shook his whole body.

He tried to get up, but once on his hands and knees, he started to retch, great convulsions that soon emptied his stomach of half-digested bacon and eggs. Dry heaves shook him and shook him until all that was left was the taste of bitter bile in his mouth.

Ray got to his feet and his mind was a blank. He left

the hammer lying on the ground next to the boards and got in his pickup. He started driving, not thinking where he was going, just driving, moving. After a while, he noticed he was going south, south and west. He kept to the rural roads, observing black Brangus and white Charolais grazing on dry brown pastures, gazing at open farmland, empty now but for an occasional combine at work.

The land grew rougher and more arid. Cattle and goat country now. Ray saw he was getting low on gas. Not country you wanted to run out of gas in. Thirty minutes later he came to a crossroads store on the edge of a small town. Ray filled his pickup, then went inside to pay.

"Let me have a beer. No, make that a six-pack. Bud Lite."

Back on the road, Ray popped a tab and kept driving. He quickly drained the first beer and opened a second. He was heading west, southwest now, more by instinct, as he kept to the small county roads. The drive was more interesting. He could keep his mind occupied looking at the lay of the land, then focusing on a particular ranch house and its corrals. He opened another beer. In the pasture to his left, white egrets wandered among a small herd of black Brangus, one white bird sitting on the broad back of a cow, searching for ticks

He was driving into the sun now. He dropped the empty fourth beer can onto the floorboards and suddenly realized he had to get something in his stomach. But he was on a long empty stretch of highway now. Finally he reached a tiny town and stopped at its only filling station, a few gas pumps outside a country store. Although he still had over half a tank of gas, he filled up. Inside, four men were sitting around a battered wooden table drinking beer. On the wall above them were the mounted heads and racks of many deer. Against that same wall was a small pot-bellied stove, cold now, its office taken by an old window unit air conditioner rattling out cold air. The men looked up with interest at the sight of a stranger. But Ray didn't look much different from them, just bigger and more powerfully built than most men. His jeans were worn, but his boots looked new, just bought. And he didn't have the thin, wiry build of men who spend much of their life on horseback. Though work hardened, he looked prosperous and well fed. Probably down to buy cattle, one of the men thought to himself.

Ray looked around the small store, a few dusty cans on a shelf, a few bags of chips. No bottles of water anywhere. But near the counter were packets of jerky. Ray grabbed a couple and some potato chips.

"Gimme a coke, too."

The old man behind the counter lifted the lid of an old fashioned metal box and pulled a coke from among the bottles of mostly iced beer and set it next to the chips and jerky. He took Ray's money and made change without saying more than he had to for the transaction.

Back on the road, Ray took a long swig of his coke, hoping it would settle his stomach enough for it to accept food. He bit into the jerky, and suddenly knew it was what his body needed. He chewed slowly, but eventually ate all of the two small packets. The salty chips were good, too. His body regained its equilibrium.

It was dusk by the time he reached Del Rio. He had bought a gallon of water, once he found a convenience store, and had drunk most of it, then turned to the now warm last cans of his six-pack. All six cans now littered his floorboard.

Ray had had no plan in mind when he had started out driving, but now that he was headed for the Mexican border, it seemed like the thing to do. He drove through the drab, dusty streets of Del Rio, headed toward the Amistad Reservoir —the Friendship Lake—formed by damming the Rio Grande, half in Mexico, half in the United States.

On the north side of Del Rio, Ray turned left on the narrow county road that led to the less traveled, rural border crossing. A bored young Mexican man walked up to Ray's window, glanced at him and his truck, asked for his papers. Until recently, no one had needed a passport just to cross into a border town. Ray pulled out his wallet, handed the young man his driver's license and a ten dollar bill. The young man looked at it for a long time, then looked back at Ray without saying anything. Ray reached into his wallet again, pulled out another ten and added it to the first.

"Buenos noches." The young man returned the license. "Provecho," he added with a little smile, and waved Ray on.

Ray's headlights illuminated the dry barren land dotted with ocotillo and cactus. The road turned south, paralleling the Rio Grande. Ray drove through the dark alien land, alert but unthinking, feeling as though he were floating through a dreamscape.

He entered Ciudad Acuña and headed for the center of town. He stopped at the first restaurant he saw, not the one farther on that drew tourists. It was as much a bar as a restaurant, but Ray could smell the meat sizzling on the grill.

There was a sudden quiet when Ray entered the adobe room. The Mexican men, small and wiry, nursing their beers at the bar, sized him up, but covertly. The few women gave him admiring glances.

Ray chose a table where he could sit with his back to the wall and survey the room. Immediately the owner appeared to take his order.

By the time his steak arrived, covered with sautéed onions and nopalitos (thin strips of pickled cactus), Ray had downed two margaritas and almost the whole basket of chips and bowl of salsa. He chewed his steak slowly, picked at the refried beans, ignored the rice. And ordered another margarita.

When he finished, Ray pushed his plate aside and leaned back. He looked up, and the bartender appeared. Ray ordered another margarita.

Ray drank slowly and steadily, keeping to himself.

Gradually the other customers left until only one or two others remained at the bar. The bartender/owner whispered to his wife, who had come to him from the back rooms that were their living quarters. She nodded and quietly disappeared. Shortly a young woman entered the bar and sauntered over to Ray.

"Buenos noches, Señor."

Ray looked up. "Evening."

"You buy me a drink?"

"Sure."

Ray motioned to the bartender who hurried over with a margarita and what looked like bourbon and water but was really just water with a little Dr. Pepper to color it.

The young woman sat down next to Ray and gazed at him admiringly. "Que barbaro," she murmured, lightly stroking his heavily muscled arm.

Ray tried to focus his eyes. She seemed pretty, with her dark hair and eyes and youthful complexion, but the outlines of her face wavered.

She moved closer to Ray until she was leaning against him. The bartender magically appeared with two more drinks.

After a while, the young woman said tipsily—though Ray was beyond noticing—"You want to come with me?"

"Okay."

The bartender appeared at the table with the bill. Ray fumbled with his wallet and tried to read the numbers. Finally he gave up and asked, "How much?" The owner/bartender told him, doubling the actual cost. Ray pulled big bills out of his wallet, not noticing that some fell on the table, where they were adroitly whisked away by a small hand. The bartender caught the woman's eye to let her know he had seen how much she took, so knew what his share was.

"Muchas gracias, Señor," the bartender said, half bowing.

Ray staggered a little, and the woman took his arm.

Outside the air was warm and caressing, and the amelioration of the heat passed for coolness. Ray stumbled toward his pickup.

"Señor," she said, putting her other hand on his arm too and pulling him toward her.

"Got to go."

"But Señor . . ." she said, looking up into his face.

"Here," he said gently, and pulled another bill from his wallet.

"Muchas gracias."

The woman watched as, after several attempts, Ray successfully unlocked his pickup door. Then she disappeared down the dark street.

~ ~ ~

The young Mexican smiled to himself as Ray's pickup halted before his small, box-like office, the pickup wheels a little across the center stripe, and just waved him on. He was listening to a futball game on the radio and didn't want to miss a play.

As Ray neared Del Rio, he looked for a motel. That's when he saw the flashing lights in his rearview mirror. He pulled off onto the shoulder, rolled his window down, and waited.

"Had a little to drink, buddy?"

"Yes." Ray fumbled with his wallet, trying to extricate his license and insurance.

"Keep your hands where I can see them."

While his partner ran the license check, the cop warily eyed Ray. He looked like a rancher who had crossed over to have a little fun and had had a little too much. But he was a big, powerful looking guy, and one could never tell about drunks. At any rate, he was certainly a hazard on the road.

He stepped back to consult with his partner, who said, "Record's clean. But he's not from around here. Better get him off the road."

The cell door clanged behind Ray. Luckily, in these early hours of a Monday morning, he had the cell to himself. Ray lay down heavily on the bare cot and passed out.

Chapter 57

Sunday, August 17, 2003, Concord, Texas

"I don't know where Ray is, honey. Get your bathing suit and we'll go to the pool ourselves, just the two of us."

Carla wore a black and white striped knit top over crisp white Capris that emphasized her slender calves and ankles. Tan sandals revealed her pearl painted toenails. She moved coolly and efficiently about the kitchen packing a small cooler with drinks, sandwiches, and fruit, but her mind was busy with an unsolved problem. Where was Ray? It was late afternoon now, and he had neither come nor called. Men were such weak, pathetic creatures. In fact, when you got right down to it, most people were weak pathetic creatures, just letting life happen to them instead of shaping their own ends. Only a few were strong and determined enough to take charge. Life was a contest, one she intended to win. It was so easy to get what you wanted if you were willing to work for it. She didn't understand why other people couldn't see that. They were so stupid.

"Ready, Mommy." Jenny stood before her with her little gym bag neatly packed with her bathing suit, towel, and flip-flops. Her straight blonde hair was pulled back in a ponytail, emphasizing the thin oval of her face. Her slender arms and legs glowed with a healthy tan.

Carla smiled down at her daughter. Jenny was a good little worker. She would be able to take care of herself.

Jenny splashed happily in the pool with several children from the neighborhood. Carla sat in the shade studying a surgical text, glancing up occasionally to check on Jenny. There was a lifeguard on duty, but Carla kept an eye out, too. She found the textbook difficult but fascinating. Already the doctors in the emergency room were impressed by how Carla always seemed to be one step ahead of the others, anticipating their needs. Carla wanted to keep it that way.

Also, she liked the challenge. It was amazing what a skilled surgeon, with all the technological advances, could do. Putting people back together who were torn apart by weapons or mangled in car wrecks or smashed in construction accidents was like solving a puzzle, but one that required immense skill and creativity. It was endlessly fascinating to Carla.

The shadows were lengthening when Carla called Jenny out of the water.

"Run put on your clothes and we'll have a picnic right here in the park."

Jenny disappeared into the bath house and Carla gathered up her things.

Outside the enclosed pool area mother and daughter sat at a stone picnic table underneath a big pecan tree. The sun was low in the west, the heat of the day lessened. A light breeze from the south stirred the leaves of the pecan tree and refreshed the two.

"Did you have fun at Grammy's?"

"Oh, yes. Jason's real bossy to Danny. He's nice to me, though."

Carla smiled, thinking about how June had always tried to boss her when they were little.

Carla and Jenny walked hand in hand down the sidewalk in their raw, new subdivision in the light of a late summer evening. Ray's pickup was not in the drive.

"It's time to get ready for bed, honey. Be sure to lay out your clothes for tomorrow. Do you know what you want to wear?"

"Oh, yes. My new lavender top Aunt June gave me, the one with the little bear on it, and the jeans that go with it, with the little bear on the cuff."

Carla had to smile to herself. Little Jenny knew her own mind.

After Jenny was tucked into bed, Carla sat on the white leather couch in the living room thinking. She rarely turned on the TV, and she hadn't let Jenny get in the habit of watching a lot of television. She thought it was a waste of time.

Where was Ray? Why hadn't he called her? This wasn't like him at all. Perhaps something had happened to him, though if he had been in a wreck, surely she would have heard by now. Maybe he was lying in a ditch on one of those county roads, undiscovered. And maybe that would be the best thing. Ray was physically strong, with a powerful masculine attraction, but he was turning out to be a weakling otherwise. Though she used them to her advantage, men's frailties disgusted her.

Well, tomorrow was a new day, and Carla looked forward to it. She stood before her bathroom mirror carefully brushing her hair until the dark ringlets shone. She gently rubbed cream into her pale clear skin.

As she snuggled down in bed, she reviewed her weekend's work. Everything had gone off perfectly. Her planning had been complete. Carla sighed with satisfaction and drifted off to sleep.

Chapter 58

Monday, August 18, 2003, Del Rio, Texas

Ray was disoriented when he awoke on the thin hard mattress, his head pounding and his stomach queasy, a little morning light trickling into the narrow cell. Then it all came back to him in a rush—the long drive, the many, many margaritas in the dusty cantina, the flashing lights of the police car, the sound of the cell door clanging shut.

It was nearly noon when Ray left the drab streets of Del Rio behind, released on his own recognizance. Clearly a substantial man, a prosperous Anglo rancher who had just needed to let off a little steam, the long arm of the law shortened for him.

He stopped at a diner on the outskirts of town and ordered the blue plate special: meat loaf, mashed potatoes, green beans, and iced tea. His head throbbed and his stomach was still queasy, but as he ate he could feel his strength returning.

The highway stretched before him, and he drove steadily across the flat arid land, into the rough rocky goat country, and finally back to the gently rolling pasture and farm land. The closer he got to Concord, the more he dreaded it.

Little things stuck in his mind. Carla's cool efficiency disposing of the body, every detail planned so carefully. Something about her behavior afterward. He couldn't put his finger on it. He just knew he didn't want to go back.

Then he remembered how she had fallen apart the next morning. She was fierce protecting her child, amazingly strong, but it had been too much for her afterward. For the first time, he realized how she must have felt when he hadn't shown up Sunday afternoon, hadn't even called. The poor thing must have felt abandoned.

How long had it been? Less than two days since . . .

No, he wouldn't think about that. The guy had it coming. It made Ray sick to even think about what that slimy bastard had done.

Ray had trouble untangling his complicated feelings. He didn't even try. He just kept driving until he reached Concord, pulled up to the house in the subdivision. Carla would still be at work, Jenny at day care. It was better that way. She would see he was there when she drove up.

Ray went into the backyard and looked around. The grass could use cutting. He found the gas can, filled the mower and checked its oil. He had almost finished the backyard by the time Carla and Jenny arrived.

The back door slammed behind her as Jenny came running across the small patio. Ray cut off the lawn mower and wiped the sweat off his face with the back of his hand.

"Hi, Ray. What you doing?"

"Making the backyard pretty for you. Did you have a good time at your grandma's?"

"Uh huh. Me and Jason and Danny found a snake, a little green snake. Jason is building a house for it. But I had to come home."

"Well, you'll get to see it next time you go."

"Mommy said to ask if you wanted some iced tea. It'll be a little while before supper is ready."

"Tell her yes, thanks."

Jenny ran happily back in the house on her errand. Ray started the mower back up and finished the last little bit of the backyard. He felt better, easing back into the routine as though nothing had happened. He appreciated Carla. Most women would have come storming out to the backyard demanding to know where he had been. After Jenny was in bed he could tell her what happened.

Abruptly, Ray looked at the finished back yard. I'll bet I can get the front and side done before supper, he thought, and kept working.

Chapter 59

Thursday, August 21, 2003, Rural Central Texas

Jim lit a cigarette, surveyed the camp, while Jeffrey loaded the roan and the palomino into the trailer. Unobtrusively, he checked to make sure Jeffrey had firmly latched the trailer gate. He had.

A few wispy clouds trailed across an otherwise blue sky that paled toward the horizon. The air was still, the dusty leaves of the hackberries and scrub elms unmoving and silent. Ten in the morning, and already the heat was oppressive. Jim didn't seem to notice, a man impervious to all weathers. Jeffrey was silently urging the air conditioner to hurry up and cool down the cab as they left camp. The caravan of pickups and horse trailers retraced their route of the previous day, but continued farther east on the county road. The road angled east southeast, not so close to the river now, only roughly paralleling it.

"We're looking for a dirt road on the left, cornfield on the west side, open field on the east side. Can't see the barn from the road, and the old farmhouse has long since fallen down. It'll be hard to see, just a field road used by the tractors. On the right, though, a couple of hundred yards before it, there's a brick farmhouse, well kept, with a big tractor barn behind."

Jeffrey nodded, stared out the window. He sipped a coke and crunched on a bag of peanuts his dad had let him buy at the Oatville Store, just before he dropped him off with Jim. It was after ten now, and although earlier than he had been getting up all summer, still it was closer to that rhythm. The salty peanuts and sweet effervescent coke tasted wonderful. It was cool inside the pickup cab, while outside, the bright sun etched sharply every detail. Corn stubble in a field that stretched toward the horizon. A newly plowed-under field where milo had been harvested. A small wood

frame house that needed painting, rusted old farm equipment
—ancient disc, harrow, planter—littering the side yard. A
few brown cows lying in the shade of a hackberry tree in an
overgrazed field.

"There it is," Jeffrey said, "the brick house and big
tractor barn."

Jim slowed the pickup, scanning the lefthand side of
the county road.

"This must be it."

He turned off on the dirt road, followed by the rest of
the caravan. The road lay silent between empty fields, the
cornstalks, stripped of their corn, waiting to be shredded, the
hayfield vacant. No gates impeded their progress.

Jim pulled off into the empty hayfield, the rest of the
rigs following.   Men unloaded horses, mounted up, and
headed down the dirt field road. Leather creaked, but the soft
earth muffled the sound of hooves.   The fancy spurs one
young man wore on his new snakeskin boots gleamed in the
sunlight.   Older men looked carefully at the surroundings,
but had little to say.

A half mile in, the road curved slightly to the right. A
sagging picket fence on the left indicated where once there
had been a farmyard. A pomegranate tree still stood in one
corner, and an ancient rosebush brushed against the pickets.
All that was left of the house were a few timbers lying on the
ground.   Farther along to the right, a well preserved wooden
barn, of much older construction than the metal tractor barns
on other farms, loomed large.

The sun was high overhead, the pale blue sky now
cloudless except for a slight whitening just above the horizon.

Jim felt a familiar adrenaline surge. He rode up to a
grouping of several hackberry trees and dismounted.

"Jeffrey, you stay here with Pete and help him care for
the horses. The rest of you come with me."

The sun was hot, the air still. The drone of crickets
and tree frogs filled the spaces of the silence. No one spoke.

Each step that brought Jim closer to the barn took effort. Time seemed to compress and expand, like a slow, off-rhythm accordion.

A wooden drop latch held the barn door closed. Jim lifted the wooden piece from its slot and pushed against the door. It creaked, then groaned and slowly opened. After the brilliant light outside, the inner gloom of the barn was disorienting, though a shaft of light from a hayloft illuminated a loose pile of hay on the floor of the barn. For a moment, Jim couldn't get his bearings. Then gradually light and shadow resolved into discernible shapes.

Almost against his will, Jim was drawn to the pile of loose hay mounded on the floor. The shaft of light poured over it, as though the sun, too, were irresistibly drawn.

A blood-spattered running shoe stuck out from the hay, a well-worn everyday shoe. It looked homey and vulnerable and completely out of place.

Jim took a deep breath and walked closer. The corpse was clearly visible, just a few wisps of hay blurring the outline from a distance. It made you wonder, why bother, if you weren't going to conceal the body. It made Jim think of a cat, scratching a little earth after doing its business. Just going through the motions, but not really covering up the feces. A kind of ritual.

The stench of death rose to meet Jim as he neared the corpse, the rot that ultimately purifies us all as we return to the elements. He gazed down at what had once been a muscular and fit young man, now oozing fluids from the decomposing body, the congealed blood on its crushed skull banqueting flies. Mid-thirties, average sized, medium brown hair, once nice looking. Jeans, gray t-shirt, worn running shoes. Everyman, soon to be composted by worms.

Outside, Jeffrey leaned up against the stout palomino gelding, taking in the scents and sounds and feel of the place: the soothing smell of horse sweat, the steady thrum of crickets and tree frogs and swell of cicadas, the plaintive cry of a mourning dove in the distance, the close embrace of the noon-time heat.

The gelding shifted his weight from one hip to the other, taking his ease while he could. The heat from his body radiated into Jeffrey's, and the boy relaxed along with the horse. There was no beginning or end, just this moment. Jeffrey was aware of everything and nothing. No thoughts passed through his mind, just the feeling of expanding until he was whirling through space, outside time.

A little distance away, Jim stepped from the barn, impaled by the fierce light. The outlines of his hawk-like face seemed sharper, the skin drawn. Success for him was seeing once again, over and over, the dark blood of evil.

He stood with his back to the barn, its fine weathered boards absorbing the heat from the sun. Under the hackberry trees, Jeffrey was leaning against the withers of the palomino, looking as relaxed and peaceful as the gelding. The call of a dove in the distance seemed to mourn the loss of innocence of children and horses, the plaintive notes a song of sorrow: this, too, is life.

The disfigured corpse in the barn was someone's son, someone's father, the center of a web of relationships now ripped asunder. Rotting now, as we all will rot, Jim thought.

He took a few steps, shook himself, pulled out his cell phone and made the requisite calls.

~ ~ ~

"Your dad will be here soon," Jim said, a hand on Jeffrey's shoulder.

Jeffrey looked inquiringly at Jim, who shook his head.

"Some things you don't need to see. Not yet, anyway."

Jeffrey wasn't sure whether he wanted to or not. Just think what he could tell his buddies. On the other hand, he had never seen a dead body before. Just looking at the barn scared him.   Now that he knew, the warm friendly barn loomed larger, housing a throbbing evil in its dark interior. Jeffrey shuddered and put his hand on the big palomino gelding, feeling its solid warmth.   A horse knew nothing of that dark roiling subterranean world just below the surface of everyday life—where things were not always what they seemed. Jeffrey wondered if the mischief his pals got into led to worse things.

Abruptly, he turned to the palomino.

"Pick up your foot, boy."

The gelding obediently lifted his front near hoof and Jeffrey checked for stones. Might as well check them all. The well trained horse lifted each foot on command. Jeffrey took the hard hoof in his hands, looking at the v-shaped frog, feeling its calloused roughness, gently setting each hoof down in turn.   He wished he had a currycomb and brush.   He scratched behind the horse's ears, and the gelding leaned into him. He breathed in the horsey smell. He wished he had a horse like this one.   He would teach it all kinds of tricks; maybe he could work up a performance for the rodeo. He had seen that once.

When Bill drove up with his deputies, Jeffrey was talking to the gelding, teaching him to hold the foot lifted on command up in the air for a longer while.

~ ~ ~

While forensics examined the body, Jim and Bill conferred outside the barn. An investigator was photographing the faint tire tracks left in the dusty road leading toward the river; then another would make plaster casts of both tire tracks and any footprints that could be found.   Carefully treading outside the tracks, Jim and Bill followed the road as it curved back left and downhill toward the line of trees marking the San Sebastian River. The heat of the sun lay heavily on them, and the rise and swell of the cicadas marked their passage. Neither man spoke.

They scrambled down the bank to the gravel bar below, Jim light-footed on the steep, rutted and overgrown road, obviously unused. Bill stumbled a little, his heft overbalancing him. A great blue heron, startled, took a little run, finally lifted off and soared above the river, squawking into the quiet.

Near the water, a patch of blackened stones indicated a recent fire. A few pieces of ashy cloth remained. Bill donned a pair of thin rubber gloves and carefully placed the fragments in a plastic bag.

"What's that?"

Jim was gazing downriver. A piece of blackened leather was caught in brush lodged against the far bank where the river curved and ran fast.

He waded into the river, thigh deep at first, gradually diminishing, then deepening once again. The water was warm, almost body temperature, and the muddy bank opposite smelled of fecundity. The outline of the trees was reflected in the water on the opposite side of the river, while farther downstream the sun lit up the fast flowing water, highlighting the ripples. It shone on the blackened and distorted leather that had caught on the brush fallen into the water.

"Looks like part of a boot," Jim called out.

"I'll send forensics down."

From overhead came the guttural whistling cry of a hawk flying high above the river, then, glimpsing them, soaring off into the distance and repeating its piercing trill.

The men were quiet walking back to the barn.

Murder was ancient, Jim was thinking, but the science of discovery modern. Murderers thought they were concealing their acts of darkness, but current technology revealed them to the light. Unless, of course, prosecutors jumped to conclusions and hid evidence that didn't fit their assumptions.

"Got good clear tire tracks," the investigator said when Bill walked up, "and a footprint."

"Send someone down to the river. Part of a burned boot is downriver. You can see it in the curve of the river from the gravel bar."

~ ~ ~

It was late afternoon when Jim and the rest of Search and Rescue reached camp. Bill had sent a deputy to take Jeffrey home; the boy had had enough for one day. Jim unloaded, unsaddled, curried, and fed the roan and the palomino. He sat down on a log a little distance from the other men who were taking down tents and packing up, and lit a cigarette, impervious to the heat. He inhaled deeply.

Always the feeling of emptiness afterward. Somewhere other families were torn apart, the murdered man's and eventually the murderer's. For he—or she or they, perhaps—would be caught. This was not the work of some anonymous loner cruising the interstate and preying on the vulnerable. The dead man had been identified: the missing realtor. This had all the marks of an amateur killing, a very personal one. The tracks would lead to the car. In all likelihood, the estranged wife and her boyfriend were involved.

Jim knew only too well the grief of the murdered man's family. But for the other family, the murderer's family, the universe was riven, too.

He carefully extinguished his cigarette, stood up slowly and walked to his pickup. He deposited the butt in an empty coke can. He leaned against the cab and surveyed his horses standing quietly in the shade of a few hackberry trees, heads lowered, eyes half-closed. The air was still, the heat palpable but lessening in intensity as the sun dropped lower in the western sky.

Somewhere in California a grown man shared his

DNA, half of it—but nothing more. The man would have nothing to do with him, and he understood that. He hadn't been there. Yes, his ex-wife had disappeared with the baby, but he hadn't really looked for him. Not until the boy was a grown man, bitter about his abandonment, and with a life he had created with no input from his biological father.

Jim lit another cigarette, then hastily put it out. He got in his pickup and drove toward town.

Chapter 60

Thursday, August 21, 2003, Rural Central Texas

A few beer drinkers had settled in at the back table of the Oatville Store near the big wall-mounted fan, but it was too early for the evening crowd. Thursday was hamburger night, and in an hour or so young families with small children, retired couples, farmers through for the day, and other groups of friends and neighbors would be coming in. Sometimes large tables were reserved for multiple generations of families and their friends celebrating someone's birthday. But for now, business was slow, and most of the ceiling fans rotated quietly over empty wooden tables.

Shirley looked up from the newspaper she was reading as a lean young man in fancy boots and new jeans walked in the store. Not from around here, she thought, looking him up and down. Outside, his white F 250, pulling a horse trailer with sleeping compartment in front, stood next to the ancient gas pump.

Quickly, she walked to the register and glanced at the gas total.

"$42," she said, examining him closely but unobtrusively. "You're not with that search and rescue team, are you?"

"Yes'm. Heading home."

Shirley took the hundred dollar bill, opened the register. She brushed a blonde strand from her face that had strayed from its moorings atop her head and tucked it behind one ear. She handed him back his change.

"Did you find him?"

The young man looked around, then leaned forward confidentially.

"I'm not supposed to say, but yes, we did."

"Was it that realtor?"

"I didn't get that part. But I can tell you somebody

really had it in for him. Crushed skull, lots of blood. Not pretty. But don't let on you know anything."

"Oh, I won't. Anything else you need?"

"Yes'm, a coke and that piece of jerky."

The young man paid again, looked around the store.

A few farmers were drinking beer at a back table, but after a quick glance in his direction, turned back to their discussion of crops and the market.

He looked once more at the rack of cast iron skillets and Dutch ovens, the fishing lures and pruning shears, then headed out into the evening heat without really noticing it. He pulled out of the parking lot and turned north for the three-hour drive, anticipating the tales he would tell his buddies.

Chapter 61

End of August, 2003, Rural Central Texas

Ray set down the rag saturated with a mixture of turpentine, Tung oil, and clear varnish and surveyed his work. The rub brought out the oak grain of the toy chest and gave the wood a subtle glow. Jenny would like it.

He glanced out the door of his workshop. The sun had dropped below the horizon, leaving behind the gentle light of an August evening.

Ray didn't want to leave. Worn tools hung on the walls and jars of nails and screws sat in orderly rows on narrow shelves. Ray could put his hand on anything he needed. But sawdust littered the floor of the shop and stains of various kinds discolored it. Dust, paint cans, and old rags covered the top of a back table, though the one next to Ray with the chest on it was relatively clear. A comfortable disorderliness overlay the careful arrangement of the workplace.

He took a deep breath, closed the shop door behind him. Evening light deepened into dusk. Venus was visible just above the western horizon. Ray looked around for something else to do. Tomorrow after work he would oil the chest a final time.

Reluctantly he started his pickup and headed down the gravel drive to the county road. A jackrabbit darted up from the side of the road, zigzagged crazily, then leapt through the fence and ran raggedly across the pasture. The old barbed wire sagged between posts. Another job for his list.

He simply refused to think about it. But in spite of himself, images arose. Carla moving quickly and efficiently about her kitchen with a self-satisfied air. Jenny playing happily with her dolls, missing her daddy but showing no conflicted emotions. Her dolls were not afraid of the daddy doll, who was invariably kind to them as he looked in on their tea parties before going off to work.

Carla never mentioned "the incident," as he had been referring to it in his mind—for which he was thankful. But at night he awakened from blood dimmed dreams, nightmares in which he heard the thunk of iron crushing living skull, like an overripe watermelon, and witnessed blood splattering. Blood rose in a tide and covered his boots, crept up his ankles, lapped at his shins, until he awoke thrashing and covered in sweat. Over and over in his dreams he swung the lethal tire iron. Over and over it connected with a living, breathing human being that crumpled into a twitching bloody mass. In his dreams the body writhed into a sitting position and stared accusingly at him from one bloody socket, the other half of his face crushed from the tremendous blow.

At the county road Ray turned left instead of right. He couldn't go home. Supper would be waiting for him, Jenny long since in bed, Carla with a smile and an inquiry about his day. But he could feel a rising tension underneath, as though she was losing patience with him and trying not to show it. At first when he thrashed awake from his nightmares, Carla would murmur soothing words and then comfort him in the way she knew best. He could lose himself in the wild passion, blot out the images that fueled the uncontrollable emotions. But they came back, with increasing intensity. Now Carla pretended to sleep, and when he looked at her, dark curls spilling across her smooth cheek, her petite body hardly visible under the covers, he felt—not gentle protectiveness flaming into desire, but . . . revulsion.

Ray gripped the steering wheel. He followed the winding country road until he reached a crossroads, turned left again. He pulled into the small parking area of Joe's Place. A table full of burly farmers talking loudly filled one end of the room. A middle-aged couple with their grandson sat at a smaller table, finishing their burgers and fries. A couple of men sat singly in the dim light at the bar, nursing their beers. Ray pulled out a barstool and sat down heavily.

Ma, Joe's wife, looked up from behind the bar.

"Why, Ray, haven't seen you in a while. How's it going?"

"Good. How about you?"

"Can't complain—except maybe about my arthritis. Just getting old, I guess."

"Not you, Ma. Still keeping everything going, I see."

"Yep, business is good. What can I get you?"

"Bud Lite, please."

Ray took a long swallow of beer. He didn't know the other two men at the bar, which suited him fine, the mood he was in. A stack of circulars advertising a farm auction sat on the bar near him. He picked one up and read down the list of farm machinery and implements, followed by household items: crockery and china, ancient radios, a meat grinder, an antique butter churn. Old couples died and the children, long since established in their jobs in the cities, sold the accouterments of a lifetime.

Ma looked Ray's way and he lifted his empty bottle. She set another before him.

The door opened and a young couple with a four-year-old and an infant came in. Slight, but sturdy and work-hardened, he held the infant carrier. The baby wore a pink sweat band with a pink bow around her almost bald head. The little boy pulled loose and ran ahead of his mother, who had been holding his hand. Carefully made up with glowing skin and a stylish hairdo, she wore tight jeans and a red, three-quarter-length tee. Already, though, she had lost the slimness of youth and carried about thirty extra pounds.

Ma came around from behind the bar. She took the baby in her arms.

"Come here to Grandma. And Jackie, look what I've got for you."

Cradling the baby in one arm, she held out a child-sized football. Jackie took it with a big smile on his face.

"What do you say," his mother said.

"Thank you, Grandma." And Jackie took off running to the other end of the store, past the table of farmers.

"Touchdown," one of the big men yelled, reaching out to ruffle the boy's hair.

Holding the little girl close, Ma scanned the room, then the bar. Ray tipped his beer bottle. Relinquishing the baby, Ma returned to the bar and brought another Bud.

By his fourth beer, Ray ordered a burger and polished it off along with his sixth beer.

The door opened again, and one of Ray's old classmates entered.

"Ray, haven't seen you in a coon's age. How you doing?"

"Good. You?"

"I'm doing great. Fertilizer business is great. Company gives me a new pickup every two years. I wear 'em out, too. But I like the traveling."

"What are you drinking, Chuck?"

"Bud's fine."

Ray held up two fingers, and Ma set two beers on the bar.

Just before the kitchen closed, the table of farmers at the other end of the store ordered steak dinners. Everyone else had left except the various men at the bar. Chuck's burger and fries arrived. The other two men, one at each end of the bar, seemed like Ray to be just drinking.

"Chuck, you ever done something you felt like you had to do, then afterwards couldn't believe you'd done it?"

Ray was staring down at his beer bottle. One of the men, the one at the far end of the bar, was paying his tab.

"I don't know, Ray. I've done things I wished I hadn't done."

"I mean something big, something you had to force yourself to do because . . . well, because you had to protect somebody."

"No, can't say as I have. My big mess-ups just

happened.   You know, something I fell into, seemed like a good idea at the time.   But that's not what you're talking about."

"I don't know how to explain it. Not even to myself."

Ray drained the last of his beer, looked around, but Ma was settling with the other man nearby.

"Come on, Ray, it's late. Ma's trying to close up."

The two men paid.   Ray stumbled on the walk outside, but caught himself.

"You good?"

"Yeah," Ray said, "don't have far to go."

He pulled out on the deserted county road and drove off into the darkness.

Chapter 62

Friday, August 22, 2003, Rural Central Texas

A pale gold sun eased above the horizon into a cloudless sky as Jim poured himself a second cup of coffee from the blue enameled pot hanging above the embers. It would be another scorcher, but for now the air was fresh and pleasant, the small fire reaching back into our common, distant past to provide its comfort. A woodpecker drummed on a nearby tree trunk, its red head bright in the early morning light. Two squirrels played tag around the bole of an elm tree.

Jim sipped his coffee, took a drag on his cigarette. The rest of the Search and Rescue team had headed back to the big city, or to the small towns near the metropolis, the afternoon before, but Jim liked to take a day to himself afterward to decompress. He watched the thin curl of smoke rising from the little fire, added his own cigarette smoke to the morning air.

He felt good about his work. There was a science to search work, research that outlined the best approaches. Jim had read the literature, mastered the techniques, and over the years gotten better and better. But there was one element that couldn't be taught. Jim didn't think about it much, but it guided him nonetheless. Sometimes he had feelings about things, and he followed them. Didn't analyze them, just acted.

He threw his cigarette butt into the fire, took a sip of coffee. The image of the body in the barn, the track down to the river, the half-burned piece of leather, all rose before him in a montage. The waste of a life, the ruin of others, the story as old as mankind. Afterwards, always, depression settled on him. Yet he knew that the adrenaline would rise, he would be compelled to search for the next body. Driven, he would pursue the next case, riding the wave of excitement and mystery to its conclusion. And afterwards, the ashes in the mouth. Yes, closure was important. He knew from his own experience how crucial it was. Yet still the person was dead, leaving unutterable grief behind. Lives wrecked, hearts wounded.

But sometimes the search found a child alive, or a wandering old person caught in time. That was unalloyed joy. Jim could live on the gratitude in a desperate parent's eyes for weeks. Whatever the search, whatever the outcome, Jim couldn't help himself. He had to do it.

Jim stood up, carefully put out the little fire, pouring water from his cooler over it, separating the wet pieces of half-burned wood. He took down his tent, packed everything in the back of his pickup. He untied the roan and palomino and led them down a winding trail to the lake. They drank deep, then began pawing with their front hooves, splashing their chests and bellies, the cascading water sparkling in the morning light. The roan dropped to his knees and half rolled in the water, followed shortly by the palomino. Jim played out the ropes and let them drink and splash their fill. They would be in the trailer a long time.

It was 7:30 when Jim pulled up in front of the sheriff's office in the county seat of Williamsville. The office didn't open until 8:00. One street over he found a long stretch of shade, parked his rig under the live oaks, pulled out his thermos with the last of the coffee, and waited.

"Come in, come in," Bill said.

He didn't remember how he had reacted the last time Jim entered his office. Jim did, but he held no hard feelings. Small towns were clannish. This wasn't the first time Jim had had to weather suspicion and hostility, but a good man always came round. And indeed, Bill had changed within hours, so completely he had no recollection of his initial reactions.

"Sit down."

"Just wanted to touch base before I headed off to the city."

"I'll keep in touch. Already we've got a match for the tire tracks, a Camry registered in the name of Carla Johnson. The estranged wife of the dead man. The boys are digging around in her past. Her first husband died, too. A young man, but a heavy alcoholic, so nobody thought too much about it."

Jim said nothing. This was not a new story for him. Every dead body told the same tale: the paucity of the human soul.

Bill broke the silence.

"Listen, I appreciate you taking the boy under your wing. It meant a lot to him."

"My pleasure. He's a good horseman."

There was an awkward silence now.

"If you're ever interested in selling that palomino, let me know."

"I've been thinking. I ride the roan mostly, don't really need two horses. The palomino was just a horse I rescued."

The two men exchanged a long look, then got down to business. Bill got out his checkbook.

"If you've got time, I'll show you where the place is right now and we can unload him there."

"I'm in no hurry. You want to pick up Jeffrey on the way, or is it a surprise?"

"It'll be a surprise all right, but the sooner the better."

"Son," Bill said as Jeffrey sat in the passenger seat of the pickup wondering what this was all about. "I've made a deal with Mr. Bowman, but I can still back out. I want to know what you think. Are you interested in that palomino gelding?"

Jeffrey turned to look straight at his father. Then slowly, as realization dawned, his face lit up with a blinding radiance.

"You mean . . . I can have the horse?"

"If you want him badly enough to do your part."

"Oh, yes!"

"It won't be easy, son, because you won't have your license for another year and a half or more, and he'll be staying at the farm.   I can get you out there a good bit of the time, and I'm sure your mother will do what she can.   But you're going to have to step up to the plate and be a man.   No more letting your mother baby you, or have to nag you to do your chores.   I can always sell the horse."

"Yessir."

It won't be that easy, Bill thought, but at least it's a chance.   If the boy's love of horses is big enough, it might work.   He'll need to get in with other boys who have a passion for horses.   There's that auction barn owner's son. He's about Jeffrey's age.

"Is that why Mr. Bowman is following us?   Are we going to the farm? Am I going to get the horse now?"

"Yes, son."   And Bill felt really good.   A surge of affection and optimism almost overwhelmed him, but he said nothing, just kept driving.

Jim followed Bill down the lane into the farm yard, then pulled off to one side into the shade of a big burr oak tree.   Jeffrey was out of Bill's pickup and behind the trailer before Jim could ease himself out of his own cab.

"Go ahead, Jeffrey, let him out."

If only adults could remember what it felt like to be a young boy, wanting something so badly without any hope of getting it, and then having it arrive as a gift, Jim thought.   He had struck a fair bargain with Bill, but the look on Jeffrey's face would have been payment enough.

"All right, okay," Bill was saying, "I'll be there in twenty minutes."   He snapped his phone shut and joined the other two, a resigned look on his face.   Jeffrey was just backing the gelding out of the trailer.

"I've got to get back to the office.   News sure spreads fast.   Mrs. Dubacek is giving my boys hell, demanding they drop everything and investigate the death of her son.   I wonder if she realizes that means his body will have to be exhumed. I'm sorry, son."

Jeffrey's face fell, but he struggled to be a man about it. His dad was deputy sheriff, and this was a murder investigation. But still . . . .

"I'm in no hurry, doesn't matter when I get back. Why don't I give the boy a ride back to town after he's settled the horse."

Bill hesitated, looked at Jeffrey's face, then looked straight at Jim.

"Much obliged. I know it means a lot to the boy."

"Oh, yes," Jeffrey breathed.

"I'll keep you posted," Bill said, as the two men shook hands in a hard clasp.

Jeffrey led the palomino into the pen in front of the saddle house and tied him. He pushed hard on the tack room door. How long had it been since anyone had opened it? Inside, everything was covered with dust, but the roof was good and the tack room tight. He couldn't believe how small his old saddle was. Two adult saddles sat on the long wooden saddle rack. Either one would need complete overhauling and reconditioning, as would the bridles hanging nearby. Jeffrey chose a currycomb and brush from the shelf.

Jim leaned against the wooden fence and lit a cigarette, inhaling deeply and letting the smoke out slowly. He noted Jeffrey's sure hands as he combed and brushed the horse. The gelding relaxed more and more, his eyes almost closing. Jeffrey brushed and brushed until the palomino's coat shone. Then he checked each hoof.

"Pick it up, boy," Jeffrey said, and then as the horse did so, "Hold." And after a few seconds, "Okay," and the gelding obediently dropped his front hoof.

Jeffrey cut his eyes toward Jim.

"I taught him that yesterday."

"You're real good with the horse."

"I want to teach him all kinds of tricks, maybe show

him."

Jeffrey could see himself in the middle of the rodeo arena, the golden horse standing proudly as the voice over the loudspeaker introduced Jeffrey Cummins and his sensational act to the huge enthusiastic crowd.

Jim stubbed out his cigarette.

"I reckon you better put him in the pasture now."

~ ~ ~

Traffic on the interstate was heavy, as usual, on the long drive back. Great tractor trailer rigs rumbled down the middle lane, pickups, SUVs, and sedans vied for position in the other two lanes, and the occasional fool, texting, wandered like a drunk across lanes. Jim was alert, but one part of his mind pondered the past, reviewed the present.

He felt good about selling the palomino. The gelding was a good horse and Jim was fond of him, but it was true he didn't need two horses. He had gotten attached to the palomino because he had saved him, but if the boy could hold to his purpose, the horse would be better off with him.

You never knew about kids, some made it, some didn't. Jeffrey at least had a chance. It certainly was better to have a stable home life and good parents, but some failed at life anyway. Some made it on their own. Like his unknown son somewhere in California. He guessed. The last he heard, and that was a long time ago, the boy had a good job, took care of himself. Was he happy? Was he a good man? Perhaps he was married. It suddenly struck Jim that he might be a grandfather without knowing it.

Interstate 35 roughly followed the Balcones Fault line. To the west, the land devolved into arid scrubland—goat country. To the east lay the long narrow island of blackland prairie. No longer prairie, of course, but the rich black loam of farmland, settled in good measure by Eastern European immigrants in the early part of the last century. But the interstate revealed none of the individuality of the country:

the small farms growing cotton, corn, and milo, wheat in the winter, usually some pasture land with small herds of Angus, Brangus, Charolais, Simmental, or various crosses.   Small wood frame houses from an earlier time, often dwarfed by a big barn; newer brick houses with great metal barns to house ever larger machinery.   An occasional quarried stone two-storey house.   Gone the Old World farmyards with their rectangular stacks of square bales topped by a rounded pile of loose hay to shed rain, the whole looking like a giant loaf of bread; gone the big black cast iron pots to boil corn for hominy and on another day to make soap; gone the family milk cow with its big brown Jersey eyes and rich creamy milk. Instead, along the interstate, mile after mile of the flat sameness: Anywhere, USA.

Jim took the next exit—Gas, Food, Lodging—got gas and a coke from a large station whose layout was replicated everywhere.

The miles passed.

Take this Carla woman. The case hadn't been proved, but if she did it, how do you explain that?   How do you explain Ted Bundy?   People who worked side by side with him couldn't believe it: not that handsome, personable, charming young man!   This Carla was from an ordinary family, church going, hardworking all of them, part of the community.   The bonds that knit kin to kin, family to families, family to church and friends, shattered.

The stone hurled into the pond rippling out not only concentrically, but also vertically into an unknown future and an unseen past.

Jim finished his coke, placed the empty bottle in the cup holder. He lit a cigarette. A Honda sped past, weaving in and out of traffic.

It was always like this after a search that ended in a dead body. Jim knew the feeling would pass. You just had to wait it out.   He stubbed out his cigarette in the ashtray and started looking for his exit.

Chapter 63

Late August, 2003, Concord, Texas

"I love your kitchen," Rhonda said. The two women were sitting at the kitchen table, Carla sipping coffee, Rhonda with a mug of rose hips tea before her. Out in the back yard, Jenny was playing on the swing set with two neighbor girls.

"Thank you. I'm so glad I had today off. I never know what my schedule will be." Carla smiled at her friend. "I can't get used to seeing you like this."

Rhonda laughed and shifted her weight. Seven months pregnant, she had gained all over, but her large-boned frame carried the weight well. She was wearing dark rose capris and a loose multi-colored top in a swirling pattern of rose, pink, and black. A black flip-flop with a thick comfy sole dangled from one foot crossed over her leg. She grew serious.

"But Carla, this is terrible about Frank. Who could have done such a brutal thing?"

"I just can't imagine."

"Tell me, what happened between you two? I know I'm not very good about keeping in touch, but I feel so bad about not knowing all you were going through. What with my first year of teaching, marrying Bob, and now this—" Rhonda put her hands around her big belly and smiled—"I've just been so wrapped up in my own life I haven't been a very good friend."

"Well, I haven't been any better. I know how it is. Work is so demanding, and then I have Jenny to care for. But we're together now."

"So tell me, what happened with you and Frank?"

Carla looked down and played with her coffee cup. Her shoulders slumped. Then she looked up at Rhonda.

"You know, it was never the same as with Joe. I think I jumped into the relationship too soon. I was just so lonely, so desperate really, after Joe died."

Carla's voice broke and Rhonda reached over and squeezed her hand.

"Anyway, Frank just moved in and swept me off my feet, insisted on marriage. Don't get me wrong. I'm not sorry. I have Jenny. But . . ."

"But what?"

"Well, you know what a downturn there's been in the real estate market?"

Rhonda nodded. Carla pointed to her tea cup and Rhonda shook her head.

"Some men, you know, can't handle their problems well."

Carla moved to the stove to pour herself another cup of coffee. She stood with her back to Rhonda, hiding her face and the fire that burned in her eyes every time she thought about Frank daring to strike her. He would never do it again.

"Frank tried to take it out on me. And you know I would never put up with that."

Carla sat back down with her coffee and smiled at Rhonda, fully in control of herself now.

Rhonda looked at her petite friend. Carla was wearing faded jeans with a pink t-shirt. Her hair was pulled back in a ponytail, and her fresh clear complexion needed no make-up. Rhonda smiled back.

"I know you wouldn't. I wonder he even tried."

Carla looked down, held her coffee cup with both hands. After a minute she looked up.

"There was more to it than that. I really didn't know Frank well enough, but he was persistent, used to getting what he wanted, and I was so lonely, so vulnerable. He rushed me into marriage, but he was no Joe. No one could ever be. But it's over now. Thank God I have Jenny."

"Such a shocking murder. Someone must have really hated him. I can't imagine bludgeoning someone to death. How's Jenny handling it? Her father's death, I mean."

"I haven't told her yet. She just thinks he's on a long trip. She misses her daddy, but she'll get over it."

Rhonda looked at her friend strangely, but just then there was a noise at the back door and Jenny came running in, followed by her two little friends.

"Mommy, I'm going to get my tea set to take outside so we can have a tea party, but can we have some real cookies to go with it?"

"Yes. I'll get the cookies for you."

The three little girls ran giggling to Jenny's bedroom. Carla carefully arranged some of the oatmeal cookies she had baked early that morning on a plastic plate.

"Maybe I'll have a girl next time," Rhonda said, laughing and holding her big belly. "I don't think this little monster is going to be interested in tea parties. I've got to go now. Mom and Dad are expecting me for lunch. You would think this was the first pregnancy in the history of the world the way those two act."

"No, I'll carry it," Jenny was saying as she clutched the tea set tighter and entered the kitchen. "You can carry the cookies."

Carla smiled to herself as she handed the plate of cookies to the little neighbor girl.

"Thank you, Mrs. Johnson."

The third little girl ducked her head shyly and followed the other two out.

Rhonda patted her swollen belly and smiled the soft knowing smile of all expectant mothers.

"This will make Bob happy, but I want a little girl, too. Jenny is so pretty, but with nothing of your coloring. She's got your take-charge attitude, though."

"Jenny is such a joy."

"Can you and Ray join us for dinner tonight? I'm dying to meet him, and it will give Bob someone to have a drink with. I'm such a stick-in-the-mud these days. But you know, I don't even miss it. All I care about is food. You wouldn't believe how much I eat. I always wondered how you could have any fun not drinking, but now I know. We can keep each other company while the men have their booze."

"I'd love to, but we already have plans for this evening. I know Ray will be sorry to miss meeting my oldest and best friend. He's heard so much about you."

"Well, there will be other times. I promise to do better. We won't go so long without seeing each other again."

Carla stood on the sidewalk for a moment after Rhonda had driven off, feeling the hot sun on her back. Ray was a mess. She wasn't sure what to do about it. Surely he would settle down after a while. How long did it take? At least he worked hard, often coming in after Jenny was already in bed, tired and hungry and not wanting to talk much. Well, he would get over it. It was just a matter of time.

Carla closed the front door behind her and stepped lightly into the bright kitchen to begin making lunch.

Chapter 64

September, 2003, Rural Central Texas

No one else was in the Oatville Store when Laura stepped into its cool dimness to pay for her gas. Shirley was sitting at the back table working on the books, but she came forward when she saw Laura enter. Laura lived just three miles away to the north and was a frequent customer. Often they went to church together. The younger woman had introduced Laura to her church after Ben died. The energetic and compassionate members of the new church had helped her a lot.

"Did you hear?" Shirley said. "They identified the body they found at the old Wentrcek place. Bill was in here again this afternoon, but still wouldn't tell me anything. I got mad because we need to know, us women living alone."

Ever since Ben's death, Laura had also lived alone. Sometimes when her old joints were acting up, she walked with a cane, but for the most part she carried on as always: working in her garden, pickling and canning, baking her own bread, cleaning her house. Keeping busy helped.

"But I know somebody in the sheriff's office, I'm not saying who, and she told me. It was that man from Concord, the one that was missing."

"Who is he? Anyone we know?"

"I don't know him, but his mother is Lucille Johnson. You know her. She's from Wirtz, but goes to our church in Graylor. They say he's a realtor—or was. You've seen little Jenny with Lucille at church."

"Johnson. My niece went with a Johnson from Wirtz years ago, but he was killed in a car wreck. Jimmy Johnson. He was drunk and missed a curve. Thank goodness Daisy wasn't with him that night."

"That was Lucille's younger son. It liked to killed her. It was after that she helped start up the church. People are saying Frank—that's his name, her other son—was murdered by his ex-wife and her boyfriend."

"Why?"

"Seems it was a custody fight over Jenny, their little girl. The hearing was coming up. You know the Dicksons in Graylor?"

"George and Sharon Dickson? He died of a heart attack."

"That's the ones."

"Oh, sure. June was a good friend of my youngest daughter."

"Well, Carla, the middle daughter, was Frank Johnson's wife."

"I can't believe it! I remember her, such a pretty little thing. A twirler, wasn't she? And June was so nice, so thoughtful. She married badly as I recall. Had to go back with her two sons to live with her parents. After Julia went off to college, we didn't see much of June."

"They're saying now that Carla may have poisoned her first husband, Joe Dubacek."

"No! How can that be? The Dicksons were such a good family, didn't have much but were hard workers, good church-going people. I remember Sharon did some sewing for my girls."

"No one knows. She always seemed like such a sweet thing. Made good grades, never got in trouble. Now they had their hands full with that youngest daughter, Patty. But I hear she finally settled down, grew up I guess."

"Her first husband, what Dubacek was that?"

"Anton and Charlene. Their farm is about halfway between Graylor and Wirtz, not too far off the highway. She's the one always won first place for her kolaches."

"I don't know her, but I remember those kolaches. Every time the Brethren Church had a bake sale, Ben insisted I be there first thing in the morning to be sure and get a dozen of her kolaches. He sure did like his sweets." Laura looked wistful, remembering.

"Charlene Dubacek still bakes for all the church sales. You know, she never did like Carla, but then she wouldn't have liked any woman Joe married. She babied that boy so. She took his death real hard. No telling what her state of mind is now. And poor Lucille Johnson, losing both her sons. All she's got left is her little granddaughter Jenny. Frank may be dead and Carla in jail, but you can bet that custody fight isn't over yet."

"It's so sad. I just can't believe it about Carla. She was such a cute, pretty child, with those big dark eyes. Poor June was the plain one. It just doesn't seem possible."

As soon as Laura left, Shirley went back to her books, but she sat thoughtful for a moment first. It was hard to believe. Life was strange. The oldest of her three sons had had a crush on Carla back in junior high, but she was going with some older boy and probably never even knew. Thank God! Shirley turned back to her accounts.

Chapter 65

September, 2003, Rural Central Texas

Leroy looked around the kitchen as he sat down at the breakfast table with the sandwiches and iced tea he had made for his lunch. It was brighter and seemed larger than when it had been his mother's. He liked the changes his wife had made, and he was proud that they could afford to remodel the old farm house, even if just one room at a time. The window over the sink had always faced west and it was big enough to let in a lot of natural light, but the cream colored walls now heightened the effect. His mother had always loved watching the sunset as she made supper. He wasn't sure Cathy took the same pleasure in nature—it had been the very fabric of his mother's life—but she knew how to preserve some of the charm of the old house while adding modern amenities. He had to admit that the granite counter tops were practical as well as pleasing to look at.

The ringing phone interrupted his reverie. Cathy and her sister had taken all the children to the water park for the day, and it took a moment before Leroy realized he had to answer the phone himself.

"Leroy?"

"Yes."

"This is Rhonda. Rhonda Jefferson. Well, Michaels now. I know we haven't seen each other since high school, but I just have to talk to you."

There was a long pause, but Leroy said nothing. Yes, he remembered Rhonda, only too well. The sound of her voice brought back vividly the pain.

Rhonda took a deep breath and started over again.

"Leroy, did you know that Carla and her boyfriend have been arrested for the murder of her estranged husband?"

"What!"

"I know. I saw her not too long ago. We've stayed

friends all this time. I mean, we haven't seen much of each other recently, what with my living fifty miles away now, but I saw her through the death of her first husband and her marriage to Frank. . . . Oh, Leroy, they're saying she may have murdered Joe, too. I just can't believe it. Please, tell me, what really happened between you and Carla?"

Leroy didn't want to talk about it. He didn't want to hear any of this. Feelings he had long buried arose sharply. He gripped the telephone stand hard.

"I know this must be hard for you, Leroy, but I don't know where else to turn. I just can't make sense of it."

There was a pleading desperation in Rhonda's voice. She, too, was suffering. He thought a moment.

"You know what Carla meant to me, the whole world. I nearly lost my mind when I found out she had planned to marry another man all the time we were engaged. I couldn't believe it. You know how strict she always said her father was? Well, when I wanted to speak to him about our marriage, she claimed her father had tried to molest her all those years, but her mother didn't know. I had complete faith in her, but she was a total liar."

"Leroy, she and Frank had a daughter, Jenny. She told Ray, her live-in boyfriend, that Frank molested Jenny and that was the only way to stop him."

Rhonda was crying now.

"She always told me that she and Joe were destined to be together, that it was something no one else could understand. He was her soul mate." Rhonda was sobbing so hard she could hardly talk. "She used his . . . insurance money . . . to go . . . to go . . . to school on. . . . She was . . . my . . . friend. . . . "

Rhonda was crying uncontrollably now. Leroy waited until her sobs had subsided.

"I don't know what to say, Rhonda. It's just too terrible to think she could be a murderer, and yet . . . . I don't know. . . . It took me a long time to regain my faith in people. I'll never be the same. Who can explain it? What in nature could make such monsters? We just have to keep going."

After he hung up the phone, Leroy looked out the window above the sink at the fields beyond. Half the near field was already shredded, dry brown cornstalks in orderly rows filling the other half.

Yes, he had made a life for himself, after all. Cathy was a good woman, a kind-hearted heavy-set woman who had few interests beyond her family and friends. Clerking at the bank was just a job to her, something she had to do. She was happiest decorating the house and caring for the children. And of course he loved little Ann as though she were his own. Every time he looked at Tommy, at his round face and sturdy little two-year-old legs, his heart swelled. True, there was no poetry in his marriage, but on the whole he was happy.

Thirty-five or forty acres of the cornfield still remained to be shredded. Time to get back to work.

The level field stretched out before him under a vast sky as he shredded up and down the long rows. Unbidden, memories arose before him: The last rays of the sun lighting up the old pomegranate tree, touching the orange blossoms. The wise old rose bush spilling petals on the ground. From the weathered barn the hoot of an owl and Carla startling, her slim supple body melting into his strong lean one in perfect faith. Carla, so beautiful in the moonlight, dark ringlets tangling on the white pillow case, her pale skin so perfect to the eye, to the touch, there in that abandoned house in fields not so different from this one. Carla, whose body leapt to meet his, who seemed to give her whole self, whose every breath met his. Leroy saw once again the life he had envisioned: Carla so brisk and efficient, but lighting up his kitchen with her charm, her kittenish ways. He had imagined her, so petite, surrounded by a bevy of dark-haired children, the little girls with errant ringlets. He could see her teaching the girls to cook from scratch, the kitchen filled with the aroma of fresh-baked bread and hot cinnamon rolls, teaching them to pickle and can, to churn butter and make cheese. She would have disciplined the strong-willed little boys, too, quietly but sternly. They would have adored their mother.

And at night, after the children were in bed and the dishes done, Carla responding to his every caress, every lover's gesture, in a wild crescendo, two hearts pounding as one till they fell both together and stilled. And yet again, as Carla nipped and played, so enchanting, weaving fantasies, perhaps her petite self as a dominatrix, or yet again, as a passive sleeping beauty needing the prince's kiss to awaken—to awaken the turbulent passion roiling inside.

The old pain burned in his heart. He would have done anything for her.

The orderly rows of cornstalks fell to the shredder. A fine dust rose in the air. Leroy was at one with the roar of the tractor and shredder, the dome of deep blue sky, the gradually receding rows of cornstalks falling like dominos behind him, the flat land before him.

The red sun rested momentarily on the edge of the horizon, looming large as a backdrop to the wide empty fields. Leroy whipped the tractor around and swept down the last rows.

He began to think of a man in a cell somewhere, one who had done the ultimate for her. Someone who had believed, as he had believed, in her. Someone whose suffering went far, far beyond the heartache of lost dreams.

Chapter 66

September, 2003, Williamsville, Texas

Ray sat where the guard told him. His shoulders were slumped, his face haggard. Finally he raised his eyes and looked at the man on the other side of the partition. The man was lean and work hardened, his face clearly accustomed to all weathers. About six feet tall, he seemed taller because of his rangy build. His regular features were handsome, but there was a hawk-like keenness in his eyes and stern lines around his full mouth that made him look older than his years.

Both men sat silently for a moment, sizing each other up. Finally the visitor said, "I'm Leroy Machu. You wouldn't know me, but I felt like I had to see you."

Leroy paused but Ray said nothing, just stared blankly before him.

"Carla was my high school sweetheart. We were engaged to be married."

A tremor ran through Ray. He sat up straighter and shook. For the first time, he looked Leroy in the face, but he still said nothing.

"I would have done anything in the world for her. I worshipped the ground she walked on."

Leroy paused. Ray was visibly agitated. He looked like he wanted to leap up from his seat.

"Carla was the most beautiful woman in the world to me, so sweet and vulnerable, but with an inner strength. I know now she was a liar through and through. But it's still hard for me to believe she's evil."

Ray groaned but seemed unable to speak. He looked straight at Leroy, and his eyes were filled with an unutterable pain.

"We had always gone out on the sly because Carla said her father was so strict he wouldn't let her date. But by the time she was about to graduate, I was making a good living farming, and we were to be married that summer. I wanted to go to her father, man to man, to speak to him. That's when she told me he had tried to molest her ever since she was thirteen. I would have gone after him myself, but she said her mother didn't know and it would kill her. Turns out Carla was marrying someone else right after she graduated. They had to put a restraining order out on me."

Ray dropped his head onto the ledge and his great shoulders heaved, his massive body shaken with sobs. Finally he sat back up and looked Leroy in the eye.

"I killed a man."

He looked down at his big hands, and his voice was hoarse. "She said he raped Jenny . . . gave details . . . said it was the only way to stop him . . . ." He paused for a long while. Then he looked straight at Leroy, his big face open. "Why?" And in that single word was unbearable pain and bewilderment.

"I was lucky," Leroy said. "She broke my heart, crushed my dreams. I will never see the world the way I saw it before. But I was lucky. It could have been me sitting where you are."

Both men were silent.

"Come on, time to go," the guard said, walking up.

"I appreciate it," Ray said, looking straight into Leroy's eyes, and his large calloused hand wanted to reach right through the heavy Plexiglas and clasp Leroy's.

Chapter 67

September, 2003, Graylor, Texas

"It's not true," Momma said. She looked suddenly very old, and though her figure was solid, frail. She clutched at her Bible.

June felt sick. In fact, she had been retching until she had had the dry heaves. She couldn't believe it, either, and yet, there were the clues, the little scenes when something didn't seem quite right. Now they were saying she had poisoned Joe, too. The man she had claimed was her soul mate. For that, for her whole life, to be a lie . . . . Her sister couldn't be such a monster . . . Carla, so pretty and even tempered, such a good mother . . . June wanted to scream and fall on the floor in convulsions.

She looked down at Momma, shrunken in her rocking chair.

"I'll make a fresh pot of coffee."

June returned to the parlor with two steaming cups. Momma was staring at nothing, her hands resting on the Bible in her lap.

"Momma," June said gently, "Momma, here's your coffee."

Finally the old lady turned her gaze toward June, but her expression was blank.

I've got to get her talking, June thought.

"Here, Momma."

June took her mother's hand and put it around the cup.

"Why, thank you."

"Momma, we've got to think of Jenny."

"That poor child."

"Lucille Johnson will want to get custody."

Momma sat up straighter. "Lucille Johnson will teach that child to hate."

"She's her grandmother, too. She'll continue to be a big part of Jenny's life. But we have to raise that child. I'll have my teaching certificate soon, and I've been promised that fourth grade class for this fall, on a temporary certificate. You could look after Jenny as well as the boys after school?"

"Of course I can."

Momma sat erect. She carefully placed her coffee cup in its accustomed place on the little table beside her rocker. She looked at June. Then her shoulders slumped, her face fell forward into her hands and she shook with sobs, tears running down her fingers into the palms of her hands. "My baby," she wailed, keening back and forth in her rocker.

June ran into the kitchen. She clutched the rim of the sink and stared out at the side yard.

Chapter 68

September, 2003, Williamsville, Texas

Carla sat on the hard seat before the Plexiglas partition, her hands resting in her lap. Her pale face, framed by the shoulder-length dark curls, was expressionless. A white knit shirt tucked into white pants emphasized her petite slimness. On the other side sat Momma in her Sunday best, navy blue dress with white trim, a navy straw hat, and sensible shoes. June stood beside her, wearing black pants and a gray and green knit top. Her face was pale and drawn and she looked like she hadn't slept in a week. But she was neatly dressed and her dark brown hair carefully brushed.

Why were they here? Carla didn't want them.

"Carla . . . What happened?" June wanted to hear something . . . anything . . . a reason . . . an explanation . . . something that might hint at extenuating circumstances.

Momma leaned forward.

"My baby."

She reached out, as though her gnarled old hand could penetrate the thick Plexiglas.

Carla stared coldly back.

"Don't ask me anything. Whatever you know, you know. I have nothing more to say."

She stood up and turned her back. She motioned to the guard, who immediately leapt to his feet and came to her. She walked away, the guard following closely behind. The heavy metal door clanged behind them.

Chapter 69

September, 2003, Dallas, Texas

"Jim? Bill here. How you doing?"

"Good. You?"

"Fine. Listen, just wanted you to know. Looks like the estranged wife, Carla Dickson Johnson, and her boyfriend, guy named Ray Olsen, are the ones. In fact, he's confessed. Won't implicate her, but it's pretty clear. They've both been arrested, bail set high."

"What kind of guy is he?"

"Big guy, six four, two fifty. A rancher, solid man. It doesn't add up."

"And the estranged wife?"

"Local girl, good family, though they never had much money. Real pretty. A twirler in high school. A trauma nurse now. Doesn't make much sense. Sure, she wanted full custody of the little girl, but that hardly seems motive enough. And money doesn't seem to be involved. She must have really hated the guy."

"The mystery of the human heart."

"A few little stories about her have come out. You know how people talk. In hindsight some people say she was cold-hearted. Seems she dumped her fiancé just weeks before she married someone else, right out of high school. He had no clue. And now it looks like she may have killed her first husband for the insurance money, enough for her to finish her associate's degree. Mrs. Dubacek—his mother—has agreed to have the body exhumed for toxicology tests."

Jim sat silent for a minute. Some murders were crimes of passion, committed in a white-hot moment of fury. Some were the acts of a lone killer prowling the highways and thrilling to the surge of power over the vulnerable and terrified. And some killers just got off on the orgiastic convulsions of death. Other murders were carefully plotted out schemes for money or acts of personal revenge. On a larger scale, some murders were politically motivated. Harder to understand in some ways. The prime example the Holocaust. Today, the terrorists who wanted revenge against us for invading their country and killing their people. Those drone strikes that wiped out wedding parties and created terrorists out of the remaining kin. An eye for an eye, a tooth for a tooth. Or tribal loyalties, ethnic and religious hatreds, that drove groups to slaughter each other in terrifying genocides. Jim remembered his high school history, how over a century ago the invading European countries had settled their differences by carving up Africa and the Middle East according to the territory each country had won. Never mind what tribes occupied what land. Or what their religions were. And then there were the impersonal deaths, caused by corporate greed. Drugs tested on unwitting third world people. If too many died, well, scratch that drug. Garment factory fires killing hundreds, because Western clothing retailers were trying to squeeze the last penny out of unscrupulous factory owners so rich nations could buy cheap clothes. Cancer researchers vying for grants to fund the search for a yet more potent and patentable toxin to kill the cancer—or the patient. Companies genetically modifying food crops so they could be drenched with weed killers, then patenting the seeds and forcing farmers to buy them, and then selling more and more toxic chemicals that end up in the food, the air, the water, to slowly poison us all.

"Jim? You still there?"

"Yeah. Just thinking. Makes you wonder, doesn't it? They say there are some people without a conscience. I don't know if they're born that way or something happens to them. But they have no remorse, no feeling for others. It must be very lonely."

"I guess you see a lot. But this is about the biggest thing to hit this area in a long time. I'm ready for things to settle down."

"How's Jeffrey?"

"Doing good.   Spends a lot of time with that palomino.   Has got some new friends that are into horses, too."

"Glad to hear it. He seems to have a gift with horses."

"You know, I didn't realize it.   Sure appreciate you taking him under your wing like that.   You should see what he has that horse doing."

The pride in Bill's voice was unmistakable.

After Jim hung up, he stepped out onto his patio. The sun was low in the western sky, but the September heat enveloped him like a soft warm blanket.   High overhead a lingering jet trail faded into a band of cirrus clouds.   Next door the neighbors were having a cook-out.   Momentarily he visualized icy margarita glasses rimmed in salt and could almost taste the tart citrusy drink, but quickly dismissed the image.   Only seldom now did he long for alcohol.   He could smell the rich scent of grilling steaks, hear the shouts of the neighbor boys and their friends splashing in the pool.   That was something he had missed.

He thought about a man in California who might or might not look a little like him, or might not be in California at all, who might be married and have children—or who might be a loner, filling his life with a computer screen.

And then he thought about a boy training a stout palomino gelding, a boy whose dad was proud of him and rooting for him to make it.

Chapter 70

Sunday, Late September, 2003, Graylor, Texas

Bright sunlight poured down on the church building, reflecting off the exposed metal of the unfinished sides, the heat as oppressive as that of August, but the slant of September light subtly different. There was a raw feel to this place of worship, in spite of two large pecan trees that had been allowed to remain even when the site was anonymous farmland lying next to the state highway, the trees now shading asphalt parking lot instead of struggling corn.

Inside the church, Laura sat next to Shirley on the hard metal folding chairs. Laura's was the aisle seat. Across from her on the other side of the aisle, little Jenny sat by her grandmother, Lucille Johnson.

"Does Lucille have custody?" Laura leaned over to whisper to Shirley.

"Just every other weekend, like Frank had. The custody suit hasn't been settled yet. Of course she wants full custody, can't stand to see Jenny go to 'that house that produced the viper.' She's becoming bitterer and bitterer. Can't blame her, but it's not good for Jenny. Poor child. June is young, raising two boys of her own. In spite of the sorrow, it's a happier home."

"Lucille looks like she's aged ten years."

"Losing Jimmy all those years ago. Now Frank. And Frank's the one who built her house, took good care of her. All she's got left is Jenny. It's hard on her."

The women fell silent as the praise and worship team entered and began to sing. Soon the whole church was clapping. Some were on their feet, arms lifted heavenward as the spirit entered them.

An aged woman leaning on the arms of her daughter and granddaughter, one on either side, hobbled down the aisle between the rows of ecstatic parishioners, to seats near the front.

Then the minister entered and the congregation quieted as he reached the pulpit.

From time to time Laura glanced across the aisle at grandmother and granddaughter. It was hot and stuffy in the church, and Laura could see Jenny beginning to fidget. Lucille put her hand on Jenny's arm, and the child stuck her bottom lip out.

The choir and the whole congregation launched into a passionate rendering of Amazing Grace.

That's what it will take, Laura thought, amazing grace, to bring that child safely to shore. Laura hoped June would get primary custody. If anyone could do it, she could. She felt so sorry for Lucille Johnson. Hers was too much to bear. But the child couldn't thrive in the vinegar of an old woman's bitterness.

Just as the minister was telling all to turn and greet their neighbors, a commotion broke out across the aisle from Laura.

"No, I won't," Jenny yelled, breaking away from Lucille, who had grabbed her arm. "I hate it here!"

She ran down the aisle and into the vestibule while Lucille was struggling to her feet. It took a moment for her arthritic legs to move, and as Lucille limped down the aisle past the silent congregation, the slamming of the outer door echoed through the church.

"She reminds me of Patty," Shirley whispered to Laura, "the youngest daughter."

"Poor Lucille. How embarrassing for her," the older woman said. "But it's better for the child to have these outbursts than to keep it all in. Do you think Lucille can see past her own grief to understand?"

"I don't know. She never got over Jimmy. Frank was all that saved her. That and the church. But after Jenny was born, Lucille just blossomed."

"I heard June has Jenny seeing some child

psychologist."

"Yes, and the woman is supposed to be real good. I don't know what Lucille thinks about that. She's old fashioned."

The hot noonday sun beat down on the two women as they exited the church. A truck rumbled down the state highway, followed by several pickups and the occasional car. Across the parking lot, Lucille was talking earnestly to Jenny, whose tear-stained face was turned to her grandmother.

"I don't know who to feel sorrier for, that child or Lucille," Shirley said.

"I'm thinking about Sharon Dickson. She worked so hard to raise those girls, and June is a wonderful person. She was a good friend to my Julia. I'm sorry the two girls drifted apart. And Carla now, she might not have been selfless like June, but she was such a pretty, sweet girl, always cheerful and cute. Sharon is a God-fearing woman. What could have happened?"

"It's strange how different those three girls were, June the responsible one, Patty the drama queen, and Carla the quiet, determined one. Who could ever have imagined . . . ."

"Do you remember that radio program, The Shadow? You're probably not old enough. Anyway, the program always began with a deep voice saying, 'Who knows what evil lurks in the heart of man? The Shadow knows.' It always gave me chills, but I never really believed in that kind of evil. I mean, in anyone I knew. It was always some imaginary stranger. I still can't believe it."

"You know, my oldest son had a big crush on Carla in junior high school, but she never gave him the time of day. Thank God!"

The two women stood for a moment longer in the shade of a pecan tree, then braved the heat to settle themselves in Shirley's SUV. Across the parking lot, Lucille Johnson carefully buckled the seat belt around Jenny and slowly drove off.

Chapter 71

October, 2003, Graylor, Texas

The sound of children laughing rose from the backyard. Late October was one of the best times, June thought, at least in Central Texas. Crisp mornings, mild afternoons, the intense heat that lasted deep into September just a memory now. She carefully arranged the stack of papers she had finished grading in a folder and put it away. Deep satisfaction flooded her. Teaching fourth grade was the work she had always wanted.

She looked out the window at the two little girls swinging side by side on the old swing set. The big hackberry tree shaded them on the back swing and then they emerged into bright sunlight on the forward motion. Shade and sunlight, shade and sunlight glistening on a mop of curls and on silky straight hair, while the girls kicked their feet and imbibed the afternoon, as unselfconscious as the sparrows twittering in the branches above them.

June worried about Jenny. Seeing her playing with the little neighbor girl, one would never guess that anything was wrong. But she had lost both parents, and in a small town couldn't be protected from the accusations that her mother was a murderer. Nor could anyone stop Lucille Johnson's bitter words. June felt Mrs. Johnson's deep sorrow. To lose both sons. How could she bear it? All she had left now was little Jenny. Yet if Jesus' words meant anything at all, one was compelled to forgive. Religion was both a comfort and an iron discipline. She, herself, was still struggling, and always would be.

June left her neat desk and her finished work behind, walked down the hall to the kitchen and across the worn linoleum to the battered old refrigerator. She took out a pitcher of lemonade and filled two plastic glasses with ice. On the pitted and scarred counter top sat a Tupperware box of cookies she had baked the day before. She arranged several on a small plate, then stuck her head out the back door.

"Would you girls like some lemonade and cookies?"

Jenny leapt from her swing, and taking Pam by the hand, raced to the back door.

"Yes, please."

Seated at the rickety old kitchen table, the girls provided a striking contrast in coloring. Jenny, with straight blonde hair framing an oval face, promised to be a beauty, if one could tell at such a young age. Pam, with brown curly hair and a snub nose, was cute as a button, June thought. She was a happy, outgoing child, the same age as Jenny, and promised to be her best friend. It was a stroke of luck, June thought, that the family had moved in next door. The father's job was in Concord, some twenty miles away, but they wanted to raise their family in a small town. The mother was a teacher's aide in the middle school where June taught. Sometimes what looked like a small thing could make a big difference in a child's life. This family was a stranger to the complex web of loyalties, hostilities, and grudges that often underlay the life of a small town.

The screech of bike brakes and the sound of tires skidding on gravel announced the arrival of Jason and Daniel. June filled two more glasses with ice and put more cookies on the plate, a lot of cookies.

"I'll tell them," Jenny said, jumping up from the table and running to the back door.

June was filling the coffee pot. Mama would be getting up from her nap soon and would be wanting her cup. June, too, liked her mid-afternoon coffee.

The boys burst into the kitchen, drained their glasses of lemonade, and demolished the plate full of cookies.

"You children run outside to play. Grammy will be getting up soon and you know she likes her quiet time."

All four children ran outside, the screen door banging behind them.

The aroma of fresh-brewed coffee filled the kitchen as the old percolator wheezed and burbled. As if on cue, June heard Mama shuffling down the hall. June filled two cups, carefully sugaring one, and headed for the small living room. Mama was already settled in her chair, gazing out the window, the closed Bible in her lap.

"Why, thank you," she said, taking the proffered cup. She turned back to the window, staring vacantly at nothing. She had lost weight, and her face appeared far more wrinkled. Her once gray hair had whitened.

"The boys are back. Do you still want them to clean your flower beds this afternoon?"

Mama looked vague.

"What's that?"

"Your flower beds. You want the boys to work them this afternoon?'

With an effort, Mama turned toward June.

"Why, yes, yes, I do."

Mama took a sip of her coffee, then resumed looking out the window.

June cradled her cup in her hands, her eyes filling with tears. Mama looked so old and frail. She sipped her coffee and thought hard, but nothing came to her. In half an hour she would call the boys in and try to get Mama interested, but it was clear she was drifting away. The boys knew what to do now and would do a good job, but Mama no longer cared about her flowers. She had quit going to church—she couldn't face people—no longer baked for the sales. She loved the boys, but now retreated from their vitality and wild energy. Sometimes Jenny could bring a smile to her face, but then she would turn vague again.

June took a deep breath. It all rested on her shoulders. She didn't know if the money from Carla's house would pay for her lawyer. And what could the lawyer do, other than avert the death penalty? June's shoulders slumped. It was all she could do to pay for a therapist for little Jenny.

But the woman was good, and June could see how it was helping Jenny. She sat up straight, drained the last of her coffee, and headed to the kitchen to put on a pot roast.

From outside came the muted sound of children's voices, then Jenny's rose high and clear.

"No, Daniel, that's not the way you do it."

June smiled as she sealed the foil over the meat and vegetables, and closed the oven door.

Chapter 72

Late Spring, 2004, Graylor, Texas
Already at the beginning of June the mild air of mid-morning had begun to heat up. From the backyard came the murmur of children playing on this Saturday at the end of the school year.

A light breeze fluttered the curtains and ruffled the paper on the desk where June sat. She would not turn on the old window units until the heat became oppressive. June had just finished averaging grades and had completed her folders, one for each child in her fourth grade class. The folders were neatly stacked on her desk, pens and pencils put away. She took a sip of iced tea.

Her students had done well and she was proud of them. Already she was contemplating ways to individualize instruction even more next year. Someday she wanted to get a master's degree. But one step at a time. She was thankful for the summer break.

"You're not the boss of me, Jason Jackson!"

"I am, too. I'm the oldest and besides, you're just a girl."

"So what? You don't know anything!"

"Shut up!"

Both children were shouting now. Jason stepped menacingly toward her, but Jenny stood her ground, glaring at him.

June sighed and stood up. As she stepped into the kitchen, she heard Daniel's voice.

"Look, why don't you divide this row in half and each tend it your way. Then we can see what works best."

Who would have thought it, June mused. She paused at the back door.

Pam from next door had trotted into the yard, her

brown curls bouncing and her brown eyes twinkling.

"Hey, what's going on?   What's all the shouting about?"

June opened the screen door and stepped out.

"You kids ready to go swimming? Would you like to come with us, Pam?   Then check with your mother. Afterwards we're going by the nursing home."

~ ~ ~

The nursing home had been built in an earlier era and showed its age, but still served the town well. A great open hall held a giant TV at one end, inconspicuous because of the spaciousness of the area. Four wings at the four corners fed into the open hall. At its back were the dining tables. Each holiday and every change of season was celebrated by a complete redecorating of the hall, which because of its height was quite an undertaking. At Christmas time, a giant fir tree dominated the center. At Valentine's, red hearts and red and white crepe paper festooned the large common area, and Thanksgiving brought its pumpkins and paper turkeys, Halloween its skeletons and black cats. The decorations were extensive and elaborate.

Almost every evening local musicians set up in the front of the hall to perform: Country Western singers, church groups, Czech chorales with accordionists and electric piano, a duo singing mellow rock from an earlier era. Some quite good, some indifferent, some off key, but all volunteering their time. Family members, sometimes singly, sometimes with the whole family, including babies, were in and out at all times of the day. Sometimes a spouse brought in the family dog. The parade of visitors made the nursing home a good place to catch up on the local gossip.

Some of the residents had started kindergarten together, married right after high school, raised their children together, bragged about their grandchildren to each other.

Now they rolled their wheelchairs up to their assigned places and ate together.

Mama was in her Geri-chair out in the big main room when June and the children clattered in. She smiled when they gathered around her chair, but in a moment her face went blank, like a shutter closing.

"Mama, I brought you some ice cream."

June wheeled Mama outside into the courtyard in the shade of towering pecan trees. Old fashioned hollyhocks—white, yellow, rose and red—half concealed the low rock wall at the far end of the courtyard. Purple verbena bordered the two side walls. The four children sat crowded together on a wide porch swing suspended from a broad pecan limb, savoring their little tubs of ice cream and licking the little wooden spoons clean.

"Pretty flowers," Mama said, as though she had never seen them before.

June pulled the tab that lifted the cardboard lid off another individual container of ice cream and handed Mama a real spoon.

"I'll be right back with your coffee."

Back inside, June took Mama's favorite cup, the one with yellow butterflies on it, from her purse, filled it with coffee, and added two spoonfuls of sugar.

"Why, thank you," Mama said, cradling the cup in her gnarled old hands.

A ray of sunshine slipped through the pecan leaves and lit up Jenny's golden blonde hair. On her right, Pam's lively brown eyes were checking everything out even as she steadily ate her ice cream. On Jenny's left, Daniel was totally absorbed in his ice cream, not once looking up until it was, lamentably, gone. Jason had already finished. He was wondering how hard it would be to leap the stone wall, the part bordered by verbena. Easy, he thought. You couldn't jump it at the end where the hollyhocks grew without smashing some. But then maybe you could vault over the wooden gate in the middle.

"What pretty children," Mama said, "especially that little girl with the golden halo."

"Why, Mama, that's Jenny, Carla's . . ."

June stopped herself, but it was too late. Mama's eyes glazed over and she forgot about the cup of coffee, which fortunately had grown cold, so that she scarcely noticed when it toppled over and pooled in her lap.

Chapter 73

January, 2005, Dallas, Texas

A rare winter snow had lightly covered the North Texas plains. Jim looked up from the files spread across his lap, leaned back in his easy chair, and stared out at the snow-covered dry brown grass on the other side of his patio. At the back of the small yard, a little yaupon tree grew against the wooden privacy fence. A few faded red berries still clung to its limbs. The bleak landscape was otherwise almost colorless beneath a lowering sky.

He turned back to the last file, opened the folder labeled Frank Johnson Murder. He could almost feel the stifling heat as images from that summer rose before him. A shaft of sunlight illuminating a bloody running shoe that stuck up through wisps of hay partially covering a stiffened corpse. A charred and blackened piece of leather caught in the debris at the bend of a river, the water riffling against it. The smell of river mud. The sounds. Murmur of the river, the cry of a mourning dove, the swell and fall of the song of the cicadas.

The insistent ring of a telephone. Startled from his reverie, Jim turned toward the phone on the nearby end table. He stared at it a moment before picking up.

"Bill Cummins here. Thought you might be interested in an update."

"Yes, indeed. I was just looking at that file. What you got?"

"Jury reached a verdict. Guilty. Sentencing handed down yesterday. Carla got ten years. Could get out sooner. Of course, she hasn't been tried in the Dubacek case yet, but it probably won't go to trial. If Charlene Dubacek had any say over it, it would, but the evidence is sketchy."

"Could hardly reach any other conclusion in the Frank Johnson case, though I guess you never know what a jury will do."

"That's for sure. You know Ray, the live-in boyfriend, confessed and got twenty years. Such a brutal murder, but he had been an upstanding citizen. He refused to testify against Carla. It's hard to understand. He seems shattered by the whole thing. It's like she had him bewitched. She claimed that it was his idea, that he was desperately jealous of Frank and that he wanted sole control of the little girl. But with the footprint forensics got from the path down to the river, it's clear she was there, an accessory. I don't know what to make of it."

"What about the little girl?"

"It looks like June, Carla's older sister, will have primary custody. Some people are angry about that. You know how it is in a small town. Lucille Johnson, Frank's mother, will have Jenny part of the time. But I don't know if those wounds will ever heal."

Twice Bill had had to break the news to Mrs. Johnson that a son of hers had died. Once as a young man, standing on her porch, never having performed this duty before, as the rain dripped from the eaves, gently, steadily. And then on that hot day in August, when she ushered him into her parlor, knowing from his very presence, but fighting against the knowledge, refusing to believe what every fiber of her being knew. It wasn't any easier for him the second time.

"The whole town is riled up, but I guess things will settle down after a time. But on a happier note, Jeffrey's got that palomino doing all kinds of tricks. I'm pretty amazed."

Bill didn't say that Mary Kay still called to complain about Jeffrey and that Linda still gave him the silent treatment if he spent too much time with the boy and that he didn't know what would happen once Jeffrey got his driver's license.

"Just wanted you to know that I appreciate all you and the Search and Rescue did for us down here."

"Glad to do it.   Hope you won't be needing our services again."

"Me, too!" Bill said, signing off.

Jim replaced the receiver, closed up the folder, stood up and stretched. He looked out the picture window into the back yard. In the fading light, the sparse covering of snow grew whiter and the few bushes darker. The living room was warm, but the bleak outdoors seemed to bring in a chill.

He made a cup of coffee, sipped it slowly.

It grew later. The sky cleared and the temperature dropped.

Jim slipped on a jacket, stepped out on the patio, and lit a cigarette. The air was bracing. The stars, not so bright as when he had gazed at them from the wilderness area, glittered coldly down on earth. He could just make out Orion's belt. As a child he had been fascinated by the multitude of stars visible on clear summer nights, and amazed when his uncle pointed out the constellations. The Big Dipper, yes, but twins and hunters, bears and dragons? What imagination, he had thought then, to be able to see kings and queens and princesses, heroes, hunters, and animals, in the vast canopy of stars scattered at random across the face of the universe. Now he saw it as the human need to impose order on chaos, to illustrate familiar stories on the distant stars of a cold and impersonal universe.

He stubbed out his cigarette and stepped inside, into his warm and comfortable living room.

The phone rang once again.

"Jim here."

"We've got a missing woman, mid-forties. Last seen walking back from a convenience store near her house. Northwest side of Houston. We'll have a command post set up at the Ebenezer Baptist Church tomorrow. The automated calls will be going out shortly."

"Be there first thing in the morning."

Jim looked out at the darkened landscape.   The

yaupon was no longer visible against the fence. Black night pressed against the fragile light illuminating the room. Jim felt like a captain poised against a sea of darkness.

The unrelenting mystery of the human soul. Once more the dark flame sucked him into its swirling blood-red depths. He strode into the bedroom and began to pack his gear.

www.ingramcontent.com/pod-product-compliance
Lightning Source LLC
Chambersburg PA
CBHW020751250626
47155CB00003B/1019